I0549699

Modern Sacrifices

Jan Osborne

Modern Sacrifices
by Jan Osborne

Signalman Publishing 2011
www.signalmanpublishing.com
email: info@signalmanpublishing.com
Kissimmee, Florida

Cover design by Kate Danailov

ISBN: 978-1-935991-28-1 (paperback)
        978-1-935991-29-8 (ebook)

Library of Congress Control Number: 2011939530

1

Six of the girls from her class were standing in a circle outside of the school, discussing the previous weekend in graphic detail. "He was so drunk that he threw up all over me!" one of them said, followed by shrill laughter from the others in the group. When Mary walked by, there was an awkward silence. Most of the people in the school, including this group of girls in Mary's senior English class, considered Mary a "goody-two-shoes," and did not socialize with her.

Although the girls stopped talking while Mary was directly beside them, she could easily hear them as she walked toward her father's faded blue, ten-year-old pick-up truck, which faithfully waited on her every day at 3:30 pm.

"She is so weird," said Phoebe, the apparent leader of the pack. "She never goes to parties or does anything that normal people our age do. She goes to church all the time, has that stupid little virgin boyfriend, and actually likes – and hangs out with – her parents! Get a life!" The other girls laughed and nodded in agreement as they began walking towards the football field to watch the day's practice and pick out their next weekend's prospects.

"So how was your day?" Mary's father asked as she threw her backpack and jacket in the backseat.

"Good, Dad," she replied as she kissed him on the cheek and smiled wearily after a tiring day of education.

It was a beautiful winter day, about thirty-five degrees, but sunny enough to trick you into thinking it was warmer than it actually was. Mary smiled as her father started down the familiar road that led to her welcoming house. She liked the simple things in life, like driving towards her house on a beautiful winter day.

"Joseph is playing tonight," Mary told her dad as they turned into their driveway. "Are you and Mom going to come?"

"Well of course," he told her. "We wouldn't miss it for the world,"

1

Mary had known Joe since they were in the third grade. Although he went to a different school, about twelve miles from the school she attended, they had gone to church together since they were small, and had officially been dating now for about four years.

Mary and Joseph shared the same values and views of life that are rare in twenty-first century teenagers. They understood that there was more to life than parties and popularity. They were happy with each other and with God, and that was all that mattered.

The other students at Joe's school looked at him the same way Mary's peers looked at her. They had both learned that most high school students don't want anything to do with you if you have a reputation for being a person of high moral values. This is not seen as a "cool" trait among teenagers.

The church that Mary's family had attended all of their lives was the place that both Mary and Joe felt like themselves. Joe played in a band, which usually led the song worship on Wednesday nights, and he and Mary were both very involved in the youth group.

"How was your day?" Joe's voice came through Mary's cell phone.

"Pretty good," she replied. "And yours?"

"Alright. My acceptance letter from Mountain Junior College came today. I wasn't worried about it, but it is good to know that I got accepted, you know? So I guess everything is still going according to plan. Mountain Junior College for two years, one year in the ministry, two years at a university, and then we get married. Looks like we are still on track." Mary loved how Joseph always had a plan. He was the kind of person that would not just plan out his entire life, but he would also *stick* with that plan.

"Good deal," Mary said with a smile. "What songs are on the play list tonight?"

"Elijah wants to play 'How Great Thou Art,' but Malachi and Jeremiah vetoed that on account of 'God is so Good' is more appropriate for the season, so it looks like we are going with 'God is so Good.' I really don't care what we play as long as I get to play my guitar and worship God. See you there?" he asked.

"Of course," Mary replied.

"I love you." And with that, Joseph was gone, probably to practice for his performance later that night.

Mary laid down her cell phone and picked up her Bible and began to read. She turned to Psalms and picked up where she had left off. Mary had always been a person who cared more about pleasing God and herself than caring what anyone else did or thought. Just how her classmates could not fathom her love and devotion to her church and God, she could not fathom their dedication to drugs, alcohol, and sex.

In defense of their lifestyle, they always used to tell her, when persuading her to come to parties or other social events, "Oh come on, Mary. You only live once." Mary always found this ironic, because they thought that they were using this statement as a justification of their actions, but really this statement only proved the fact that you should try your hardest to live your life right the first time around. Some people don't get a second chance.

Thirty minutes later, Mary put down her Bible and went into the kitchen to see if her mom needed any help with supper. They always ate supper early on Wednesdays so that they could get to church early and visit with other members.

"Need any help?" Mary piped up to her mother, who was just starting to wash her hands for the nightly cooking. Mary was an only child and felt it was her duty to help out whenever she could.

"Sure, honey," Mary's mother said with a large smile. "How was school?"

"Oh fine. Same as always. I think we have already learned everything that there is to learn. They are just keeping us hostage until we graduate." Mary smiled as her mother laughed.

"Well, you only have three and a half more months until you are free from your holding cell," her mother laughed. "Did Joe ever hear from Mountain?"

"Actually, he just told me that he got his letter today," Mary replied, with a mouth half full of apple. "He says our plan is still on track."

Mary's mother smiled. She loved that her daughter had such a kind-hearted boyfriend who treated her right and had plans for their future.

"Have you two decided where you are going to go after Mountain Junior College?" she asked as she began to boil the noodles for spaghetti.

Mary began to get out the hamburger meat and brown it in their cast iron skillet. "We haven't decided yet. Africa or the Middle East. There are ministries set up in both places, but we can't make our minds up. I guess we have two more years to think about it, though," she answered.

"Have you decided to stay at home or live in the dorms at Mountain?"

Mary loved how her parents, especially her mother, let her make her own decisions. She trusted her enough to treat her with respect like an adult and have faith that she would make the decision that would be best for her.

"I'm going to stay at home, I think. It is only a twenty-minute drive, and I think the car option would be better for the future. I could still have it even after Mountain, but the dorm would only be for those two years, you know?" Mary's parents had given her the option of staying in the dorms at Mountain Junior or getting a car that cost the equivalent of the dorm.

"That is what I would pick too," Mary's mom said with a smile. "We will find you a dependable car that will last a long time, hopefully."

"Are you still going to major in education?" Mary loved the small talk that her mother made, and loved how her mom asked questions that she already knew the answer to.

"Yep. Nothing has changed."

When supper was finished, the three of them ate and got ready for evening service. On the drive over, Mary thought about Phoebe and Joan, and some of the other girls that she had grown up with. She wondered how you could drift apart so quickly, and how their childhood bond of friendship was practically non-existent. She silently prayed for her peers, that they might become more concerned with their relationship with God than their relationship with other teenagers, and hoped that their attitudes towards life would change. Mary hated the thought of people around her, or anyone for that matter, not knowing or caring about God. It deeply saddened her to even consider the possibility that all people might not join her in heaven. She let her mind drift to another subject before she got upset.

Joseph and the other band members were already at church when Mary and her parents arrived. They were setting up their equipment when Mary snuck over to Joe while her parents went to get a seat in their usually pew.

"Hey," Mary said softly. Joe smiled when he saw her and asked how everything was.

"Same as always. Are you guys ready to play?" Mary loved that fact that Joseph respected her beliefs and never tried to hug or display affection to her in public. She would be mortified if her parents or anyone else in the church witnessed Joseph and her hugging. This was one of her best qualities, in Joseph's opinion.

Mary gave Joe one more quick smile and a, "Good luck," before going to take her seat. On her way to meet her parents, the youth minister stopped her to talk about ministry options. Everyone in the church knew of Mary and Joseph's plans to join the ministry, and appreciated the rare dedication of young people.

The youth minister told them that the next two years would fly by, and they needed to go ahead and plan out their destination and purpose. Mary decided that she wanted to go somewhere in the Middle East, and her minister had printed out pamphlets about all of the programs offered there.

Mary took her seat as the preacher started asking for prayers and concerns, and started to look at the brochure. She smiled to herself as Joseph and the band started to play, knowing that Egypt was the place she really wanted to go. She could feel it in her heart, and knew that Joseph would agree with her.

Mary listened intently to the message that night, and felt as if her pastor were preaching directly to her. He spoke about witnessing to others and how rare is the sharing of God's word in our society today. Mary felt as if she should apply that to her situation with the girls at school.

After the casual Wednesday night service, Joseph asked Mary if she wanted to go to the Dairy Queen with the other band members and him, and they could run her home later.

After telling her parents, the five of them loaded up in Joseph's 1998 Toyota Corolla and headed west. It was late for a school night, about 8:25, and Mary was already yawning.

"You guys are getting better every time you play," Mary told the group as they pulled into the parking lot.

"Yeah, I just wish that we weren't all splitting up after this summer. It will kind of feel like a waste of three years," Malachi said.

"Our colleges aren't that far though. It's not like we won't hang out anymore," Jeremiah piped up.

"Yeah, yeah. It just won't be the same, though," Malachi said with a sigh.

Surprisingly enough for a late Wednesday night, the parking lot at the Dairy Queen was overcrowded. Some of the cars were recognizable from the two different schools that the people in the car attended.

Mary yawned as she got out, and Joseph laughed. "Quit that, you party animal," he joked.

"It is almost past my bedtime," she kidded back.

Other than a couple seemingly in their late sixties with children who must have been their grandchildren, the fast food restaurant was full of high school students. Just as most people do, everyone looked up when Mary and the band members walked in.

A group of about eight high school kids were sitting at a circular table adjacent to the counter. Mary and Malachi were laughing about a joke the preacher had told when they walked by the table. All of the students got very quiet and glared at the five. Oblivious to the stares, Joseph began to place their order.

"Steak finger basket, chicken strip basket, hamburger combo, popcorn chicken, and another steak finger basket," Joe told the girl, kind enough to pay for everyone's meal. He had a lawn mowing business that had really grown in the past couple of years, and he actually made a substantial amount of money that lasted him throughout the year.

The group paid, got their order number, and went to find a seat. Naturally, the only one available was beside the large group of their crude high school classmates. Not bothered by this, they sat down.

Malachi and Elijah went to school with Mary, so they were very familiar with the tactics of some of their peers. Joseph had the same problems at his own school, but was also familiar with this particular group of kids.

"Ok, tell us one of your corny jokes," Joseph said to Jeremiah, and the other four started to smirk while they waited for their number to be called.

Jeremiah was known for his goofiness and fun-loving attitude. He always told the corniest jokes, and the only funny part about them was how he laughed throughout the entire punch line.

"Why did the cop stay in bed all day?" Everyone else could not help but smile as he started to giggle like a little schoolgirl.

Suddenly, he burst into laughter, almost not able to catch his breath in-between gasps for air. The others could not help but smile and laugh. "Why?" Elijah finally said when he had had enough. He was the serious and straight laced one. Mary loved how every one of their friends had such different personalities.

"Because he was undercover!" Followed by uncontrollable laughter. Everyone laughed, not at the joke, but at his silliness.

"Forty-seven," the cashier called out. Joseph walked towards the counter to pick up everyone's food. He stopped by to grab some ketchup and utensils, and then placed the food on the table.

Until this point, the other teenagers in the restaurant had not even acknowledged them, but when Mary, Joseph, Elijah, Jeremiah, and Malachi bowed their heads to pray, the other high school kids took their cue to mock and publicly humiliate them.

They all prayed silently to themselves, thanking God for the food in front of them, as they did every time they ate. Faith that strong in young people is very hard to find in today's society, but they were strong enough in their beliefs to know that believing in God and trusting him was better than any party, cuss word, sexual act or drug.

"Look, they are all praying. How sweet," mocked Sarah, loud enough to interrupt the five of them and get the attention of some others close by.

"Have you ever seen anybody so dorky?" Another said loudly.

Mary and Joseph cast low looks to each other, and then they all began joking and carrying on with their conversation as if no one was bothering them.

"Don't you EVER do anything wrong?" Susanna seemed to genuinely ask. Mary had seen her at school, and she did not seem to fit in with the others. She did not intentionally make fun of people simply because she was considered "popular," and Mary often found Susanna staring at the floor when her so-called friends were mocking or laughing at others.

"Of course we do," Mary responded, though Joseph had given her a look that said, "Please just ignore them."

"We sin every day, just like everyone. The good news is that God forgives us."

"Whatever. They probably party like crazy every night after church and get drunker than any of us," one of the boys said, followed by laughter from everyone at his table, along with some of the other tables listening in.

Joseph cringed in pain as the words were said. It physically hurt him that others would consider him a false prophet, only worshiping God during the day and mocking him by night.

Mary was usually a very quiet girl, and never spoke up—especially in situations like this. But here in the Dairy Queen, with many her peers listening, she was overcome with the feeling that she needed to defend God and stand up for him.

"Proverbs 20:1 says, 'wine is a mocker, strong drink is a brawler, and whoever is led astray by it is not wise,'" she said loudly, stopping everyone mid-laugh. No one had ever quoted the Bible at these partying teenagers and they did not quite know how to respond.

Suddenly, one of the girls blurted out, "Well you know, Mary has sex with all those boys and that is the only reason they hang around her. They probably all tag-team," she said loudly enough so that even the cooks, with the deep fryers rolling and the vent hoods on high, could hear.

Everyone at Mary's table was silent. The words not only hurt them, but also humiliated them. Realizing that his girlfriend and band members wanted to disappear at that very moment, Joseph followed Mary's faithful example.

"First Thessalonians 4:3 says, 'For this is the will of God, your sanctification: that you should abstain from sexual immorality.' And none of us would ever participate in sexual acts like you, for some reason, want to believe. I don't understand why you people can't lead your life the way you want to and just leave us alone." He was not angry when he said it, but was very direct.

Mary, Malachi, Jeremiah, and Elijah began gathering their food up to finish in the car. They could see that this would not be an enjoyable place to eat.

Mary got the rest of Joseph's food while he finished his lecture. Solemnly, they all walked towards the door and outside. Mary and Joseph were both very Bible oriented, and could quote many verses, especially the ones that were closest to their heart, and lead them through their lives.

As they were almost back in the car, the loud bell on the door could be heard, and Mary looked to see who had come out. Probably someone coming out to mock them some more before they left.

Mary's heart went out when she saw that it was Susanna, the girl who had asked about their faith.

"I really want to apologize," she said. "You guys don't deserve to be treated like that. You are such good people, and I just want you to know that I can't believe some of the things that were said to you. I don't know why those guys do stuff like that; I guess it makes them feel better about themselves." She paused. "I wish I had the faith and convictions that you all do. You should be proud of yourselves." Susanna looked like she was about to cry.

"Susanna, you are a good person too," Mary condoled. "You don't have to hang around with them if you don't agree with their lifestyle. I know that we would be more than happy to hang out and socialize with you."

Susanna looked down at the ground. "Thank you. You are very nice. Even though I don't like the way those guys act, and I know they are in there making fun of me right now because I am talking to you, I like the way I feel when I'm with them. Most of the time." She paused. "Being popular is really important to me. Do you understand?"

She was obviously torn on the inside. Elijah nodded at her and she walked back into the restaurant with a hanging head.

"What was that all about?" Phoebe asked when Susanna walked back in.

"Nothing," she replied. "I just told them that there was a party on Friday night with lots of alcohol and loose women if they wanted to join us."

Everyone laughed.

2

After Joseph had dropped off the three other guys at their houses, he headed south towards Mary's house. Her parents were already asleep when they walked in at 9:04. Mary smiled at their consistent schedules. Up at five and down at nine.

Joe walked back towards Mary's game room. Since her parents had a three-bedroom house and were only able to have one child, they had turned the other room into a "game room," equipped with a futon, lots of board games, and a TV for watching movies. Mary's parents did not have a TV in their living room, nor did they have cable or satellite. This worldly possession took time away from their family and their opportunity to pray and think of others. They had, although, given Mary a TV a couple of years ago so she could watch movies.

The two of them plopped down on the hard couch and turned the radio on.

"That was pretty intense tonight. I can't believe you stood up for all of us like that. I am really proud of you. You know that the life we live is not a popular one and that people don't understand it. We will be mocked forever, and I really admire your conviction to stand up for yourself and the rest of us," Joseph told her lovingly.

"I just don't understand it. If they want to lead a life of sin, fine. But why feel the need to make fun of our lifestyle?" she asked rhetorically. "Oh well," she sighed. "I say forgive and forget. I don't want to waste my time worrying about it," she said wearily.

"I have the best girl in the world," Joe said as he kissed his girlfriend.

They kissed for a while until Mary finally pulled away and simply laid into him, with her back against his chest. They had spoken about many times about where they stand and decide to draw the line in their physical relationship.

Just as in Bible times, in today's society, everyone has physical needs that they wish to fulfill; that is human nature. But God tells us to suppress those needs until we are bound by marriage, and that is exactly what Mary and Joseph intended to do, until they were married. Until then, kissing was a great way to show affection.

When Mary had fallen asleep, Joseph tried to ease out without waking her up. He shifted his weight from under her and gently laid her head under a pillow. He kissed her on the forehead and eased out the garage door, locking it as he went.

The next five months flew by, as time seems to do in our fast-paced world, and Mary found herself staring at her image in the mirror. The long maroon robe was huge on her body and hung all the way down to the ground. The diamond-shaped hat did not cover her ears and her long brown hair humped up at the earlobe. For the first time in her life, she had on high heels.

Practicing prior to today, she had only fallen four times, which she considered a success. Her mom had insisted on the heels, especially since she would be the most-looked-at graduate.

As Mary waited for Joseph to arrive and for her family to drive towards the school auditorium, she went over her speech in her mind. She could not believe that her twelve years of public school were over with, and that all of her hard work had actually earned her the 4.0 grade point average and Valedictorian title she had hoped for.

With all of her classmates and their families, many of the town elders, and other random people who give anything for a chance to get out of the house in attendance, Mary knew that this would be a great moment to witness to her community.

Mary smiled as Joe walked into the house, greeting everyone as he did. At first, she had been furious when he told her that he planned on skipping his own graduation to come to hers. He had explained that he would be just another face in the crowd, but she was the valedictorian. That was much more important to him.

After a couple of hours of trying to convince her, Joseph finally told Mary that he was coming and there was no stopping him. And a couple of weeks later, here he was, walking in the door in his khaki slacks and blue button up shirt.

"Are you nervous?" he asked as he kissed her on the cheek.

"Well I wasn't. Thanks for bringing it up, though," Mary joked.

"She's going to do absolutely great," her mom said.

"And even if she doesn't, I guess we will still keep her," Mary's father joked. With a more serious tone, he added, "We are so proud of you, sweetie."

Mary was oblivious to the small talk going on around her in the car on the way to the school. She felt like she might throw up. She had never been one who was that comfortable giving public speeches, and got pretty nervous when she had to speak at church or school. This was different, though. Her whole town and community would be there, not to mention all of the family members of the other students. Her stomach rumbled.

"What do you think, Mary?" Joseph asked.

"Huh?" She hadn't heard a word they had said. They all laughed, noticing the daze she was in.

Meeting with the other graduates, lining up in alphabetical order, walking onto the stage, taking their seats. Mary was panicking the entire time, and seemed as if she were not doing these things, but someone else was and she was watching from the ceiling.

The national anthem was sung and Mary literally thought she might throw up right there on the stage. She didn't like people looking at her or giving her attention, and as she scanned the crowd, she was once again hit with the realization that two thousand people would all be looking at her and giving her their full attention.

She could feel the color in her face leave and the overwhelming urge to pass out was creeping up her spine. When her name was called, she did not even know if they wanted her to give her speech or receive her diploma. Her heart raced.

She could not do it. Looking into the crowd made her knees buckle, and she silently prayed that God would help her get through these next seven minutes.

Once she watched herself walk to the podium, she remembered what her mother had said about the crowd. She had told her to close her eyes and pretend no one was there. She had said that the lights would be so bright and the seats were so far away, that no one would be able to see if her eyes were open or closed.

It took a year and a half for Mary to get to the podium, or so it felt to her. For the first time since she got to the school that day, she felt that her mind and body were on the same track and no longer felt like she was in the ceiling, watching herself move.

Mary closed her eyes, said another short prayer and started the speech that she had spent two months memorizing.

"Wow. I cannot believe that the past twelve years have gone by so quickly. It seems like just yesterday that we were in elementary school, and now we are being thrown out into the world to prepare a way for ourselves. The friends and memories we have made will stay with us forever." Mary peeked her eyes open, and quickly shut them tightly again at the sight the auditorium with standing room only, and people crowded around the doors and exits.

"We had the privilege of attending this quality school, and have all received a quality education. While an education is good and essential for a successful life, what is the purpose of this life? What is the point of trying to succeed and making a substantial life for yourself? I mean, we are just going to die in a couple of years. Right?"

She heard the shuffling and gasps of the audience. She knew what they were thinking. Was she really saying there was no point in living a fulfilled life? She paused and smiled to herself as she hoped that this approach would really get their attention for what she was going to say next.

"Why do we try so hard to make good grades, get into the right college, get a job, start a family, and raise more humans in this cycle of living and dying? What is the point?" She paused for dramatic effect.

"The point of living and of life can be summed up in one person's name. God. He is the way, the truth and the life, and through him, we are offered eternal life." Mary opened her eyes now. She felt more comfortable talking about salvation and decided to leave them open for the duration of her speech.

"When I started thinking about what kind of speech to give and what was important enough to say to all of my peers and fellow town members, I realized that nothing is more worth saying than the grace and salvation of my lord and savior. Yes, high school was great and we are all lucky enough to live in a country that allows us to receive such an education. But the bigger picture here is how much God has blessed us all, and how lucky we are to receive his grace and forgiveness for our sins.

"No matter what you have done in your life, no matter how unforgivable you think you are, God forgives you and asks you to give it all to him. Many times, we get caught up in the hustle and bustle of our measly little lives and forget about the bigger picture. If you get nothing else from this speech, I at least want you to think about the fact that you are forgiven no matter what you have done in your past. Once we realize and understand that forgiveness, we can start to forgive one another and begin to live for God instead of the worldly things.

"For those of us here who are parents, imagine raising your child to the best of your ability. Always giving him the essentials that he needs, plus more. You nurture them spiritually and mentally. You give him or her the best games, clothes, and toys. You treat the child like he or she is a king or queen. Then they grow up and decide they are going to kill four people and take their own life. I want you all to stop and think about how that might feel.

"The feeling that I hope you are experiencing right now is how God feels every time we sin against him. Now I want you to imagine the forgiveness you would feel toward your child who had killed and taken his own life. Though he or she had done a terrible act, a loving parent could find it in their heart to forgive.

"God offers each one of us forgiveness like this, but many of us are too busy with our own lives to ask for that forgiveness. If we try to live a life according to God and his word, we will be rewarded with things finer than you could imagine.

"No, you will not be the coolest or most popular person. You can ask my classmates that," she paused. Some of the audience members laughed at the joke, but most of Mary's peers were staring at the floor.

"But your relationship with God is incomparable to the relationship you will have with the other people on this earth. If nothing else, I hope that each one of you here might think about where you stand with God, and consider how your own father feels about the decisions you make in life. You might not be a murderer or a killer, but chances are there are many things that we all need to seek forgiveness for and repent.

"If you feel the need to pray with someone or talk to someone, any of the preachers at church or myself would be glad to discuss the love of God and pray with you.

"Although this was not the graduation speech that everyone was expecting, with stories about their high school experience, plans for the future, and how we will never forget the memories we made, which speech do you think made a bigger impact? And if someone here has never heard the word of God, then maybe I did the right thing. Please be in prayer for yourselves and your neighbors. If you are willing, I would like to close with a prayer. Everyone please bow your heads." After a short pause, Mary began to pray.

"Dear Lord, please let the words spoken tonight touch everyone and lead us closer to you. Please forgive us where we fail you and help us to stay on the path to righteousness. We know that through you, all things are possible, but please help us to trust in you and put our lives in your hands. We pray for all of the ill and injured and hope that you will heal them. In your name we pray. Amen."

Mary sat down and every eye in the entire auditorium was upon her. She could feel the stares and realized that no one really knew what to do next. She had shocked everyone with her words; she only hoped it was a good shock that would help people understand God.

Slowly, the principal got up and quietly said, "We will now hand out the diplomas to our graduates." The graduation ceremony continued with ease and soon Mary was a high school graduate.

"That was great, honey. We are really proud of you," her mom said after the caps had been thrown and the graduates were allowed to mingle with their families.

"Sure glad I came to your graduation instead of mine. No wonder you wouldn't tell anyone what you were going to say. What a great surprise." Joseph smiled supportively.

"I think you deserve dinner at your favorite place tonight," Mary's father said as they walked towards the car and headed to their local restaurant that Mary loved.

After dinner, all of them were so tired that they went home and went straight to bed. Mary had big plans of sleeping in, and enjoying being a functional adult in society and no longer a child. Around nine o'clock though, she could overhear voices in the living room and was quickly awoken.

3

No one ever came over on Saturday morning this early. Either something was wrong or someone needed to talk to her family. She quickly put a short blue robe on top of her argyle patterned boxer shorts and summer camp T-shirt and walked the short distance to the room to see what the commotion was all about.

Two men in suits were standing there with papers in their hands, and Mary's parents looked very flustered and upset. Mary's head was spinning and did not comprehend what was going on.

The words "civil suit" and "separation of church and state" and "all over You-Tube" were thrown into their faces like swords cutting stone. More arguing. More questions. The men were so hostile.

Mary suddenly started to cry when it hit her that all of this was her fault. The state was taking her to court over her prayers and "sermon" at a public school graduation. Apparently, this was illegal and since Mary was eighteen, she was to be tried as an adult.

Mary's mother was crying and Mary kept saying, "I was just trying to get people to come to God."

After the third time she said it, one of the men turned to her and said, "That is against the law. You cannot force your beliefs upon anyone, and everyone has rights to go to a public place and not worry about someone forcing religion on them. How would you feel if someone told you about Buddhism at your own graduation? Your little stunt is all over the internet, and if you would turn on the news, it is there too. You will be tried as an adult because you are over the age of eighteen. You are to appear in court on July 22. You need to have yourself a lawyer. And if I was you, I would get a good one. Do you understand?"

How could anyone talk so rudely? Mary was a sweet and innocent girl, and these two men were mocking her and yelling at her as if she had just committed murder. She did not know what she had done was even an issue, much less illegal. Why were they worried about her little words anyways, when there were real thieves and murderers out on the streets?

Mary started to panic. Her mind was spinning and she could feel her throat closing up and her face go pale. She felt that she could throw up at any minute. What had she done? Her parents could not afford a lawyer. They must be expensive. They did not deserve to go through this. What about her plans for the future? What would Joseph say? Would she go to jail? Can you still go to college if you have gone to jail?

All of a sudden, sitting in the living room with her parents on either side of her and tears in her eyes, Mary had an overwhelming sense of calm. All of her fears were gone and somewhere deep down inside, she knew that it would all be OK. God would take care of her and no matter what happened, and everything would work itself out.

She couldn't explain it, but Mary knew when God was talking to her. So many times in today's society, people expect this huge scene where the clouds open up and a huge, booming voice comes out to tell them what they want to know. But God does not work like that. If you are quiet and willing enough, he will speak to you. You just have to open your heart and allow him in.

Mary could not believe how fast the last two months had flown, and how much media coverage she had gotten. All because of a seven minute speech to a small community of people.

She constantly wondered why so many people were concerned with what she did or said and why everyone was still talking about her words. Words are just things you say. More important things could be on the news. Like actions. Actions of violence, actions of hunger, actions of leaving small children outside in the cold.

Though Mary refused to look at any of it, her speech had been filmed and put on You Tube, facebook, myspace, twitter, and all of the news channels. She really did not know it would make such a big stink, or she would have spoken on all of her wonderful memories from high school like every other valedictorian in history.

Although she did not wish to get too involved or engulf herself in this case that she was in, she did understand that she could be sued, fined, or at worst, put in jail. The first one made her laugh. She hoped they would sue her. They might get a whole twenty dollars.

The fine scarred her a little more because she worried that her parents would be obligated to pay it, and they did not need any more bills. She would not let herself consider going to jail, because that was unfathomable to a sweet young girl like her. She just prayed continuously that God would take care of her.

She could not believe the turn of events and everything that had happened in such a short time. Mary had planned to spend her summer getting ready for college and hanging out with Joseph, but that was yet to happen.

Joseph. He had been so supportive of her. Never once left her side, despite the fact that she could go to prison for a short speech at a small town graduation. Mary started to get angry at our stupid laws and the people who are trying to throw her in jail while thieves and murderers walk the street.

But she would not allow herself to lose control. Harboring anger only hardens your heart and eventually turns you away from God. She needed God more than ever now.

"Do you understand?" The judge's words jerked Mary out of her thoughts. She nodded, though she had no idea what had just been said. She wanted to keep it that way for most of the trial. Listening would only cause anger.

The man sitting adjacent to her had on a dark black suit as he stood up to represent the civil rights of Americans. Had they really polled everyone in America to see if it personally offended them, what Mary had said? Was everyone as concerned with her as these official court people seemed to be? Mary said a short prayer for her safety and her future.

The lawyer seemed to have rehearsed his speech. "Imagine your son or daughter, after eighteen years, is finally graduating high school. You have prepared for this moment since they were born, invited all of your family and friends, and have plenty of batteries in the video camera." He paused for dramatic affect and looked each jury member in the eye.

"You get there early to get a good seat, and get ready for an even that will change your and your child's life. All of the late nights helping them study and going to football and cheerleading practice. The valedictorian gets up to give her speech and you are still beaming with pride.

"Suddenly, this seemingly sweet little girl," he turns and looks at Mary, "starts her valedictorian speech. Instead of the inspirational words and wisdom you were expecting, you find yourself at a church, and this young girl is the preacher.

"She talks on salvation and coming to know God, and how wonderful he is." He stopped once again and glared at Mary.

"Now imagine you are Buddhist." And that was it. He sat down.

Mary could sense that about half of the jury was on her side, and the other half was glaring at her with hate in their eyes. She was asked if she would like to make a statement before recessing the court.

Mary's knees almost buckled as she started to stand up. "Yes. Thank you sir," she said in almost a whisper.

"I really want to apologize for what I said, but I cannot. I did not realize that speaking about my wonderful Lord and savior was against the law, and I would like to say that given the chance, I would not do it over again. But that is not true. I probably would. I just really don't understand why I am in a courtroom right now, facing possible jail time simply for speaking at my high school graduation." She spoke so softly that many had to strain to hear.

"If you want me to say that I am sorry, I just can't." She looked extremely sad, knowing what was probably about to happen to her. She still could not believe that civil rights prohibit you from speaking your mind in public. And her country is famed for being the best country in the world? Maybe people needed to rethink that.

The judge cleared his throat, not sure how to take this innocent young girl before him. He excused the courtroom and called a recess for the jury to deliberate. Outside the mahogany room, Mary's parents and boyfriend hugged her and tried to convince her that everything would be fine.

Outside the courthouse, they could hear the reporters anxiously waited for a verdict. Mary had already planned an escape route out the back of the building, hoping to avoid them.

She decided that for now, it would be best to sit on the hard wooden benches outside of the courtroom. Shortly after Mary and her closest loved ones took a seat, the judge walked by on his way to his chambers. He passed them, and then seemed to have a quick thought. He turned around and walked towards Mary, with her eyes wide and scared at the sight of him.

"Young lady," he said in a gruff voice. "I have never had a case quite like this one, and I just want to tell you that I agree. Our justice system seems to be focusing on the wrong kind of 'criminal'. I wish that I had the faith and convictions that you do. You are facing fines and prison, and you still held strong to your faith. You have no idea how much I admire you." He smiled and walked away.

Mary did not know why, but she suddenly began to cry. It took over her body, like the enemy force taking over a small country, and although she fought back the tears, they came anyway.

Joseph, not saying a word, simply put his arms around her and let her lean into him on the uncomfortable bench. They did not move for forty minutes. Suddenly, scuffling of feet and opening of doors meant that the jury had made a quick and hasty decision. That could mean one of two things: that they were unanimously against Mary or unanimously for her.

After the court was called back to order and everyone was settled down, the judge asked the jury to read their decision to the court. A small lady, seemingly in her sixties, stood up slowly. Mary felt like eight years were passing before her eyes.

She could not breathe. Could not move. The same queasy feeling that had overcome her before giving her graduation speech was moving back into her stomach, up her throat, and washing over her head, turning it pale white. She considered how ironic it was, that the valedictorian speech that had given her the same nauseous feeling was the reason she was here.

The petite lady took an eternity to open her mouth and speak. "We the jury, unanimously find Mary not guilty of civil rights crimes against the people. We furthermore find what a disgraceful country we live in, where someone would force this sweet, kind, faithful girl to experience this," she glared at the prosecuting attorney, and Mary had a feeling that wasn't part of the jury's decision, as much as the individual lady's.

"I am embarrassed for my own country and sad for Christians everywhere. Do you even know that we do not have other faiths, besides Christianity, in our community? The funny thing about this is that you were fighting a case for people who were not even at this graduation." She was really giving it to him now.

"Never in my life did I think I would see the day that a crude man would convict a young girl of talking about God. Lord have mercy on your soul." At the end she was yelling, taking her anger out solely on the poor lawyer, who was simply assigned to the case and did the best job he could.

Mary knew she should feel happy, but she suddenly felt overcome by sadness. During the last two months, she had continuously thought about what would happen to her personally, in addition to fighting to keep the thoughts from entering her head.

She hadn't really stopped to think about the bigger picture. She had been on trial for speaking the word of God. She had faced jail and prison for attempting to bring people to God. What kind of world was this?

Mary could feel Joseph on her right side and her father on her left help her up after months and months of agonizing mental stress. As they neared the back door, she could hear the reporters' cameras and their feet shuffling around to get the best angle.

They walked out the door, into the bright flashing lights and were bombarded with questions. Mary was still in a daze when she heard her father saying, "God was the one delivering the verdict today."

4

The weeks following Mary's trial were spent finding ways to fight off the reporters and questions. Why had she done it? How did it feel? Was she simply making a statement? She could hardly bear to walk out her back door.

"Hey," Joseph said, walking into her house one afternoon. He could sense the tension and turmoil in her head, even now, weeks after the hectic events. "Guess what? I have some news for you." He smiled when she looked up, the same sad and depressed look she had had since she left the courtroom that rainy July day.

"Don't be mad, but I sent all of your transcripts and information, along with mine, of course, to Centenary Junior College. I thought that, with everything that happened, it might be nice to move away to go to college. Everyone here still mobs you with questions and stares, and I know how much it bothers you. I figure that three hours away is better than twenty minutes.

"Now we only got a couple hundred dollars in scholarships, so we will have to take out students loans and probably pay on them the rest of our lives," he grinned, jokingly, "but I definitely think it would be worth it. Just to get away from the craziness, you know?

"It wasn't hard to be so sneaky with you in a daze all the time. Your parents think it is a good idea too, in case you are wondering." He winked at her.

Mary looked up at him from her permanent spot on the couch. She stared at him for a long time, and then, ever so slowly, started to smile. How was it that he knew just what she needed? She could not handle the public attention anymore and wanted nothing more than to go with Joseph to Centenary.

"I take that as a yes?" Joseph laughed.

For the first time since the fast, head-spinning turn of events, Mary felt like her old self. Back to normal, and uncontrollably happy.

The next week was spent in a hectic rush. Mary and her mom had so much to plan. They were type A personalities to a T, and did not do well with last minute changes. After seven full days of buying dorm room items, visiting Centenary, registering for classes, buying books, applying for student loans, and getting the dorm room situated, August 25 rolled around.

It was harder than Mary could imagine, saying good bye to the people would had raised and loved her. Even though she would be home every weekend, breaks, and holidays, she was still experiencing agonizing pain and guilt, leaving them at home to deal with the reporters and media while she whisked away to Centenary.

Tears covered Mary and her mother's eyes as her father put the last of her suitcases into Joseph's trunk. After the world wind spring of events that summer, buying the car had been put on hold, leaving Mary to rely on Joseph, who wouldn't want it any other way.

It seemed as if they were driving west before Mary really even had a chance to replay the summer in her head. So much had happened. The preparation for the trial, fighting off reporters, stares from her old friends and townspeople, late night talks with her preacher, Joseph, and her parents, deciding to go to a different college, getting ready for that college, and now this. Mary stared out the window in amazement at house fast things happen in life, and how things can change before we even know it.

She turned her eyes to Joseph and smiled, knowing how lucky she was. He told her how much he loved her, and for the first time in a long time, Mary was truly happy.

College was much different that high school, and Mary and Joseph found themselves loving every minute of it. Right after settling into their dorms, before classes even started, they found their way to the FCCS, the Fellowship of College Christian Students and feel in love with the people there.

There had been a poster with the letters FCCS on it beside a table and two people with FCCS T-shirts on. It was in between a sorority and a fraternity table, and they were all trying to recruit the new freshmen.

The sorority and fraternity tables were full of young people, but Mary and Joseph walked directly to FCCS, and were greeted with smiling faces. They were given brochures and information, and told to come by anytime.

They met every Tuesday and Thursday, and Joseph started playing in a new band with some of the other guys. He loved playing again, and Mary loved to be able to listen to his Christian rock. She forgot how much she missed their band now that they were all at different colleges.

Monday and Wednesday and Friday afternoons were spent playing on the FCCS's intramural sport teams. Mary and Joseph had joined the volleyball, basketball, and tennis teams to stay in shape, but realized how much of a blast it was.

The FCCS players, along with everyone that they played against, were just as untalented as they were, making every one of them laugh at all of their athletic mistakes. Mary and Joseph had never felt this at home in high school and could not believe all of the wonderful friends they had already made.

Everyone at college seemed to have their own priorities, and the clichés and clicks and popularity contests that Mary and Joseph had witnessed in high school were non-existent here.

Students focused their energy where their interests where, with no concern about what others were doing. Mary and Joseph had one out of their five classes together, and loved how much more open college classes were for discussion. People would just give their opinion while the professor was speaking, instead of having to raise their hand.

The couple both fell in love with this style of learning and thoroughly enjoyed all of their basic classes. Many times, while studying together at night, the two would lose track of time and simply discuss the conversations and arguments that were held in each course.

By October of their freshman year, Joseph decided that they should each get a student job to initiate the pay-off of their future debts. "We will have a lot of loans to pay off when we graduate. And even though the finance companies don't start billing you until six months after graduation, just imagine how ahead we would be if we started paying now," he had told Mary. He was so smart about worldly ways, and Mary felt so naïve and uneducated about it all.

Joseph got a job at the school library, and Mary started tutoring students in reading. Student jobs were really a great way to earn money, while working around your class schedule and staying on campus.

Mary thought that everything about college seemed to be wonderful and perfect. She and Joe were as much in love as they had ever been and did not seem to notice the pressures of living on their own. They kept their relationship the same as it had always been and keep living in love with each other and with God.

Many of the people Mary tutored were athletes, struggling to balance school and their individual sport. During football season, she tutored baseball and softball players, and vice versa in the spring. With practice every day, there was no time for tutoring, so they focused more on their studies in the off-season.

Joseph got most of his homework done while working at the library, as most of his job was sitting and waiting for people to come and check out books. Between classes, work, intramural sports, the band, and FCCS, Mary and Joseph found out quickly that there was a lot less free time than they thought there would be.

They definitely did not go home every weekend like they had originally planned. Mary felt guilty, until Joseph convinced her that her parents were fine without her.

One early November night, Mary and Joseph were sitting in the common room of Mary's dorm, sitting around and talking, Mary's back leaned into Joseph's, as his legs came up around hers. Of all the Armani couches and Italian silk loveseats, there was no better place in the world than right there, in Joseph's embrace.

Joshua, the young FCCS minister, startled them as he walked in.

"There you two are," he said as he plopped down on one of the rock hard sofas. "Been looking for you all afternoon."

"We are pretty hard people to find," Joseph joked. "We usually hide out all day from people like you." They all smiled. Mary loved how close they had gotten to Josh in such a short time, and how they always teased each other.

"So, how is everything going?" Josh asked as he tried to get comfortable in the unmoving chair.

"Absolutely wonderful," Mary said as she looked up at Joseph.

"Joe, I put your guitar behind the stage today, so if you go to looking for it, you can blame me," he winked at him.

"Mary, I'm going to quit making small talk and ask what I came here to ask."

Mary tensed up, getting a little concerned with what he would say.

"I know that you guys came to this school to get away from your conviction and what happened back home. I know that you hate attention on you and don't want people to make a fuss over you." He paused. "But I am still going to ask you to give your testimony at our convention next week."

He did not even give her a chance to utter a word. "Before you say no, I just want you to think about it and look at the bigger picture, Mary. You were a martyr for God, and did not deny Him, even with the risk of going to jail or getting fined because of it. There is no better witness than you, and I really think it would help others' faith if they heard your story."

"I'll think about it," Mary said after a long time.

Joshua smiled. "Well, I can't ask any more than that. I think God will lead you to do what needs to be done." He winked at Joseph. "I'll let you to get back to your cuddling," he joked and was out the door with the comment.

"Let's not talk about it right now," Joseph said before Mary could begin with the questions and thoughts that he knew were coming. "Just pray about it tonight and see how you feel tomorrow."

The mere thought of getting in front of other students and describing the agony she went through was unfathomable. Just as Mary was thinking about a way to get out of the task, she suddenly felt compelled to tell her story. It just might make someone understand God's grace, and if only one single person came to God, it would be worth bringing up the past torments of media and reporters.

The convention had a huge turnout for the small campus. Miraculously, five hundred people showed up. There were only one thousand enrolled in classes.

After prayers, singing, and someone else's testimony, Joshua got up to speak and announce Mary.

"Many of you heard about the civil rights case that was held this past summer. A young high school graduate had spoken at her graduation about God and his wonderful grace. For speaking those words, she convicted of demeaning the civil rights of the public, and slapped with a lawsuit. Facing being sued, heavy fines, and even jail, she stood up before the judge and jury and said that she could not be sorry for what she had done. Because it was the right thing to do."

Joshua motioned for Mary to come towards the stage, and she was astonished at the fact that the queasy feeling was not present. Not today.

"Hi. He makes me sound like some kind of saint," she joked while quiet laughter spread.

"I am not a saint. I am just a person who believes in the greatest God there is, and who wants others to experience the joy that I do in that faith." Mary paused and thought about the speech she had prepared.

Suddenly glancing at Joe, sitting in the front row, she was overcome with the feeling that she did not need to speak. She needed to answer.

"I had my testimony all memorized and rehearsed. But I suddenly feel that more people will get more out of this if they simply ask questions and I will answer them." She felt a feeling of calmness with her decision.

There was silence for a solid two minutes. Finally, a voice from the front row asked, "Why did you give your valedictorian speech on God?" Mary looked down at Joseph, grateful that he was willing to get the questions rolling.

"Uh hum," she cleared her throat. "Every one of us is given talents. I was given the talent of academics and excelling in the classroom. If we are not using our talents to serve God, then what are we using them for? I used my valedictorian ship as a way to serve God and witness to him. What better way to tell people about God than when your entire community is sitting still, listening to you?"

Before she could even finish, someone else shouted, "How did you not know about civil rights and the laws that correlate with that?"

"My family does not own a television, nor do I get on the Internet much. I find that it just uses my mind space up when it could be channeled for more important things. So when I say that I did not know it was illegal to speak religion in public, I honestly did not."

"Why do you think the jury let you go?"

"I think God took control of the situation and took matters into his own hands."

"How are you such a good Christian? Are you not tempted with the ways of the world?

Mary looked down in the first row. "I am extremely blessed to be surrounded by people who love and support me despite the evils and pressures in the world.

One after another the questions came. Mary felt like she had stood on the podium for two days, in what had really been two hours. She felt that not only did she help some people understand what she had done, but also helped herself understand.

The whole experience had been a negative one in Mary's eyes that she had never stopped to think about the whole picture. She really had been a good witness for God, maybe even had a big enough impact on others to make them question their faith.

That day, through Mary's testimony, twelve people professed their faith to God. Eleven of them belonged to sororities and fraternities with hard-core partying reputations, proving to Mary and everyone else that the sins of the world do not bring you true joy. Only through trusting and serving God do we have eternal peace and purpose. Mary finally started to see the good she had accomplished in God's eyes. Joseph just laughed when she told him. He had known all along.

5

Mary could not believe how fast two years could fly by. Her experiences and friends she had gained at college were all wonderful, and she could not bear to leave them behind. Still, she stared at the Associates Diploma she held in her hands, knowing that it signaled the start of a new chapter in life.

Over the past two years, Joseph and Mary had grown together in love, and made some lasting memories. Joe was the leading musician on Wednesday nights in FCCS and the local church they had begun going to, after the price of gasoline went up and the idea of going home every weekend slowly dwindled to about once every three months.

Mary had seen fourteen athletes pass their classes since her tutoring job began, and Joe swore he had every book in the library memorized. The couple stayed in shape by keeping busy with their intramural sports, and being involved in almost every activity on campus.

The college was small enough that most people knew Mary and Joseph by name, except for the newest students on campus. Mary loved the fact that no one judged them, but were usually nice, said hello, and then left them alone.

Centenary did not have a traditional graduation for Associates recipients, but they did have a small ceremony to commemorate the success. Mary's parents, alongside Joseph's, were sitting in the front row, and Mary smiled as she thought about how lucky she was to be blessed with them.

Finally, the Dean of Students was done with his speech. Everyone stood up in their alphabetic spot, and were allowed to slowly walk off of the stage into the arms of their greeters, as the graduation hymn played softly in the background.

Mary had a huge smile on her face when she spotted her family in the crowd. Joseph had already found them and was waiting patiently on Mary.

"I can't believe you two are college graduates!" Joseph's dad said.

"Well, not technically," Joe smiled. "We still have to go two more years before we get our Bachelor's degrees." He winked as his dad his head got put into a playful headlock.

"Good…Stay out of the real world as long as possible," Joseph's dad joked.

"Alright kiddos," Mary's mother always referred to them as her kiddos. "Tell us where you want to eat. You'll have to show us around this town. I always get confused when I come here. That square messes me all up." Mary and Joseph's parents had both visited the young couple about a dozen times in the past two years, but always loved to let Mary and Joseph feel like real grown-ups, showing them around their own town.

"How about Hershel's? It will probably be crowded though; it is cheap, therefore popular with students." Mary smiled at Joseph's suggestion. He always knew the perfect place to go.

"Hershel's it is!" Joseph's mom shouted, a little too eager. The drive over must have been unusually long, because she looked extremely hungry for her petite frame.

Over dinner, Mary and Joseph discussed with their parents the events of the last couple of weeks, since they had seen them last. After all of the intramural trophies and FCCS events were discussed, there was a huge silence that overcame the table.

Neither Mary's nor Joseph's parents liked the idea of the journey that they knew their children were about they embark on. All four of them had tried to talk Mary and Joseph out of going overseas next month. With the fighting and the confrontations constantly happening in the Middle East, their parents knew of the danger that they could encounter.

But, as Mary and Joseph tried to convey to their parents, they truly felt led to go, and knew that God's word was needed there. Needed to be heard and spread. They knew of the dangers, but also of the great rewards possible. Even if they only brought one person to God over their next year, then it will have been worth it.

"Let's not worry about our mission trip, but instead celebrate what we came here to celebrate." Joseph's kind voice of reason seemed to agree with everyone as the subject was changed.

"Well, do you guys feel like functioning adults yet?" Mary's mother joked.

"Functioning adults? They are barely even out of high school. They are too young to know what is best for them," Mary's father said sadly, disobeying Joseph's requests. He was scared at the thought of his daughter going away to a war zone, even if it was for the church.

Joseph's father smiled. "I don't know. If they have made it this far with the good heads on their shoulders, making the good decisions they have, I think we should trust them."

The mothers nodded in agreement, but Mary's father still looked questionable.

"We are not leaving for three weeks, Daddy," Mary tried to console him. "We will be very careful and God will watch over us."

"Well, I still don't like the idea of you two hopping around another country sleeping side by side." Mary's father was trying to find negative sides to this mission trip, in a last attempt to keep them here.

"We have promised not only God and you guys, but also ourselves that we are not going to do anything sexual until we are married. We sleeping side by side in our bed rolls should be a comforting thought for safety and closeness, not a worrisome thought about our hormones and the pressure associated with them." Joseph was such a kind and just man to be only twenty years old.

Mary's father sighed. "I know, Joe. I am just worried about you guys. I wish you would stay here, safe with us. But if you really feel led to go, I will really try to understand and be supportive."

Mary's mother gave him a quick hug and Mary held his hand. "Everything is going to be fine, Daddy. This one year will go by quicker than the past two have and we will be back in college before you know it," she said. Her father smiled at her and kissed her on the forehead.

"Now then," Joseph's father chimed in. "Who wants ice cream? I hear they have the best in town." He winked. Joseph's parents, along with Mary's parents had numerous phone conversations with their children while they were here, at their favorite restaurant in the town. It was cheap enough to attract the college kids, yet nice enough for all ages. And the food was delicious.

Mary did not even have to speak. She jumped up and raced towards the counter so she could beat everyone else. Ice cream was Mary's weakness. Especially in the early spring and summer. Nothing came close to the taste of it on her tongue, not even Joe's kiss, she had joked with him.

There was a long line, as Hershel's was extraordinarily packed after the many ceremonies from the different degree programs that day. Joseph squeezed behind Mary in line and gave the small of her back a pat.

"It really is going to be OK," he said softly to her. "As long as we have each other, what could go wrong?" Mary gave him her questioning look, but Joseph whisked it away with a soft kiss on her forehead. He then turned her around and put his arms around her as they waited in line, with their parents patiently waiting on the sweet dessert.

Joseph knew that Mary was beginning to worry as much as her father about their trip. She had never been more than three states away, and now they were going to another country for a whole year. And not just any country, but a hot, Middle Eastern country in a time of war.

Mary had prayed countless hours about their mission trip, and finally came to the conclusion in her heart that Egypt, Israel, and Jerusalem was where they needed to go. Now she just had to convince herself.

Joshua, their FCCS leader, had finalized the plans for them. They were leaving June 6, headed for a Christian mission in Egypt. They were going to be rebuilding houses destroyed by the war, and witnessing to the people whose houses were rebuilt. Four months all over Egypt, another four in Israel, and another four in Jerusalem.

Mary's thoughts were luckily interrupted as her turn at the counter approached. The less she worried about the trip, the better. The couple ordered everyone's favorite ice cream and headed back to their corner booth.

"This is the only reason I come to this town. Sorry, guys. I hope you didn't think it was to see you. That is just one of the perks." Joseph's dad winked and everyone smiled as they licked their ice cream cones dry. It really was the best in town.

After they had eaten all of their food and finished off their dessert, the six people stayed at the family owned restaurant another hour, talking about the kid's accomplishments and memories from Centenary.

When they were the only ones left in the place, Mary's mother stretched. "Well kiddo, we better go get your dorm room packed up. We have a lot more to do and a long drive home."

They had brought the truck so all of Mary's things could go in the back, under the camper shell. Since Joseph's family did not own a truck, they would be carrying most of his things home also.

They slowly got up to leave and headed for the door. Loading the truck took a lot less time than unloading all of Mary's stuff had. She was simply taking it and chunking it in, with little concern about organization. She would worry about that when she unpacked.

Joseph, on the other hand, had everything already packed and ready, with labeled boxes and neatly placed dorm furniture. Mary's mom smiled to herself as they helped load everything up. Maybe opposites really do attract.

An hour and a half later, Mary and Joseph were turning in their dorm keys, and heading back to their childhood home, another chapter in their life closing while a new one was about to begin.

Mary slept the whole way home, after an exhausting couple of days. She made herself comfortable in the back of her dad's truck, while a packed car of Joseph's parents followed closely behind, tailed by Joseph's car, also loaded with stuff.

Three hours later, Mary felt the truck stop and sat up with squinty eyes and deep breaths. "Are we home?" she asked half asleep.

"Yes," her mother said cheerfully. Too cheerfully after the long day, Mary thought.

"Are we going to unload now or later?"

Mary looked at her mother as if she were crazy. "Definitely later," she replied.

Mary and Joseph had taken a vow to spend every waking moment of the next three weeks with their parents, friends, and extended families. They knew how worried everyone was about them going overseas, so they wanted to make their three weeks at home really matter. Besides, they would be together one hundred percent of the time for the next year. Three weeks was nothing compared to that.

Since most of the public schools were also out, Mary got to spend time with her younger cousins, who she had not seen since Thanksgiving. They were fifteen and seventeen, and of course thought Mary hung the moon. They spent their days laying out by the pool, shopping at the mall, and going to the movies. In the evenings, when Mary's parents got home from work, she spent the nights with them, going and doing whatever they wished.

After her parents went to bed, Mary would call Joseph and catch him up on the events of her day until she got so tired she fell asleep. Only to wake up and do it all over again.

Joe's schedule was about the same, hanging out with his old band members who were also in from college, old high school friends, and family members who had lacked his presence in the past two years.

Later, Mary and Joseph would crave these easy summer days with little responsibility. They sped by so fast, no matter how long they tried to drag them out. It seemed like only four days when Mary, a procrastinator, finally had to sit down and pack her looming suitcase.

Her heart started racing and she felt light headed when the task of packing was finally, actually at hand. That meant it was all real and she really had to leave this life of luxury she had become so accustomed to.

Mary tried to pack, but there was so much she would need. So many clothes and necessities; there was absolutely no way it would all fit in her three suitcase limit.

"Let me guess…you are done?" she answered the phone.

"And let me guess? You haven't started?" Joseph laughed. "Good thing I am about to be at your house to help organize your suitcase."

Mary's head popped up from the bottom of her closet at the sound of the doorbell. She hung up the phone and walked gloomily towards the entrance way.

Exasperated, she swung the door open. "Help," she said sweetly, hoping to get Joseph to complete the task for her.

"Now dear, how would you ever learn to pack for yourself if I did it for you?" Joseph smiled at her. "I am simply here for support." He kissed her on the cheek and headed towards her room.

"I figured you would say that," Mary gave him the eye as she shut the door. "What if I don't want to learn how to pack myself? That way, you will always be guaranteed that I will keep you around. I'll always need you for something," Mary jokingly tried again.

"If you whine just a little more, maybe I'll say yes." They both laughed. "You do realize we are leaving tomorrow, right?" Joseph added, seriously.

"Yes. I just kept thinking that if I put off packing, the trip would also be put off. I'm really scared, Joe. I've never been to another country. Maybe our parents are right. Maybe we are too young to be traveling around the world by ourselves. We could always to back to school in the fall and just get jobs this summer." Joseph could see the legitimate concern and worry in her eyes. He knew that she was scared of the different cultures and the war that they would encounter during their year.

Joseph took Mary's hand and his joking demeanor left. "Mary, I know you are worried. I am too, even though you think I don't show it. But we have talked about this trip for years now, and we both know that it is what God wants us to do. Yes, it is a big sacrifice, but just think about all of God's work that will be accomplished. I would never, never let anything bad happen to you, Mary. I love you. If I even had the slightest doubt that something would go wrong or you would be hurt, you know I would not suggest that we go. But I have this feeling, deep down inside, that everything will be OK." Joseph looked deep into her eyes with a love that is unexplainable. A love that normal twenty year olds do not experience.

"I know," Mary said softly. She looked up at him. "I love you too."

Joseph smiled. "Now, where do we start?" he gestured towards the mound of clothes that Mary had attempted to take out and sort between "taking" and "not taking."

Mary shrugged, and then smiled as Joseph started to organize her piles and neatly pack them into her suitcase.

6

The car ride to the airport was silent, other than random small talk. Mary and Joseph had already shared tearful good-byes with church members, friends, and other family members, and were now down to the four. The hardest four they would have to say good-bye to. Mary's eyes started to tear up as she looked from her parents, to Joseph's parents, and to Joseph.

The two hours was the longest, most awkward time Mary could remember. She wanted everything to be normal, but it wasn't. Nothing would ever be normal again. She suddenly had the urge to crawl up on her daddy's lap, like she did she did when she was a little girl, and let him rock her to sleep on the back porch rockers.

Her thoughts were interrupted as the car came to a stop, and the silence grew thicker.

"Well, here we are," Joseph's father finally spoke up.

"Let's unload your bags." Mary's mother added to the short, hard conversation.

The six of them got out of the cramped space and started getting whatever bags they could grab. Getting into the busy door was difficult with all of the luggage and people. Mary even dropped all of her bags after the door stop caught the wheel on her suitcase and flung her backwards. When they finally got inside the crowded doors, Mary started to bawl uncontrollably.

Joshua was standing there with a big smile on his face, along with Mary and Joseph's preacher.

"After all of the work we have done with you two, you didn't think we would let you leave without seeing you off, did you?" Joshua smiled. "After all, Brother James and I set this whole thing up, right?"

The older, more serious man spoke up when Mary's tears were not ceased with Joshua's laid back humor.

"Mary. Joseph. What you are doing is a great sacrifice, and great in the eyes of God." Now the mothers started to cry. "It will not be easy, this trip

33

overseas. You will be in a war zone, in a different culture, where people might not be as accepting as they are here, and you will not be able to talk to your friends and family except through the internet. You have already accomplished so much. The people in these places need to hear the word of God. They need peace and forgiveness and are seeking it. I hope that you bring it to them."

Mary's tears stopped as the considered the big picture and the group all stopped to talk with the church men about the young couple's trip. They had arrived three hours early to the airport, leaving thirty or forty minutes for the parents and children to talk with the preachers about their mission trip.

After everyone felt some-what at peace with the decision, Joshua and Brother James said their good-byes. This time, it was Joshua who teared up. "I don't think you two know how wonderful you are," he told them.

Once they got to the metal detectors, Mary and Joseph's parents knew that they could no longer go with their children on their journey. Mary tried to be strong for her parents.

"I will email you guys every day. And we will use the web-cams we bought. I love you guys so much." She squeezed them as hard as she could.

Joseph was saying his last good-byes with his parents when they were rushed and shoved by others standing in line.

"We'll call you when we land in Georgia. Then in Italy. From there, we'll see," Joseph said before they were rudely shoved on down the line.

It was the first and only time Mary had ever seen her father cry.

Mary and Joseph took everything out of their pockets, belts off, shoes off, and anything else that would set off the detector. After being rudely shoved quicker down the line and redressing and situating themselves, the couple was handed their tickets and left alone, not sure where to go.

Mary and Joseph had both flown before, but with families that said, "Go this way," and "Sit here." Now where were they supposed to go? Who was going to tell them what to do? They had spent so much time preparing for what it would be like during their mission trip, they hadn't really thought about learning how to get around an airport.

After asking a substantial amount of people, they finally found their gate. Mary thought that arriving at the airport three hours early was crazy, but after they went through security and walked half way around the airport, their plane was already loading.

"Less time to sit and think about it," Mary thought. "Just do it."

They walked right up to the flight attendant, who tore their tickets and asked them to walk forward.

Once they got on the plane, Mary relaxed a little. Joseph gave her a sweet kiss and they started to play rock, paper, scissors, Mary's favorite time passer.

It seemed like time stopped and endless, boring airports lasted forever before the couple arrived at their final destination. Five airports and twenty-eight long hours later, Mary and Joseph were standing in Egypt.

Joseph looked at the papers in his hands. They were directions on how to contact the mission once they arrived, although he was obviously feeling the stress of responsibility and unsure ness now.

"Where do we go?" Mary asked, cautiously.

"I don't know, Mary." She didn't know if his tone was irritability or scared. Because of his sureness, his maturity, and his attitude, Mary sometimes forgot that Joseph was only twenty, the same as her. Only twenty and in a foreign country, not sure where to go or what to do.

"The instructions say 'Walk out the doors, and look for a white van, with "Christian Ministries" written on the side,' but I don't know which doors. It also says not to ask civilians directions, and to try to only have contact with people in the ministry until they tell us otherwise. Some of the people are not very welcoming to foreigners." Joseph started to panic. "Which doors, Mary?"

Mary felt like the calm one now. "Here," she said as reassuring as she could. "Let's try these to our left. Surely the people who wrote the directions knew which gate we would have come out of, right?"

Joseph looked questioningly. He shrugged, and they walked toward the doors, holding onto each other's hands almost in a death grip, as they drug their entire luggage along behind.

They walked out the door and were overwhelmed by the mobs of people, cars and buses flying by, and the stench that hovered over the area. Mary forgot that she did not live in airports, as she felt like the last day had been her entire life, and was not prepared for this.

Joseph's grip tightened even more, if possible, as people were shouting in another language and talking loudly all around them.

Someone bumped into Mary's luggage and almost knocked her off of her feet. Joseph looked around, expecting an apology, but people were everywhere. No one was concerned about them.

Finally, after twenty minutes, Mary pulled Joseph's arm with force he had never felt from her.

"Look!" she shouted at him with such glee and joy, he knew she had found the van. It was just pulling up to the loading and unloading area, and Mary and Joseph raced towards it.

The door swung open and faces, similar to theirs, appeared.

"Sorry it took so long," a young man said. "Traffic around here is unbearable. You can never get where you are going anytime soon."

A woman smiled. "Let us help you with your things, and we will head back to the house," she said nicely. Mary did not think she had ever felt safer.

"Thank you," she said, exasperated after the long trip and scary experiences.

"It can be overwhelming, but I promise, you get use to all of this. I have, after twenty-two years," she winked at Joseph.

"It's a lot different than this, back at the house," the man said. "There are twelve of us in the mission, and we are all good, Christian people. Easy to get along with. And we love the work we do for people. They are really very appreciative of their new homes, and open to the words we bring them."

After all of their baggage had been lugged into the back, Mary and Joseph seemed to slowly start to relax a little, and feel safe in the comfort of their own culture.

"It was pretty scary back there in the airport, with all of those people milling around. I was half thinking of getting back on a plane and heading back home," Mary told the group to break the ice.

Everyone smiled. "That is how we all felt our first time out," the woman said. "Don't worry; after a couple of weeks, you will forget what home is." She winked at Mary.

During the two-hour ride to their new home, Mary and Joseph learned about their new roommates, along with learning the answers to the seeming thousands of questions they had. Many of their twelve housemates were not from America, but from Europe, Italy, Australia, and Canada. Mary found it interesting to have to chance to meet and live with such a wide variety of people.

They learned more about how to communicate with the people who they would be helping, and what exactly they would be doing at the construction sites, since they had no previous carpentry skills.

"Manual labor," Mary thought. "Fun, fun."

Joseph smiled at her, as he knew what she was thinking. He, on the other hand, was excited at the prospect of learning something new.

The mission house was more like a hotel, which Mary decided was probably what the building was used for before this retched war. There were thirty rooms with bathrooms, and a kitchen and common room downstairs. And WiFi, the most important contact tool with the outside world.

Mary's laptop was the first thing out of her bag. Since there were no cell service or land lines, her only contact with the ones back home was the internet. She turned on her laptop and sent her and Joseph's parents a quick e-mail telling them that they had arrived safely and met some extremely nice people.

Then she logged into her facebook and myspace accounts to greet her friends and let everyone know that she had arrived at her destination. Before the left, Joshua had advised Mary and Joseph both to open a public networking account, as this would be another form of communication with friends and loved ones.

They created one together, and had obtained four hundred and fifty-one friends after a couple of short day on the sites. All of their family, college friends, church friends, and associates from high school apparently already knew about this new technology, and were avid users.

After updating everyone on the status of their trip, Mary closed her laptop and started to consider unpacking her other items. She was still sitting on the soft bed, staring at the unopened suitcase when Joseph looked up.

He laughed at her. "Wow, you have really made a lot of progress. Let me guess, already e-mailed the family and gotten on the silly sites to post your status?" Joseph knew her too well. Mary smiled as she considered the fact that she also knew him too well. If she played her cards right, there was a large possibility that he would do all of her unpacking.

"Yes," she yawned. "Everyone says hello, and that they love you." She kissed him on the cheek. "Can you believe we are really here? It still seems kind of surreal to me."

"I know." Joseph started unpacking Mary's things without even realizing what he was doing. "It seems like an eternity ago that we left home. I guess twenty-seven hours of traveling will do that to you." He paused. "Everyone seems really nice. What do you think so far?" His concerns were legitimate, as he wanted her to be as happy as possible.

"I think we are doing a good thing, Joe. The people will be so appreciate. And like you said, even if we only touch one person and bring them closer to God, all of this will have been worth it."

"How was I every lucky enough to find a girl like you, Mary?" Joseph looked lovingly at her.

"Same here, dear." She sweetly smiled and hugged him, as he left her clothes in a pile and they feel asleep on the bed, exhausted from the long day.

The couple soon awoke to the sun streaming into the windows, unable to believe that they had fallen asleep at six o'clock in the evening, in their clothes, and slept straight through until eight o'clock a.m. Mary suddenly realized what it meant to have jet lag.

A knock on the door soon signaled it was time to get ready to go to their job site. They drowsily started to get up, as Joseph walk to the bathroom to get ready. Chivalrously, he shut the door, keeping to their promise to each other to stay private, as to not be tempted in the ways of the world.

After he was dressed and ready, Mary waddled into the bathroom, still half asleep, to get ready. Mary had never worn make-up on a regular basis, and simply fixed her hair in a pony-tail, so she was always a quick one to get ready. Brush her teeth, change clothes, pull the hair up, out the door.

They walked downstairs and greeted everyone for breakfast. Half of them were perky morning people, like Joseph, and the other half were not yet speaking, like Mary.

When everyone was down, they held hands to give thanks for their food before eating. Mary's favorite: fruity cereal with ice cold milk.

Throughout breakfast, numerous conversations were ablaze, from politics, to philosophy, to culture and religion. Mary finally started to transform from her sleepy, groggy self to her normal, sweet self, as she always did around 8:30, and joined in the conversations.

Mary and Joseph learned that they would be traveling to a site today that was half way complete. It would take them about another two weeks to finish, and the family had opted to be part of the entire process, wanting to experience each stage of the building process.

The mission house was about twenty minutes from the job site, and all fourteen of them piled up in a cramped van to make the trip.

The weeks ran into each other as Mary and Joseph worked on various job sites, cleaning up trash, handing men boards, holding boards in place while they were nailed together, bringing men water, and so on. Mary concluded that all of their boring, monotonous work paid for itself when the owner finally got introduced to their completed abode. Words could not describe the gratitude the people felt and the joy that overcame the mission workers.

After the shock of seeing an amazing home, Mary, Joseph, and the others always offered to pray with the family and speak with them about the wonderful works of God. About half of the time, the people wanted to listen, and the other half did not.

Over a span of four months, Mary and Joseph had the privilege of witnessing eight new homes, made amazing friendships, and brought four gracious hearts to God.

They could not believe that their time in Egypt was up and they were moving on to their next destination. Their past lives seemed like a blur in history, like a story they had once heard someone else tell.

Their current living conditions and jobs seemed to overpower their memory, seeming to forget all about their young lives in America. Now, they were nomads, traveling abroad, holding boards to be nailed, and spreading God's word.

Mary was very sad on their last day in Egypt. She had made some true friends there, and was scared of the unknown in Israel. She hoped the mission there would be as wonderful as this one had been.

Mary and Joseph were not, in the least bit, frightened in this foreign airport as they had been the first time they were there. Now, this country seemed to be all that they knew, and the scary things that had overcome them four short months ago were oblivious to them now.

7

Mary and Joseph napped while they waited on their flight to take them to their next destination. They had been assured that the people in their next home would be as wonderful as the home they just left, and Joseph found himself excited for a change.

The hours ran together as the young couple boarded their plane and flew to the next location. Mary seemed to have lost track of time when they found themselves off the plane and loaded into another van, full of extremely friendly people, taking them to the mission house.

Israel proved to have almost the same experiences as Egypt, only with different faces. Mary and Joseph really enjoyed the people they met and worked with, although the work got boring after a while.

Everyone in this country was also just as appreciative of the wonderful generosity that Mary, Joseph, and the others were dishing out, and the mission workers were happy to do it.

Mary and Joe had been in Israel one month when they were suddenly in real danger for the first time since they had left America. They had been lucky to dodge the harsh military leaders in both countries so far, but that rainy spring day proved to be different.

The mission workers had left the house at 9:00 a.m., as they always did and turned east towards the house they were working on that day. No farther than a mile down the road, they were stopped by a barricade, guarded by uniformed men with guns.

Mary squeezed Joseph's hand as Lucas, the driver, rolled down the window. They had apparently put the barricade in place over night, in attempt to control the area.

"Identification, please," the uniformed man said in a thick accent, with no expression. Their work was not appreciated by everyone in the country, and Mary started to worry about what these military leaders would do to them.

"What is your purpose here?" the soldier asked after studying the ID very carefully.

"We are doing mission work about four miles from here. Rebuilding houses and helping the people," Lucas said sweetly.

"You need to stay in your own country," the man said. "You are not needed here."

Lucas's eyes got a little wide when the barrel of the man's gun was shoved into his chest.

"I do not like you people being here, bringing your silly God to my people. They do not need to hear your nonsense." With that, he jabbed the end of the gun into Lucas's nose, instantly producing a steady flow of blood.

"Get out of here before someone seriously gets hurt. But be warned, I am the least of your worries. My brothers will do much more damage that me." Mary could barely understand what he said through his broken accent and poor English, but the gun spoke loudly enough to her.

They quickly drove away towards their job site, and pulled over when they were out of sight of the soldiers. Mary surveyed Lucas's injury and decided that he needed stitches. The soldier had shoved the end of the gun so hard on his nose that it caused it to separate from his face.

Blood was pouring out of the wound faster than Mary and the others could clot it. They decided to go the long way back to the mission house and lay low for the day, seeking the needed medical attention for Lucas.

It was about twelve miles to get back to the mission house, with the route they decided to take. Mary kept casting worried glances in Joseph's direction, but he continued to smile at her, to keep her from worrying.

Once they arrived back at the house, the older woman of the house called the appropriate doctor and began to bandage Lucas's nose best she could.

Joseph had a feeling Mary would want to talk about their recent danger in private, so he followed her into their room when she went.

"I don't think I have ever been that scared, Joe." She was almost crying. "Sometimes I forget we are not in a safe place, and anything could happen to us. Do you realize that soldier could have injured him more, even killed all of us, and no one would even care?"

Mary really was crying now, worried for their safety. Joseph hugged his wonderful girlfriend and kissed her on the forehead. "I know, sweetie. I am just glad we are safe for now." He was about to pull her body down on the bed with him and cradle her in his arms when Mary suddenly had a confused look on her face.

She ran into the bathroom just in time for her vomit to hit the inside of the toilet. Worried, Joseph followed her and held her long hair while she threw-up.

"What is wrong, babe?" Joseph was really worried, and it showed on his face.

When Mary had finished emptying the contents of her stomach into the commode, she looked at Joseph.

"I don't know." She looked confused. "That was the weirdest thing. I don't feel bad or anything...I just all of a sudden had an overwhelming urge to throw up."

"Huh," Joseph said. "That is weird. It is probably just your nerves. You know how worried you get about things, and what just happened to us could have definitely triggered that."

"Yeah, I guess so," Mary agreed. Since she did not feel sick anymore, they both laid down on top of the covers in the comfort of their safety net.

About ten minutes later, Mary ran to the bathroom again. Joseph started to get concerned for her health then. She could have picked up any disease that her body was not immune to.

"When Doc gets here to stitch up Lucas, I am going to have him check you out," Joseph told her when she was finished vomiting in the bathroom.

"No, I'm fine. Really. Probably just something I ate." Mary hated to have people fuss over her, especially doctors.

"I'm not going to argue about this with you, Mary. Sometimes you forget all of the diseases and uncooked food that run rampid over in this part of the world. I just want to make sure nothing is seriously wrong. Better safe than sorry." At the protesting look of his girlfriend, Joseph added, "Don't make me call your parents." That shut Mary up for the time being, and as if on cue, they heard the downstairs door open and a loud, thick accent, signaling the doctor had just arrived.

Mary and Joseph met the doctor last week, when he came to their job site to fix another mission workers arm that accidentally drove a nail gun through it. He was a dark skinned man of very small stature, about four foot ten. His English was so broken and his accent so thick, one had to strain to hear what he was trying to say.

Despite the language barrier, the local doctor and the mission workers hit it off instantly, due to the professional's hilarious sense of humor. He stayed around the job site the previous week, talking and laughing with the Christians.

Joseph left Mary upstairs on the bed while he went to check on Lucas and talk to the doctor about Mary.

Lucas had to get nine stitches in his nose to connect if back to the rest of his face. He didn't even flinch when the doctor stuck the needle in his flesh and weaved it through his skin. Joseph hoped he was as strong as Lucas was.

"You be lucky," the doctor said, serious and worried. "My people no nice. They hurt people different."

"This 'different' person is going to need a lot more than a few stitches to kick me outta here," Lucas joked.

After giving him the proper follow-up care, the doctor was gathering his things when he got pulled to the side. Joseph did not want to worry the others, and tried to keep the matter of Mary between the two of them. The rest of the mission workers were busy checking out Lucas's new addition to his nose, so Joseph considered this his opportune time to approach him.

"Hey, Doc," he said in a low tone. "Do you mind coming upstairs to check out Mary? She just started getting sick when we got home, and I'm kind of worried about her. She says she doesn't feel bad, but I want you to check her out if you have the time."

The doctor's face became worried. "Oh no," he said shaking his head.

"What?" Joseph almost shouted in anticipation of what he would say.

"She may be turn into fish," he said, making a fishy face with his mouth, and then bursting into his funny laughter.

Joseph tried to laugh, but did not consider what he said funny, for he was really concerned about Mary.

After the petite man walked up the stairs, he finally got to Mary and Joseph's bedroom. He performed his normal checkup procedures on her, and when he found them inconclusive, he asked if he could take a blood sample.

"Derinphia starting to be in country. Make you very sick. Maybe what have you. Only in blood can I find. If have, I can fix. But if no fix, maybe die." At the look of Mary and Joseph's worried faces, he added, "No die if I treat. Even if I no treat, no die for years. Not to worry. I give test scores tomorrow after lab give me."

He told Mary to rest until they found out for sure if she had this rare disease.

"Great," she told Joseph. "One more thing to worry about."

"It will all be OK," he told her as he kissed her forehead. "Let's just take a nap for a while and take it easy today."

The next twenty-four hours seemed to drag on into the endless circle of time that was surrounding Mary as she lay around in bed and played on the internet. Ignoring Mary's pleas to stay with her, Joseph had gone with the rest of the crew to their job site. He insisted that they would drive the back roads and be safe.

Mary did not want to lay around by herself all day, but she also did not want to bring Joseph into her day of boredom, so she finally gave him her blessing to leave her alone.

She slept in while Joseph got dressed and explained to the other workers that she was sick and would be staying in bed today. He then assured her that he would be home in time to talk to the doctor about her illness.

Just as Mary was drifting back off to sleep, around 9:00 a.m., she felt it again. She knew she was going to be sick, and ran to the bathroom to catch the bodily fluid. She could not understand why she kept throwing up, but did not feel sick. She had unfortunately caught the flu eight times in her life, and remembered the intense pain and weak feeling that overcame her body. But this time, she did not feel weak or sick at all. Maybe she did have this odd disease Doc had told her about. Either way, she did not want to worry about it, and tried to take her mind off of the issue.

Mary passed the hours by catching up on her e-mails that hadn't been checked in two days, getting on her networking websites, and reading news stories. She looked at two hundred of their friend's pages, checking on their new statuses and photos on facebook and myspace.

Although Mary was not raised with a television and did not rely on cable shows to fulfill her life, she did enjoy a good movie every once in a while, and decided to go downstairs and rummage through the movies.

After selecting a good love story from the 90's, she settled into the couch to watch it, realizing that this was the first time since they came on the mission trip that she was completely alone.

It was rather nice to simply sit on the couch and watch the sappy story line with no one to worry about but herself.

After lunch, Mary felt sick again. "Well," she thought, trying to look on the bright side, "Maybe I will lose some weight, seeing how I can't keep anything down." She smiled to herself at the thought, knowing that her body was the perfect size and did not need to be slimmed down.

Finally, after a long and tiring day, Joseph arrived home early just like he promised he would. He had driven one of the mission worker's cars so that he could come home early in anticipation of the doctor's phone call. He was supposed to phone the mission house at 3:00 p.m. to give the couple the results of the blood test.

"Are you relaxed?" he asked as he walked in the door and spotted her on the couch. He went and grabbed a sandwich from the kitchen and plopped down on the furniture beside her.

"Bored, actually." Mary looked up at him with a weary look. "This is going to sound weird, but I think I am actually more tired today, from just sitting around, than I am after working on the houses."

"Yeah, I have always been that way. I hate sitting around with nothing to do. It wears me out," Joseph said. Then he cut his eyes at her in a playful look. "You are not tired from worrying all day about this test result, are you? We made a deal, Mary."

"I know, I know. I've tried to not even think about it." She tried to please him with her answer.

Joseph relayed the morning at the job site to Mary and filled her in on the events that she missed. He also assured her that no soldiers had stopped them, and no locals had seen them.

By the time they looked at the clock again, it was three-thirty and Mary cast a scared look at Joseph.

"Babe, you've met that doctor. He is goofy. He probably just forgot or lost track of time. Don't assume that just because he hasn't called yet, something is wrong." How did he know her so well? How could one person know what another was thinking? Did he know her that well, or was she just that predictable?

As if on cue, there was a knock on the door. Since the other workers would not be back until after five and there were no mumbled conversations to mask other sounds, the knock could be heard loud and clear.

Mary threw Joseph a look. She did not have a good feeling.

"Hello, hello," the doctor said in his weird way when Joseph opened the door.

"Hey. How's it going?" Joseph tried to lighten the mood.

"I good.I great.How you?" He asked both of them.

"I would be better if I knew what was wrong with me." Mary had never been ruder in her life. For some unexplainable reason, she seemed a little more moody and on edge than usual.

"I know I say I call, but I come instead." The small doctor smiled wide and large.

"I tink you be happy with me news. No derinphia. No derinphia at all."

Mary and Joseph both had a wave of relief wash over them.

"So what is wrong with her? Just a stomach bug?" Joseph asked.

"You no know?" He started laughing and smiling and his little body hunched over his shoulders, leaning forward to pat Joseph on the back.

"You have baby." He thought the news would be accepted gladly, as recreation is in his country.

Mary laughed out loud for a long time. Joseph also smiled at the joke, but was ready to hear the real news.

"Doc, seriously, what is wrong with her?"

The old doctor stopped smiling and took a serious tone. "No joke. Blood test no lie. Mary pregnant. If no believe me, go another doctor. You be happy. Babies good." He seemed a little hurt that they did not believe him.

"But doctor, it is absolutely impossible for me to be pregnant. I have never had sex," Mary told him precisely.

"Maybe in you sleep. Because you have baby in belly."

Joseph, who had been taking it all in, stopped and looked him in the eye. "Doctor, this is seriously no joke? You really believe that Mary is pregnant, even though she is not sexually active and could not have possibly conceived a baby?"

"I no know Mary sex life. Only know what test say. I give you number for different doctors in town. Go there and they tell you same thing." With that, the doctor wrote down the addresses of several clinics he recommended and left.

Mary and Joseph looked at each other when he left and laughed at the doctor's stupidity.

"Can you believe he really thought that?" Joseph laughed. "Maybe he is not as respectable as our crew thought. Come on, let's go check out some of these clinics and find someone to tell us what is actually wrong with you."

"Oh, Joseph…it is probably just a stomach bug. I'd rather just stay here. I 'm sure it will get better in a couple of days," Mary protested.

"Mary, we are in a different country and I'm not risking anything. I promised your parents I would watch out for you and I intend to keep my word."

Knowing that there was no use arguing, she followed him to the car they had borrowed and rode along to the first clinic.

The first clinic ran a series of tests on Mary and gave them the same results Doc had. Stunned, and wondering what was wrong with this country's medical professionals, they traveled to the next clinic.

Four different clinics from four o'clock until seven thirty told them the same thing, over and over. Mary felt like she was in a dream or floating through someone else's life whom she did not know.

8

What was wrong with these people? Didn't they know that Joseph and her had taken a vow to each other and God and would never break than vow? Didn't they know that Joseph was such a strong willed young man that he kept a layer of covers between Mary and himself when he slept, and still kept much privacy between them? Didn't they know that there was no possible way Mary could be pregnant?

Joseph was silent on the way home, and when Mary tried to speak to him, she could tell his mind was troubled.

The silent car ride seemed to take an eternity, and finally they arrived back at the mission house.

Before they got out of the car, Joseph finally spoke up.

"How could you do it?" he bared his teeth and clenched his fists. "We took a vow to each other, Mary. Was I not good enough for you? I am not worth waiting for? Who was it? Who did you have sex with?" He was screaming at the top of his lungs now, an uncontrollable anger rising up in his face.

"You made a promise to me. To God! Do you have any idea how I feel? And to think you sat there and acted like was impossible! You knew the whole time that you were pregnant! Who was it, Mary? Did you like it?"

She was bawling and he was screaming.

"I guess kissing isn't enough for you! I thought I knew you better than this! I don't even know who you are. You might as well be one of the whores we went to high school with."

Joseph did not even give Mary a chance to speak before he slammed the door so hard it broke from one of the hinges and started walking in circles outside the car.

Mary did not know how to react. They had never even fought, much less yelled at one another. She was hurt deeper than imaginable and felt her heart tear apart and her body go numb. She suddenly felt like she might pass out, and her face flushed as white as a sheet.

She stumbled out of the passenger side door and walked towards her pacing boyfriend.

"How dare you?" she asked, barely able to speak as the emotions overwhelmed her.

"You know me better than that. How dare you call me those things and treat me that way. After everything we have experienced and been through together. How dare you call me a whore?" She was bawling and her anger showed through her tears.

Joseph stopped and let the entirety of the information sink in. He did know her better than that. He knew, in the bottom of his heart, that she had not broken their promise and that she would never do anything he had accused her of. He had been with her every waking moment for the past five months, and there had never been a time when she was alone or with another male.

"How do you explain it then?" he asked her, still not sure whether he was ready to apologize.

"Do you think I have multiple personality disorder, like that female doctor suggested? Maybe I am me most of the time, but sometimes during my sleep I am someone else and I have sex?" Mary started bawling at the thought.

"No, Mary. I would know if that were the case. Look, I know you have not done anything wrong, and I am really sorry for lashing out at you. I just don't understand what is going on and I'm mad at the situation." He looked at her and pulled her into his chest. "Not at you." He kissed her on the forehead while his troubled eyes were deep with distress.

"Please forgive me," Joseph whispered into Mary's ear while he caressed her head and hugged her as tight as he could.

"Look, Joseph, these doctors are not like the doctors back home. It is not humanly possible for me to be pregnant. There is some freak thing that I have caught, and all of the tests here are picking it up as the pregnancy hormone. That is the only reasonable explanation for all this." Her voice of reason made sense to him.

"We should go get some sleep tonight, and tomorrow we will make plans to go home. We shouldn't be here while we deal with this. We will go home and find out what is really wrong with you," Joseph said.

He hugged her for a long time before he started to cry, something Mary had never seen him do. She pulled away from him and gave him a puzzled look.

He could barely speak through his hard, thick sobs. "I...I can't believe I said those things to you. I...am...so...sorry." He could not catch his breath, and Mary instantly forgave him.

"Joseph, you were just mad. It's OK," she tried to comfort him.

"It's not OK. It's never OK for me to talk to you like that. I just don't understand," he sobbed.

The couple tried to compose themselves before they went in and faced their colleagues. They had agreed to tell everyone that they had gone to eat at the local restaurant, and after talking with their parents tomorrow, they would decide how to tell everyone they were leaving for good.

Exhausted from confusing and strong emotions, Mary and Joseph went straight upstairs and went to bed. That night, Joseph allowed them to sleep under the same level of covers, allowing their bodies to touch while they slept. Not in a physical aspect, but so that Joseph could hold Mary all night and protect her in his arms.

Mary and Joseph both reached their REM level of sleep at the same time, and began tossing and turning as they dreamt. Mary did not usually dream, and Joseph rarely remembered his dreams, but this was unlike any dream they had ever experienced.

Mary fluttered her eyes, rolled over, and kicked her legs as her dream began to act out in her mind. Most dreams are pieced together with no sequence or relevance to the previous scene, but this dream was so real, so alive, that Mary did not know if she was asleep or in another realm.

Everything was white and Mary was as wide-awake as she could be. Someone was walking toward her, with a light reflecting off of his clothing. He wore a white T-shirt and blue jeans and had dark brown hair.

"Hey," he said in his dreaming, but ever-so-real, voice. "I'm Gabriel."

Mary looked around inside her head, as her physical body turned over, obviously connecting with the dream. "Um...Hi."

Gabriel grabbed a stool from nowhere and sat down, as Mary was apparently already seated.

"Here's the deal, Mary." She noted how normal and easy to talk to he seemed. "All of these doctors are telling you that you are pregnant, right?"

In shock, Mary nodded to the young man and wondered if she was really still asleep or if she was talking to someone in another one of the other personalities that she apparently had.

"Mary, there is no need to go home." He smiled at her. "You in fact are pregnant. You have been chosen by God to carry his son into your world."

Mary laughed in her dream-laugh and looked him in the eyes. "Ok, dream boy. This is really weird and I'm just trying to wake my body up so that you will quit freaking me out. I am not pregnant, and if God wanted to choose a person to carry his son, there are plenty of other women who are better than me, so tell them to do it."

Gabriel laughed. "Oh, Mary, you are so modest. There is no one better than you. You have been chosen to deliver God's son. You will not understand until it is finished, but he will deliver you and the world around you.

"You are to have this baby, with Joseph by your side, and name him Jesus. You do not need to go home, for God has a plan for you. You need to stay here and finish your mission work. Do not worry of the things that will happen to you, for you will be rewarded in the eyes of God. You will be mocked and humiliated, for people will not understand God's plan. Do not worry. Be content with yourself, Joseph, and your baby and do not worry about other people. Your own family might even forsake you, but do not worry. You have found favor in the eyes of God and will be rewarded soon." With that, Gabriel got up and walked away.

Mary sat straight up in bed, shaking from the intense dream she just had, trying to decipher between reality and the dream world. The clock read 2:37 a.m. and she noticed Joseph shaking violently beside her.

Before she had a chance to wake him up, he jerked up the same way she had, pouring sweat down his forehead and gasping for air. After a solid two minutes, Joseph, ever so slowly, turned his head to look at Mary.

He looked scared to death, and as he looked at Mary, he realized that the dream had not been a dream.

Without saying a word, she started nodding her head, somehow knowing that Joseph had experienced the same phenomenon.

"Why us?" Mary asked.

With new, unexplainable understanding and excepting of their situation, Mary and Joseph lay in the silence and tried to understand what was going to happen to them over the course of not only the next nine months, but their entire lives.

"How can one dream make us both understand what is going on? And how did I somehow know you had the same dream? And how are we going to explain this to our family and friends? No one will ever believe us. God doesn't perform miracles like this anymore. What are we supposed to do?" Mary's concern was evident, and although Joseph had the same worries, he tried to stay positive for Mary and follow the instructions in their weird dreams.

"I don't know. I guess we just have to tell people the truth and expect them to believe us. If they don't, we can't worry about it. We know the truth and I guess we have to be happy with that," he said with conviction.

Mary started to cry. "What are my parents going to say?" she suddenly started to hyperventilate at the thought of telling her parents that she was pregnant.

Joseph stroked her back and pulled her close. "I don't know, Mary. I am so confused. Like you said, God doesn't perform miracles like this anymore. This is 2011." Joseph paused and looked at his lovely girlfriend and promised wife.

"I think he was some sort of angel, Mary. I always pictured angles wearing long robes, with halos and white light surrounding their bodies. And flying. But he looked just like any old guy. White T-shirt and jeans. No flying, shining light, or halo. Weird." He was half way talking to himself, when his thoughts were interrupted by Mary.

"I don't know, Joseph. I just have this unexplainable feeling that everything is going to be OK and that we shouldn't worry about it."

"Yeah, me too," her boyfriend responded. "I guess we did vow to give our lives to God. I just didn't expect something like this to happen." He stopped and looked her in the eyes. "Whatever happens, you know I'll never leave you or treat you like I did last night. I love you, Mary."

Mary smiled. "I love you too."

Mary perked up. "Maybe coming on this trip was a blessing in disguise. We wouldn't even have to tell anyone that I am pregnant so that they cannot judge us. We could just stay over here a little while longer and then, when we go home with a baby, tell our friends and family that someone abandoned it and we took it in." Her eyes lit up with possibility.

"That would be wonderful," Joseph said. He got quieter. "But I'm afraid that is not what God intended when he planned this path for us. Somehow, I feel like we are supposed to be martyrs and tell everyone what has happened to us. Don't ask me how I know this, I just fell it deep down." He sighed. "But we definitely don't have to tell anyone until it is more definite and certain. We will just keep on living our normal lives until this pregnancy begins to sink further in and become reality. Until then, we act like nothing else changed." He looked at her for agreement. "OK?"

Mary sighed. "Yeah, OK."

Mary could not believe what was happening, and how she and Joseph both seemed to understand it and accept it. Shouldn't she be mad? Shouldn't she hesitate about sacrificing her life and everything that she had planned for it? She could not explain it, but somehow she knew that doing God's will would be better than anything plan she could ever make for herself.

9

Five months later, when Mary and Joseph had finished their jobs in Israel and had moved on to the mission house in Jerusalem, the twenty-one years old's ever growing belly made evident the fact that they could not hide the pregnancy any longer.

They had not told any of their co-workers in Israel, and decided to wait until absolutely necessary to tell their friends and family. But with Mary's five-month-old child growing inside her, they could no longer hide her big stomach with baggy T-shirts and loose fitting jeans.

Even though they had secretly been going to a doctor once a month for pre-natal care, Mary and Joseph both hoped and prayed that they were doing enough to nurture its growth. Neither one of them had ever known much about pregnancy or childbirth; they never thought they would have to experience it first hand, at least not for ten years or so.

The night before they decided to tell their friends and family the news, Mary broke down.

"What's wrong?" Joseph's concern was evident in his face. The procreation had caused Mary to be sick quite regularly during the past five months, and Joseph worried about her and the baby boy each time.

"Joe," she said through her tears. "I just can't believe this is all real. But more than that, I can't believe that you have stayed with me and supported me through all of this. I didn't ask or want this to happen to us, but it did. I am just now excepting the fact that this is the path God chose for us, but I just can't understand how you have been so patient and nice about it." She paused and looked at him in awe. "Do you have any idea how amazing you are? Most guys don't even hang around pregnant girls when they are the father of her baby, but you have been by my side through everything. How are you such a good person?" She was crying now.

"Mary," he said, stroking her hair and kissing her forehead. "I can't explain it. I just know that this is what God has planned and that he will take care of us. You underestimate yourself; you are an amazing person yourself, you know?"

They both held each other and cried in preparation of the heartache soon to come. The heartache that they knew would accompany their sharing of the news.

They decided to first call their parents, then their co-mission workers, and finally post if on their facebook and myspace accounts. There was no better way of spreading news than on the internet social networking sites.

Mary's hands were shaking and her tears would not stop as Joseph picked up the phone. He was such a just and honest man; he had agreed to make the calls. He knew his girlfriend could not bear to do it.

Mary sat on the floor, curled up in a ball, rocking herself and covering her ears to stop the screaming that she could hear on the other end of the line. She hummed to herself to drown out the hate.

"WHAT?" her father shouted, obviously crying. "SHE IS PREGNANT?! I TOLD YOU THIS WAS A HORRIBLE IDEA. YOU TOOK HER OVER THERE, IN OTHER COUNTRY, AWAY FROM HER PARENTS AND MORALS AND VALUES, AND FORCED HER TO HAVE SEX WITH YOU!"

Joseph had prepared himself for the complete blame and anger that he knew would be placed solely on him. He stayed calm and tried to explain how this situation arose, and about the dreams that had both had and the indescribable feeling deep down that he believed what was happening.

"HOW DARE YOU, JOSEPH?" Mary's father was still screaming at the top of his lungs, obviously trying to hold back sobs. "HOW DARE YOU BLAME YOUR MISTAKES ON GOD? BE A MAN AND TAKE RESPONSIBILITY FOR YOUR ACTIONS! I CANNOT BELIEVE I EVER LET HER GO WITH YOU TO THAT GOD FORSAKEN COUNTRY. I CAN'T BELIEVE I EVER TRUSTED YOU WITH HER WELL-BEING. WE THOUGHT WE KNEW YOU, JOSEPH. I FEEL SO BETRAYED RIGHT NOW. HOW COULD YOU?!" He was ranting and raving beyond control, and Joseph sensed that his face was probably beet red and the veins on his neck were probably protruding like a snake on the riverbanks.

Mary's mother obviously jerked the phone out of his hands, because she cut in abruptly.

"Joseph," her voice was calm, but saddened. "Why did you not tell us before now? I can't imagine my baby in another country, five months pregnant, with no one to help her or tell her what to do." She started bawling uncontrollable, seeming to be more concerned about Mary's needs than the situation at hand.

"Joseph, you need to come home this instant," she said after she composed herself. "I am going to call the airline and get you guys a ticket home as soon as we hang up. My daughter will not suffer any longer. You bring her home now." Her passive attitude suddenly turned authoritative, and Joseph almost gave in.

"I'm sorry, we can't," he said with despair. "It is God's plan for us to stay here and have this baby. I can't describe it; we both just know and feel that this is what God wants."

This conversation and argument went on for forty-five minutes, with Mary's father screaming, Mary's mother crying and trying to convince them to come home, Joseph crying and telling them that they could not, and Mary, still in the fetal position, rocking herself and humming songs to silence the noise and yelling.

In the end, Mary's mother told Joseph that if they did not come home instantly, they would not be welcome there ever again. Mary's father was still screaming at him in the background to take responsibility for his own actions.

The phone call to Joseph's parents played out about the same as the last. The young couple could not bear hurting their parents, but they tried to make them believe and understand. Joseph's father even told him that he would believe that Mary had conceived this child by God when he saw the Easter Bunny hopping down Main Street.

An hour and a half later, Mary and Joseph had both had enough. They knew this would be hard and no one would believe them, but this shunning by their parents, their loving caretakers for eighteen years, was too much to take.

They cried and prayed and held each other. Suddenly they drifted off into a deep sleep and when they awoke, they both had a calming sense about them, and the strength to share the news to more people.

Since the couple had stayed at the mission house that day, they would have to wait until everyone else got back at 5:00 or so to tell them. Mary got out her laptop and gave Joseph a look of acceptance.

Once on the networking website of facebook, Mary knew the hate and mockery that would receive. She and Joseph were strong, though, and they were ready to face it.

On her status she wrote this quote:

"As most of you know, Joseph and I have been traveling the world doing mission work for a while now. We are staying longer than expected, and we have news to share with our closest friends and family members. I will be having a baby in four short months! I know everyone is probably thinking that Joseph and I conceived the baby together, but we did not. We took a vow to one another and to God that we would never break. This is going to sound extremely weird, and I know that most of you won't be able to fathom it, but God placed this baby in my womb for me to give birth to.

"I don't exactly know the plan for this baby, but I do know that God is sending him to save us from our sins. God loves us and wants us to be happy, rejoicing in his name. You are more than welcome to comment on this post or tell others the news. God bless!"

Mary waited for Joseph to read the words and nod his head before clicking, "Post." She copied and pasted the words and posted them on their other networking accounts, myspace and twitter.

After submitting to all three sites, Mary and Joseph closed the computer down, just as they had promised each other. They were not ready to see what everyone was going to say, not just yet. They would wait a couple of weeks, and then go onto the sites and answer any questions that people have asked. They were prepared for the horrible things that would be said of them. Everyone they knew, along with people they didn't know, were their friends on the sites, and avid, daily users of them. They knew everyone would see the post within twenty-four hours and formulate an opinion about it.

Mary and Joseph both felt calm and happy about their decision to share their joy with the rest of the world. For the next couple of weeks, they would continue working and enjoying the company of their Christian roommates.

Two weeks to the day, Mary and Joseph prayed before logging back into their websites. They had not communicated with either of their parents since the phone calls, and hoped they might also have some e-mails from them. After seeing no e-mails from parents or family in their inboxes, they sadly moved on to the websites.

On facebook alone, there were two thousand, four hundred and eighty-two comments to their post, and twelve hundred and twelve on myspace. Twitter hit the jackpot with three thousand, nine hundred, and fourteen comments.

Mary almost laughed when she saw the numbers. They didn't even know a tenth of that number of people, and she wondered who was that concerned with people's lives whom they did not even know.

Out of all of those posts, only twenty-three were positive and nice. The rest were hateful and crude, saying things like, "How dare you blame another young pregnancy on God?" and "Just admit that you had sex!" and "You two are an abomination to God!"

The twenty-three positive ones were from Joshua, their old minister, and their cousins, aunts, and uncles. Positive did not mean they believed what had happened, but they were supportive of Mary and Joseph's baby.

They read through all of the posts without a tear. They had braced themselves for the hateful words, and asked God to help them get through them. Mary and Joseph found new peace in the fact that they knew the truth, and knew that they were doing God's will, and nothing else really mattered.

Only one thing hurt the young couple more than words ever could. And that was the absence of a relationship between their parents. They could not believe that they had unintentionally hurt them, and wanted to make things right. But both parents had stopped answering the phones and e-mails. The young couple was devastated and prayed that God would open their hearts.

10

Twelve weeks later, Mary and Joseph were lying in bed when they suddenly felt the building shake and heard a piercing sound resonating through the walls. Joseph jumped out of bed and rushed to the window.

"What is it?" Mary's scared voice shook with fear.

The area hadn't been bombed in weeks, and Mary and Joseph almost forgot they were in a war zone. But as the anger between the countries intensified, so did the acts of violence.

"Mary!" Joseph shouted. "Get down to the basement and get with the other women in the house. There are bombs exploding everywhere and fires are blazing!" Joseph was terrified, and Mary could hear it in his voice.

Mary and her huge belly waddled down the hall in obedience and gathered the other women in the mission. All five of them hunkered down and tried to listen for the bombs to stop.

Joseph and the other men were outside, trying to help burning people and ones who were crushed from falling debris. Unlike their other houses, this mission home was in the center of town, an old hospital, and they were lucky to be close enough to help the citizens of Jerusalem.

It was forty minutes before the horrid bombing stopped and the cries of the innocent stopped ringing out in fear. Joseph and the other men had been lucky enough to steer clear of falling debris and fires, and were steadily helping people get to the hospitals in town.

Mary and the other women came out of the basement once the loud booms stopped and started helping whoever they could. Five hours later, the first glimmer of sunlight broke through the sky and everyone could survey the whole damage that had occurred.

The mission workers finally decided to go inside and get some rest, as they had helped all of the people they could.

Mary tried to lie down, but as soon as she did, she screamed.

"What?" Joseph asked, concern all over his face.

She stood up and tried to walk to the bathroom, but her water broke and seeped all over her legs and the floor. She panicked and Joseph stared in disbelief. He thought that maybe God would just take the baby out and they would not have to go through the grotesque scenes he had watched in reproduction class.

"Crap!" Joseph yelled, as he started getting Mary's things together to go to the hospital.

Running ahead down the stairs and outside the door, Joseph asked a roommate if he could borrow the car. When he told him yes, he asked if they wanted any help getting to the hospital.

"No," Joseph said. "I just need to get her there NOW!"

Joseph loaded the car and went back up to help Mary. After a seeming eternity, they got in and backed out of the driveway.

Now that the sun was in full view, they surveyed the damage and Joseph started to hyperventilate.

"How are we supposed to get through this rubble?" he shouted.

"Just find open roads and GET THERE!" Mary screamed as she felt a contraction coming on.

There were rocks and brick and trash covering the roads from the horrible bombings the night before. What looked like a city only yesterday now looked like piles of concrete.

Joseph swerved around and through rubble and finally made it to the hospital that they had been to many times for Mary's pre-natal checkups. From the looks of the outside of the hospital, the inside was packed. Joseph told his pregnant girlfriend to wait in the car while he ran in.

A stressed nurse told him that every room, nook, and cranny that they had was full, and they would have to go to the clinic down the road.

Joseph screamed in frustration and raced back to the car. Mary was crying and screaming in agony, and Joseph just wanted to make her pain stop.

He drove like a professional race car driver through torn and broken houses and buildings and finally made it to the clinic, which was also covered with bloody and injured people. Joseph was told the same thing at the clinic, and at three other medical facilities.

By this time, Joseph knew something had to be done, because Mary's screams were coming faster and closer together.

"Mary," he looked at her, scared to death. "There is no room in the hospitals. What do we do?"

"JUST PULL OVER SOMEWHERE! I HAVE TO GET OUT OF THIS CAR!" she could barely speak through the blinding pain.

Joseph was already on the outskirts of town, as they wondered through the civilized areas looking for medical attention. They were stopped at a place with worn-down barn. Joseph decided the owner's house must be somewhere else, because all that was there was a field, a fence, and a barn.

Joseph looked disgusted and horrified. "I don't know where else to go," he cried.

"Just get me out! Let me lay DOWN!" Mary shouted.

Joseph got her out of the car, figuring there had to be some hay or something in the barn to create a make-shift bed for Mary to lie on and be more comfortable.

He steered her into the broken and rusted door and looked around inside. There was a pile of hay on the far side of the barn and some small animals roaming around. He could not believe that Mary was going to deliver a baby here, in this filthy place.

Joseph's thoughts were interrupted with another scream, louder this time. She had never been in pain like this, and Joseph was worried sick about her. He had no idea what to do or how to comfort her. Joseph had never seen a woman in labor, and was panic stricken with fear, as he felt helpless for Mary.

He laid his girlfriend down on the pile of moldy hay and tried to make her as comfortable as he could. She was really screaming now, and he wished he had paid more attention to what the doctors had told them what to do to prepare for the birth.

At the time, Joseph still thought that God would take the baby out without Mary having to go through any of this, so he had not been very concerned with listening. Now, as he sat beside his screaming girlfriend, in a barn with no sanitation, he was terrified.

"What do you what me to do?" He was mortified just by looking at all of the pain Mary was obviously in. "Why did this have to happen to us?" he screamed loudly in anger.

In between screams of agony, Mary was suddenly very calm. "Because we were chosen by God," she responded to his question. "Don't look at this as a negative thing just because I am in a lot of pain, Joe. Everything is going to be OK. I have a feeling that for some reason, this is God's plan. He wouldn't have allowed me to go into labor when that bomb hit and all of the hospitals were full unless he had a plan. He is going to take care of us." She smiled up at him and Joseph was overcome with her faith and trust in God. He started bawling as her face began to slowly turn back to a painful look.

After about four hours of the same, continuous contractions, Mary passed out from the pain. Joseph began to panic and scream as he cried and held Mary. She was starting to shake as he realized she was having the baby. She slipped in and out of consciousness for a minute, and then was acutely aware of what was happening.

Once the little boy started to enter the world, the rest of Mary's labor one took three minutes. Joseph was screaming, and Mary was screaming, but they both were suddenly silent when they heard a baby screaming.

It had taken five long hours of excruciating pain, with no medicine or attention from doctors. Mary could not believe what had just happened, and the whole situation seemed surreal to her.

She looked up at Joseph with a horrified, scared look before blacking out from excruciating pain once again. Joseph was bawling, not sure what to do as he held this little baby boy, who was still soaked in slimy afterbirth and blood. Joseph was overtaken by a stiffening earthy smell, as the iron, blood, and placenta aroma filled the barn.

The little bundle was screaming and Joseph had no idea what to do. He tried to wake Mary, but the pain she had still had a hold on her. After a seeming eternity, Mary started coughing, as she was choking on the blood that had seeped down her huge belly, over her chest, and into her open mouth. She threw up, and then cleared her throat.

"Now what?" she asked Joseph in a tired and exasperated voice.

Joseph shook his head. "I don't know," he cried.

Mary got up and took the newborn boy, who was still crying hysterically.

She spotted an old blanket in the corner of a horse stall, and flung out the dirt and dung best she could. She wrapped the baby in it so that he would not be cold, and instantly took on motherhood as she sacrificed her own feelings and needs to care for her baby.

"We need to see a doctor," Joseph told her as he wiped the blood and afterbirth off of both her and the baby best he could, with his own shirt he had taken off his back.

"We are alright right now." Mary spoke so weakly he could barely hear her. Out of pure instinct, she began to let the baby drink his first drop of milk. It was uncomfortable, and she had not known what to expect, but she knew she must feed her baby.

"Joe," Mary said through exhaustion. "Let's pray together as a family."

Joseph nodded, thankful for Mary's calmness and faith. "Father, we thank you for this unexpected miracle. We ask that you guide us to do your will with this baby, as we know you gave it to Mary for a reason. We try not to question you, Lord, and trust that you are doing what is best. Please keep Mary and the baby safe, as we have no access to doctors or medicine. Please forgive us where we fail you, and lead us on the path to righteousness. In Your name we pray, Amen."

Joseph kissed Mary on the forehead when they heard a knock on the outside of the barn. Stricken with panic, Joseph scrambled to get up from the bed of hay. Not knowing what kind of trouble they would be in for hiding out in someone else's property, he cautiously walked towards the east end of the barn, the source of the knocking.

Joseph pulled the stable gate open to see three men standing outside, with gentle expressions on their faces. They all seemed to be in their late sixties and early seventies, and wore slacks with starched shirts.

When Joseph did not speak, one of the men offered an explanation.

"Young man, we are here in rather odd circumstances. We are elders of the local church, and we all three had the same dream and uncontrollable feeling to come here and see a miracle. God has told each of us, through our dreams and subconscious, that he has sent a little baby here to save us all. This might sound odd, and I hope we are not intruding, but is there such a miracle here?" The old man was so gentle and kind, Joseph was glad to be in his calming presence.

Suddenly, Joseph started to cry. Not tears of fear or sadness like before, but tears of joy. He knew that God would take care of them, and He had sent these men to verify this miracle. He still could not understand it, nor would he ever in his lifetime. But his trust and faith was all that mattered, and led him to do whatever God asked.

"I can't explain this," Joseph told the men. "My girlfriend just had a baby, and she was and still is a virgin. No one believes us, expect maybe you." He looked at the three men funny, still not sure if this was all a dream or reality.

"Please come in the barn and see this baby, whose name is Jesus."

The men followed Joseph into the barn, and now the mid-day light shone through the cracked two-by-fours, allowing them to fully see this young, sleeping mother and baby. They were both still covered in blood and afterbirth, and Joseph knew they needed cleaning and medical attention.

Suddenly, Joseph was taken aback. As he watched, the three men, slowly in their old age, got down on their knees and began praying and worshiping the baby Jesus. Joseph was confused. Was this God in human form? He had no considered the vastness of the situation yet.

After the men prayed and thanked the Lord, they handed Joseph gifts.

"For the mother and baby," one of them told him.

"That is not necessary," Joseph was saying when one of the men stopped him in mid-sentence. "Don't argue. Just take them."

Joseph was grateful to receive the gold necklace, perfume, and small monetary donation. He figured Mary and he could use all the help they could get, with this new addition.

Since their parents were not speaking to them or supporting them, and they were not paid for their work at the mission house, Mary and Joseph would struggle to make ends meet with a new baby. They were aware of the new added stress, but did not let their minds focus on it. They knew that no matter what life threw at them, God would take care of it.

11

After the men left, Joseph finally convinced Mary to get up and try to walk to the car. He figured that the hospitals would have an open spot now that they bombs had stopped over twenty-four hours ago, and wanted to have both Mary and Jesus checked out medically.

Without the required car seat or anything a baby would normally have, Mary slowly got up from the hay, holding on to Joseph, who was holding Jesus. She eased towards the door of the barn, holding Joseph all the way, who was carrying baby Jesus, still wrapped in an old horse blanket.

When the three finally arrived at the nearest hospital, nurses started franticly running for supplies for the new mother and baby. Joseph had told them what happened, and they didn't know whether they should be mortified or scared.

Surprisingly enough, after three hours of tests and observation, both Mary and Jesus were deemed perfectly healthy and were released to go home. Joseph had called everyone at the mission house and told them the news, so they had time to go get diapers and bottles, and the necessary baby items.

When they arrived at the house, Joseph carried Jesus in the new carrier the nurses had given them, and then went around to help Mary out of the car. She was still weak from her long hours of childbirth.

When they walked in the door, they were deafened by a, "Surprise!" and surrounded by balloons and decorations that proclaimed, "It's a boy!" Joseph smiled as he thought about how lucky they were to be surrounded by such good people, who, whether they believed the situation or not, supported them.

Mary smiled and started laughing for the first time in months. She was so happy to have the baby out of her body, and thrilled to be back around friends. Everyone started milling around them, to see Jesus, who slept in carrier as Joseph slightly swayed it back and forth.

Everyone started shouting at the couple to open presents, and Mary and Joseph felt obliged. Mary sat down, still tired after the events of the last two days, and Joseph stood beside her, putting Jesus' carrier down on the ground.

Their co-workers gave them diapers and bottles and clothes, and all of the other essentials new parents need. Lastly, Timothy told them that the best present was upstairs and that he would go get it. "It was too big to wrap," he told them.

Mary started bawling when she saw the present. She and Joseph had prayed endlessly for months on end that God give them this one desire. Though she was weak, Mary jumped up and ran towards her mother and father. Joseph's parents stood behind them, and all four of them surrounded the new mother.

"Can you forgive us for not being there for the birth of our new grandson?" Mary's mother said through chokes of tears.

"Don't mention it," Mary smiled and squeezed them as hard as she could.

"We don't know if we believe your story," Joseph's father spoke up, looking uneasy at the situation. "God doesn't usually perform miracles like this anymore. But either way, you are our children and we support you no matter what. All four of us have an unexplainable new acceptance about this situation, and we want to apologize for the way we acted."

Now Joseph was crying. "It doesn't matter anymore," he told them all. "All that matters is that we move forward."

After their greetings and hugs, Mary and Joseph's parents' attention was soon diverted to the new baby, as all grandparents do. It was love at first sight. The grandparents could not believe they missed out on the birth, and vowed to make it up to the child throughout his life.

After Mary and Joseph's parents proved that their bonds were close once again, the young family made plans to go back home and raise their new baby. They wanted to be close to their parents and familiarity, as they needed all of the help and advice they could get.

They knew that going home meant seeing old friends, and the mockery and gossip that would surround them, but being close to their parents was more important. The small, young family said their good-byes to the other mission workers and headed back to America.

Once they arrived back in the states, Mary, Joseph, and Jesus settled into Mary's parents' house. The young couple officially got engaged, and planned to marry during the following summer. Until then, they went back to school full time while both Mary and Joseph's parents watched Jesus.

The following year, Mary and Joseph were married in Joseph's grandmother's backyard, and Jesus was the ring bearer. The wedding was in the fall, when the crisp cool air set the mood for romance.

Mary wore a white, tea length dress and Joseph wore khaki pants and a white shirt. It was a small ceremony with friends and family, and a sweet reception with soft music and finger foods.

Gossip flooded the town, and the running joke referenced Mary's white dress. White represents purity, and many people crudely joked about the lack of need for a white dress in Mary's case.

On the contrary, Mary and Joseph both found it ironic that they were already raising a child that Mary bore, and yet the first time they made love was on their wedding night.

When Jesus was two years old, both Mary and Joseph graduated college and got new jobs to start their careers. They moved into their own small rent house and lived as normally as they could, with their miracle child in tow.

Jesus had a wonderful childhood and brought unending joy to Mary and Joseph. Although they had no idea how or why it had happened to them, they thanked God for him. On Jesus' fourth birthday, Mary found out that she was pregnant again.

Mary and Joseph were elated to discover that they were having another child, and could not wait to share their news. Unlike the first time they told their families Mary was pregnant, this time was filled with smiles and hugs.

The young family grew two more times during Jesus' childhood. Between work and four children, Mary and Joseph were constantly running here and there, busy, but happy. Before they knew it, Jesus had become a young man.

He went to public school just like his brothers and sister, and was blessed to join in sports, festivals, school events, and games like his peers. Although Jesus seemed physically normal for his age and size, Mary and Joseph noticed massive differences between him and their other children.

Jesus never did anything wrong, and never had, even as a toddler or young child. Their other three children lied, cried, screamed, pulled their sister's hair, beat up their brother, and were terror toddlers, as most children are.

Most children, except Jesus. He had a calming presence about him, even when he was a baby. He was so patient with everyone, and desired to help people. His teachers at school loved him and thought he was the best student they had ever had.

When Jesus was fourteen years old, he went to speak with Mary and Joseph. One night, after a hectic supper, they were all getting ready to go to a

T-ball game. Mary was dressing her daughter, and Joseph was trying to stop a fight between the boys. Jesus asked them to stop what they doing, because this would be a very serious conversation. Joseph always wondered how Jesus seemed so much more mature and understanding than he did.

"It is time for me to leave," he told them solemnly.

"Where are you going, hun?" Mary asked, oblivious to the seriousness of the matter.

"My father sent me here for a reason. I have to go where He is calling me." Jesus was begging them to understand. "Look, you didn't question God when you became pregnant with me. Just trust that this is His plan for my life. Do not be selfish, Mother. You have to let me go; it is why I was brought to earth."

Mary and Joseph started blankly at him. "Go where?" Mary finally asked.

"You cannot go anywhere without us, son. You are only fourteen years old. Are you crazy?" Joseph was firm in his words.

"Look," he sighed, knowing this was more than he bargained for. "I know that you don't understand. But this is my father's plan." Mary and Joseph had talked with Jesus a lot about his relationship with God and understood that somehow, this miracle had been placed upon them, and that Jesus was actually God's own son.

"I know you are not truly our son, Jesus. But you cannot just leave and expect Joseph and I to let you go, not knowing where you will be or for how long. Do you understand?" Mary was near tears. She dreaded that this day might come.

"Mother," Jesus took her hand. He had such wisdom for a young teenager. "I am not yours to keep. You have to let go. You have my brothers and sisters. Don't worry, you can definitely control them when they are fourteen and try to leave home," he winked at her, trying to lighten the mood.

"Where are you going? How are you going to support yourself? And what are we supposed to tell your grandparents and all of our other friends? That you just left, and we let you?" Joseph was blatantly upset.

"You trusted in my father when I was born. You are just going to have to trust him now. I was sent here to save the world from itself. You probably won't understand this now, or will you understand it during your lifetime, but letting me go is necessary."

"Well maybe I don't think the world needs saving," Mary said huffily. "It's not like everyone is dying from some wretched disease. You might be God's son, but you are my son too, and I will not let you leave our home like this."

"I'm not asking your permission," Jesus said with a sweet smile. "My father is making a bigger sacrifice than you are. You have three other children, he does not. I cannot worry about things like money and where I will live. God will take care of me, and I have to do His will, which is what I was sent here to do."

"Well, will you at least call us?" Mary asked through tears, a mixture of madness and sadness.

"Of course," Jesus smiled. "I am just going to bring the word of God to people of the world; I am not running away forever." He winked again, trying to lighten the mood once again.

"And don't worry what people think or say about you. Not even your parents, my grandparents. They will not understand, and that is God's plan. Just as you were when I was born, and when you moved back here, to your hometown, you will be mocked and shunned. People will not understand why you willingly let me leave home on my own, just a fourteen-year-old boy. This is not punishment from God; it is simply part of the package. This is a perfect example of why I have to go and preach His word. He has a plan. It will not be an easy road for any of us, but it is the only way. Remember that God has found favor in you, and this is not a punishment. Please try to understand." Jesus was sad now, knowing that he would leave his wonderful family.

"I just don't know if I can," Joseph said. "You cannot take care of yourself. You are only fourteen."

"You know I can take care of myself. I am not like other fourteen year old boys. I am God's own son. You don't really think he would let anything happen to me, do you?" Jesus joked with Joseph, which was usually their playful relationship. This time, though, Joseph did not laugh.

"I want you to go on to the T-ball game. My brothers and sisters will be sad for a while, but they will understand. God is giving them the understanding that they need. When people ask, tell them the truth. That I went to preach God's word. I will stop by every once in a while to visit and see you. Just think of it as my going to college or a boarding school. We'll keep in touch. Now go, before you are late, and I will be gone when you get back. This is God's plan. Please trust it and don't fight Him." Jesus hugged and kissed both of his parents and promised to call them every day before shoving the family out the door.

With tears in their eyes, Mary and Joseph hurried their other children out the door. They were in a daze, not sure what was happening or what they could do about it. They had feared this day might come, and now it had.

12

Jesus packed a small amount of clothing and necessities, but left all other material things at his childhood home. Sadly, he left Mary and Joseph's house, knowing that the road ahead would be difficult.

Hundreds of miles away, a young preacher named John had been getting quite a bit of media attention, due to his claims that the son of God had been sent to earth. John was a twenty-seven year old man who had been preaching for three years.

Almost one year earlier, John had a frighteningly realistic dream, almost like a message from God himself. He dreamed that God was going to have a son and send him to earth to preach his word. John did not know how to explain it, but the feeling was so strong, he felt that he had to share it with the world. He knew people would not believe him, as he would probably not believe someone if they told him the same thing.

There was no way that he could describe how he knew this information; it was just like the wind. Something you cannot see or explain, but know with all certainty that it is true. He knew that he had to share this news, and started with his congregation. After telling everyone in person about God's son coming to earth, he began to spread it by way of the Internet. He created a website, sharing his dreams and news with the human race.

Naturally, the media took the story and ran wild with it, portraying John as an insane man who was trying to take over the world. His story was on the news, facebook, twitter, google, and all other media outlets. Almost no one believed him, and his congregation had dwindled down to almost non-existent. John hated all of this negative attention, but felt compelled to tell people what he somehow knew was coming. He reasoned that if he knew a tsunami was coming, he would have to tell people about that, also.

After days of traveling by bus and car, with the help of wonderful people and preachers, Jesus finally found himself on the doorstep of John's church. He knocked on the door, but didn't expect an answer, seeing how it was one o'clock in the morning.

A couple of minutes later, a sleeping, eye-rubbing man appeared at the door.

"What are you doing here?" Jesus asked, taking John by surprise.

John stared at him for a moment. "I live in a small room in the back of the church. We don't have the money for a parsonage, and especially now, with my new-found fame." He said the last part sarcastically, and under his breath.

"Who are you?" John asked, realizing that he had not even asked what this young boy was doing knocking on the church door at such an hour. From the looks of him, the boy had run away from home, so John motioned him in so that he could feed him and call his parents.

"So," John said after he had fixed Jesus a glass of milk and made him a sandwich in the small church kitchen. "Where are you from? I need to call your parents so that they don't worry about you. Whatever you have done or whatever they have said or done to you, we'll work through it together."

Jesus smiled at John. "I have not run away from home," he told him. "Do you not know who I am? You have sacrificed your reputation and life to tell people about me."

John's eyes became wide as he stared at the young boy. "Ok, kid," he finally said. "I know I have been in the news a lot, but you are not going to get out of calling your parents by telling me that you are God's son. Now what is your name?" John was still processing the information.

"John," Jesus said with a voice years older than he was, "You have been preaching about this moment for a long time. It is time to live it. My father wants you to baptize me."

John coughed and spit up the bit of sandwich he was chewing on.

"What? You should be baptizing me! How in the world am I qualified for something like that?" John had, with some unknown understanding, believed that Jesus was who he said he was. But he could not comprehend the task Jesus had asked him.

"I don't want to negotiate it. You are going to baptize me in the name of my father." Jesus spoke so quiet and calmly, but with such authority. "And then you are going to call the news stations and post on your facebook and twitter pages what you have done. Trust me, not many people will believe you, but you need to be strong in your convictions. You know that your rewards in heaven are much greater than anything you could get here on earth."

Without any further arguments, John nodded his head. He was still confused about how in the world a small, fourteen year old boy was telling him what to do, and how he could possibly be God's son, but he decided he would rather trust in Him than question the unknown.

John told Jesus to follow him outside, to the stream behind the church. He went through his normal baptism rituals, and dunked Jesus in the water. Miraculously, when John had finished, there was a scene in front of both him and Jesus like something you would see in a movie.

Even though it was deep in the night, the stars seemed to brighten and the sky became filled with light, illuminating from the stars and moon. The stars burst with light, and John could have sworn he heard a voice, saying, "This is my son, in whom I am well pleased."

As quickly as this phenomenon began, it was over, and all John and Jesus could see was the black, starry night. John played the scene off on account of his extreme tiredness, and knew that the whole thing had to have been a dream. But somehow, he really believed that he had just baptized God's son.

The young males went back inside the small, old church. John told Jesus that he could sleep in the old nursery, which was the adjacent room to John's. Too tired to talk anymore, both of the fell into a deep sleep for the rest of the dark night.

When John awoke the next morning, he found that the old nursery was empty. Jesus had already left, although John was not sure of where he went. As he had been instructed, John retold the events of the night on his social networking websites, and closed his laptop before he could see the negative comments that he knew would come.

13

Jesus had gotten up at daybreak, and left the small church where he had been baptized. He wanted to begin spreading the word of God immediately, but felt like he needed to get closer to his father first. He would have to push himself to be sure that he would be able to withstand the humanly temptations and pressures that he would be would be faced with.

Directly behind the church were endless acres of woods, which the church owned and would soon be harvesting for timber, so that the profit could go towards their new sanctuary fund. With direction from his father, Jesus took off into the woods, where he would spend the next forty days.

The young boy felt that he needed to be alone in solitude for a while so that he could reflect on his past and prepare for his future. Since he had left his laptop and cell phone at Mary and Joseph's house, he had no way of contacting the outside world, and felt that this would be a great way to reconnect with his father.

Jesus traveled into the thick, mosquito infested woods until he found a small clearing beside a hot and steamy pond. There was a small ridge beside the pond, seeming to be formed from years and years of water erosion. Jesus decided to set up a makeshift camp and spend a month with his lesser species.

The mere teenager began living off of the land, as people once did. He found bamboo, which would make the ridge covered on all sides, but left a small doorway so that he could enter and exit. He then brought water from the pond and began to boil it over the small fire he made, which took quite some time.

After he had a safe and secure shelter and clean drinking water, Jesus began truly focusing on his mission on earth. He knew the reason he had been sent here, but still had to wrap the idea around his fourteen-year-old brain.

Jesus stayed in his makeshift cabin in the woods for over a month, not eating anything while he was there. He had made the decision not to eat, because he wanted all of his energy focused on God, not on trying to find food to eat.

During the first ten days of his hiatus, Jesus could barely concentrate for the loud, vibrating grumble coming from his mid-section. After fifteen days, his body started to rapidly lose weight, but his stomach no longer growled. It had given up on finding nourishment through noise. Jesus figured that the human body could get used to anything, given time.

Once Jesus had arrived at John's church, he had called Mary and Joseph to let them know that he was all right. He could tell from their voices that they were sick with worry about his whereabouts and well-being. There was too much evil in the world not to worry about a person living on his or her own, especially a fourteen-year-old boy.

But since Jesus left John, he had not called his parents. They did not understand that he was faithfully completing his mission here on earth, and expected a call every couple of days. When they did not receive one, they began to panic.

When Jesus had been in the woods for over a month, and Mary and Joseph had been searching frantically for him, a man who claimed that he was from John's church stumbled across the teenager.

Jesus was on his knees, praying in the stillness and quietness of nature when the man, who was dressed in black, even on the hot summer day, startled him.

"Hi there, young man," the man said in a sweet voice. "John told some of us church members that you had wandered off into these here woods, and I thought you might want some food. A boy your age needs to eat." The man smiled down at Jesus, whose ribs were bulging from his sides and his face was gruff and dirty.

"I am not out here trying to find food," Jesus told the man. "I am praying and becoming closer to my father."

"Look, son," the man started to get agitated. "You need to eat. It ain't right for a boy like you to be living in the woods with nothing to eat. Now I have brought you all sorts of different things. Eat."

"Mister," Jesus said in a reassuring voice, "People need more than food to survive in this world. Even if I died out here, due to lack of nourishment, my body would still be full."

The man cocked his head a looked at Jesus as if he were confused. "You mean to tell me that you have been out in these here woods for over a month, with nothing to eat, and you are not going to accept the food I have brought you?"

Jesus smiled. "No, sir, I am not. Maybe one day you will understand what I mean by being filled with the spirit as opposed to food."

The man huffed and stomped away, in the same direction that he came. A couple of minutes later, Jesus knew that he could leave the woods and head out into the world. He knew now that he was strong enough to stand up to any form of temptation.

14

Over the next four years, Jesus traveled all over the world, staying with different churches and in preacher's homes, preaching the word of God to anyone who would listen. He had contacted preachers during the first couple of trips, asking for a place to sleep and eat. Once the word began to spread about Jesus, he no longer had to ask for shelter and food. It was offered to him in every town he visited, by faithful preachers and followers of his word.

He went to see his parents every holiday, and other random times, as he promised, and they were always elated to see him.

When Jesus first came out of the woods and began preaching, the media had a hay day. Everyone had an opinion about this teenager, claiming to be the Son of God, and they all felt obliged to share how they felt.

CNN, Fox News, and many other news stations aired the story just weeks after the media got a hold of it. One newscaster even made a joke about the situation, saying, "Have you heard about the kid who is going around claiming to be God's son? If I were his parents, I probably would have told him the same thing. I wouldn't claim him." Jokes like this were popping up all over news stations and late night broadcasts.

Although many people were critical about Jesus and quick to judge and share those judgments, a small number of people trusted God and believed what Jesus preached. The morals and values of society were drastically dropping, and people had no regard to what was right and wrong, and simply did what was necessary to get ahead. The minority of believers believed that God would do something to turn society around, and thought that Jesus might be just that.

After spreading his preaching's nationwide, Jesus decided that it was time to recruit some men to help him spread God's word. He had just left a small, northern church with a wonderful preacher who was great company.

He started walking south, and had to smile when he saw the bumper sticker that said, "Honk if you are God's son." Although he had a good sense of humor about his naysayers, he hoped that they would change their minds before it was too late.

Shortly after leaving the previous preacher's house, Jesus stumbled across a harbor, which was directing and storing the biggest yachts he had ever seen. Jesus was suddenly saddened at the thought of how much money those massive boats cost, and all of the good that could be done with that money throughout the world.

On the side opposite the ships were the working class people, loading their shrimp and fishing boats, getting ready to head out for the day.

Simon and Andrew were loading a ten-foot tackle box into their boat, and directly adjacent to them were James and John, waiting to untie the lines on their father's shrimp boat. The four young boys ranged in age from nineteen to twenty-three, and had their lives ahead of them.

They had all graduated high school, but none of them had gone to college, instead choosing to make a living in the fishing and shrimping industry. Knowing that they would go, Jesus stopped at their boats.

"Hi!" he shouted at them.

All four males stopped what they were doing and stared at this young man, seeming to be their age or less. He stood in between their two boats so that all four of them could hear.

They immediately recognized Jesus from his appearance. His once khaki slack pants, too-big white button up shirt, and dirty tennis shoes were a dead giveaway.

James turned down the radio on his boat so that they could all hear what Jesus was saying.

"What's up?" Simon hollered down at him, shouting over the loud construction site nearby.

"What are the odds that you *don't* recognize me from the news and Internet?" Jesus asked, half expecting them to pretend they didn't know who he was.

"We've heard about you," Simon said. "Do you need a place to stay?" He was sincere in his question and would have genuinely offered him one, had that been what Jesus wanted.

"Well," Jesus paused for a minute, not knowing if the guys would even listen to what he had to say. "Actually, I really need some people to travel around and preach with me. Crowd control, witnessing to other people, things like that. Don't ask me how, but I somehow feel like you four might be willing to do that."

The brothers looked at each other from their own vessels. Simon and Andrew and James and John had always known each other, but had not hung out much, on account of the demanding time schedules of their work. They knew little about each other, but looked to one another to see what their answer would be.

James jumped down off the deck of his boat and shook Jesus' hand. "I'd be obliged," he said, followed by the handshakes of John, Andrew, and Simon.

The young men were all under twenty-four years old and had their lives ahead of them. Starting out so young in the fishing and shrimp industry, they could easily make a comfortably life for themselves and their current girlfriends, who they assumed would one day be their wives. Their children could have been raised in a life of comfortable luxury, and they could have owned a nice house in a nice neighborhood, fishing during the day and coming home to this picture perfect family at night.

Overcome by a sudden urge to join this young man in his witnessing, they left all of that behind. James and John left their boat tied to the dock, for the bank to repossess and sell to the next eager fishing entrepreneur. Simon and Andrew left theirs with their father and they set off afoot with their new leader and friend.

Simon and John wanted to stop and get their computers from their houses and tell their parents, family, and girlfriends good-bye, but Jesus told them not to.

"If you are going with me, you have to be willing to give all of that up. Look, I know that is a lot to ask, but you have no idea how much this small sacrifice is going to pay off in the end. I promise, all of these worldly things will be so meaningless, and you will wonder why you ever felt the need to have them in your life."

Although all four young men took their cell phones, all other possessions and relationships were left behind. In our world of sin and self-worth, it is unfathomable to imagine leaving everything and everyone you have worked your whole life to acquire. John, James, Simon, and Andrew did it without blinking an eye, and found that getting back to the basics was more fun than they ever would have thought.

The company and conversations they had with each other were great, and they found and created little games and riddles to pass the time, something that modern technology has steered us away from. The four young men had forgotten how fun and fulfilling the simple things in life are, things that they had enjoyed when they were children.

They four young men were not sure where they were headed, but as soon as they neared the town, they could see a huge crowd of people. They exchanged glances, realizing that Jesus must know where they were going, even if they did not.

15

When they were on the edge of the crowd, Jesus turned to his new friends. "I have been preaching God's word for years now. It is time I started making people believe me if I expect any of them come to God and start worshiping him. I'm going to go in front of this crowd and speak, so if you would, please just try to make sure people are watching and listening." With that, Jesus turned and got lost in the crowd.

After reading the signs and posters, the four young men came to the realization that the CDS (citizens with diabetes society) was protesting the new health care bill, which would prohibit working class people with diabetes from receiving government assistance towards health care, in addition to the insurance carriers being forced to drop their coverage.

Andrew heard one of the people shouting towards the government building, "WE PAY FOR TEENAGERS ON WELFARE TO HAVE BABIES, BUT YOU CANNOT HELP MY WIFE, WHO HAS LOST HER LEG AND CAN'T AFFORD A SEVENTY THOUSAND DOLLAR PROSTHETIC!"

Jesus' four new friends began to get angry as they listened to the citizen's complaints. They also did not agree with the new government bill, and thought it unfair to deny health care assistance to these hard working people.

Just when John was about to grab a poster and start protesting with the others, they saw Jesus standing on a podium in front of the crowd. Recognizing him from the media, almost everyone in the crowd began to turn their attention to Jesus, not sure what he would say.

"We're here to make a change, not listen to someone tell us about God!" someone from the multitude shouted.

Suddenly, the lady in the wheelchair who had been talking into the microphone looked up at Jesus, who was standing directly over her. Jesus leaned down and got eye level with the frail woman and touched her face. Jesus smiled and nicest, kindest smile the woman had ever seen.

After Jesus touched the woman, she looked up at him, knowing there had been a change in her physical make-up. She grabbed her instant tester and poked it into the end of her finger. Her insulin levels were normal.

The crowd slowly gained understanding on the situation at hand. "The politicians are controlling every aspect of our lives!" One of the crowd members shouted. "Now they have this monkey parading around, trying to make us believe that he can actually cure everyone. Which one hired you?" He shouted towards Jesus. "Because we're not buying it. Can't you people just leave us alone? We just want to protest this injustice. You do enough harm in the world with your lies and scandals. Just leave us alone!"

With this man's bitter anger, half of the crowd began to disperse, believing that the crooked political leaders led this man to make portray this scene. The other half stared at Jesus in disbelief, not sure what to do. After a couple of minutes, the people seemed to decide that they would rather be cured of their diabetes than argue a political battle. When one middle-aged lady walked up to Jesus, the rest of the group did also.

Jesus took the hurt and pain away from each one of the people, while John, James, Simon, and Andrew realized, for the first time, the un-humanness of Jesus. When they decided to leave their boats and lives and travel around, preaching with him, they had not totally grasped the situation.

The group stayed at the diabetic protest for hours on end while the people went up to Jesus, telling him their stories and offering their gratitude while Jesus took the illness out of their bodies.

Hours later, when all of the people were healed and gone, Jesus and his four new friends were the only people left. They all sat down on the curb, outside the massive government building, all drained and exhausted from the afternoon's events.

"So…" Simon started to ask Jesus. "Why did you do that? And how? The media is really going to run wild now."

"Simon," Jesus said in his calm, reassuring voice, "Those people have suffered for a long time. The people who have lost hope, the ones who mourn, the weak ones, the poor ones without food or water…those are the people who are blessed the most. It is easy for rich and seemingly blessed people to worship God. But people like this, who suffer, are the ones who have the strongest faith, because they trust God through everything they have to suffer. Do you understand?"

All four of them nodded.

"The people who show mercy toward others, the ones who have good, pure hearts, and the people who make peace in our world of anger and hurt-those are the ones who are truly blessed, and who will be in heaven with my father when they die."

After news of the diabetic protest got out, people started coming out of the woodworks to find Jesus. The young men kept traveling, continuing to stay with Godly people along the way. Everywhere they went, they were stalked by paparazzi.

Camera flashes and mobs of reporters attacked the five young men and chased them down. Jesus ignored them and did not seem to be bothered by this, but the other four got agitated quickly. They couldn't stand having people in their faces all of the time.

Jesus' face was on the home page of yahoo and google, and his story was on every major news channel in the country. He was the hot topic on the social networking internet sites, and everyone seemed to have an opinion about Jesus. There were more negative theories about him than positive ones, but Jesus could not concern himself with those. He simply focused on the task at hand.

Jesus and the four guys continued traveling, preaching, and healing people. Time was flying by fast, as it always does when you are busy and consumed with work. After being hounded by the media and questioned by the authorities, Jesus spoke one day on his intentions on earth. He was in a large city, with people bustling around and hurrying to work and home.

Jesus stood in the middle of the sidewalk and began to speak.

"I want to let everyone know that I am not here to break the law or belittle the rules of this country." People stopped to listen, compelled by the presence of Jesus. Someone started filming this declaration on their cell phone, and it aired on CNN two hours later.

"I do not want to disrupt the law; I am simply here to witness to others about God. He has given me an extraordinary gift, and what are we doing with our gifts and talents, if not worshiping God with them? I am not defying the laws that govern us, but I want everyone to be as concerned with the laws of God as they are with even the tiniest governmental law, like buckling your seatbelt. People who follow the rules set forth by God are much better off than a person who follows of all of the legal laws, but none of God's."

After his soliloquy, Jesus simply turned and kept walking to his next destination. James, John, Simon, and Peter were used to these tactics by now, and simply waited on Jesus to finish his preaching before continuing on with them.

Back in Jesus' childhood home, Mary and Joseph and their other children had been intently following Jesus in the news. They were happy that he was safe, but sad that he was traveling the country on foot. They offered him a car every time he called home, but he told them that he could not have any material things.

Their parents and friends had been appalled when they found out that the young married couple let Jesus leave home at such a young age, and many of them had still shunned them from society, all these years later. Mary and Joseph tried not to let the negativity bring them down, and knew that they were doing right by God. No one could see the whole picture, or predict what was going to happen.

The years seemed to speed by like a city bus spinning out of control, barreling full speed ahead. At the churches he visited, Jesus preached to the willing congregations, and hoped to bring a much-needed change about to the morale of humanity.

"Murder begins in the heart," he told a congregation one Sunday morning. "I realize most of you think that it is preposterous to think that you would ever murder anyone. But when you begin to hate someone for the wrong that they have done to you, that anger harbors in your heart and you begin wishing evil upon them. Eventually, that anger and hate might take control of your life in a way you cannot understand. You have to forgive others where they have wronged you and accept the joy that full forgiveness brings."

After Jesus left each congregation, there was a new understanding on life and sin that each person experienced. They could not explain how, but they were overwhelmed by his presence.

"How many of you are married?" Jesus asked another congregation a week later. He waited for the hands to slowly pop up. "Marriage is sanctity of God, and people must take in its seriousness. If you have inappropriate thoughts about someone other than your spouse, you might as well be having a marital affair." Many people shifted uncomfortably in their seats.

"Watching impure sexual acts on television and the internet are equivalent to acting on those impurities. In addition, divorce is unacceptable. In our promiscuous society, our ideas about marriage are that we will simply get a divorce if our spouse gets on our nerves or annoys us. But this casual attitude must change, and people have to start honoring their spouses and families just like they would want to be honored.

Jesus kept delivering his sermons, all across the nation, most of the being aired online or on television. People started to listen more intently to him and take his words to heart. He told people to love their enemies, taught them how to pray, warned them not to be concerned with material things on earth, and told them not to worry, but to be happy with their lives here on earth while they worshiped God.

He also spoke about not judging others, which was running rampid through the mouths of the young and old, spreading gossip and judging people on a materialistic basis. He warned people that this would not be the easy path in life, as many of the popular people would laugh at them and mock them for doing the right thing, but they would be rewarded more than they could ever imagine.

16

As Jesus traveled to each church, the number of people believing and following him began to grow. He was like a rock star with crazed fans following every move he made. People, many of them ones he had healed, followed him everywhere, listening to what he said and trying to abide by it.

As Jesus was on his way to the next church, he stopped by a homeless man lying in a dirty alley. He was obviously asleep, drained from a hard couple of years. When Jesus stood in between the sun and the man, they lack of blinding light suddenly startled him, and the filthy and smelly man jerked up.

His stench and odor were stouter than a waste management plant, and many of the people who had been following Jesus, listening to what he had to say, started backing away and leaving. They didn't want anything to do with someone as low as this poor homeless man.

Ashamed, the man tried to explain his situation. "I haven't always been this way," he said, sadness and regret on his brow. He knew who Jesus was, and felt disgusting to be seen like this.

"I had a good job, wife, and kids. Everything people strive for. Four years ago, my family was attacked in our own home by six masked men who robbed us, sexually abused each one of us, and shot and killed my family. All of them died except me. Now, I have HIV and am just waiting to die. If I could kill myself, I would." The man was crying. "Want to know the funny part?" his tears turned to anger and his teeth clenched and he started to shake.

"Those men who did that to my family-they only served two years in jail before they got out on good behavior!" the man started to shake, filled with anger and the hard path his life has taken.

Jesus looked at the man with complete love. He did not see a homeless man with AIDS, but a wonderful child of God. Jesus leaned down and touched the man's face. The hardships and struggles seemed to slip from the man's face as his heart was healed, along with his meek body.

82

The couple of people who had stayed with Jesus in the dirty alley, with rotting food substance and rodents, felt for the man what Jesus did. Compassion and love.

Jesus kept traveling, healing and preaching, with dozens of people in tow. One fall evening, a television show producer found Jesus and asked him if he would consider being a guest star on an episode, on a show about drug and alcohol addicts overcoming their addictions.

Jesus decided to heal the people from their addictions and poor choices, but would not go in front of the camera. Although he knew his face had been plastered all over the media outlets, Jesus did not want to purposely appear on television shows as a special guest. That would take him away from his purpose here on earth.

Traveling across the lands brought Jesus and the many people following him to a harbor with many shipping and fishing boats ready to go out to sea. For a split second, James, John, Simon, and Peter were sad that they had left and were glad to be back near their previous way of life.

Jesus turned and looked at his four closest friends and told them to get on the boat in which he was standing beside. They did what was asked of them, but some of the other people looked at Jesus in disbelief.

"Do you even know whose boat that is?" One of them asked.

"You're not going to steal it, are you?" another asked.

Jesus looked at the two doubters with sincere love. "I am not stealing. It will be put back directly where I got it. Besides, I know the owner," he winked at them.

The five men took out into the ocean, and the once fisherman were pleased to feel the ocean spray on their faces again.

After they had been on the ocean for some time, fishing and enjoying each other's company, the sky became dark. They had traveled far out into the ocean, where the massive fish lurked, in hopes of catching a monster.

Soon, it started to rain, and then hail. Lightning and thunder started flashing all around them, and the waves started rolling into the side of the vessel, violently trashing it about.

Jesus' friends exchanged worried glances and suggested they head back to the harbor, but Jesus did not agree. The storm raged on for almost an hour before they went to him in horror.

"Jesus, this boat can't take this beating. I told you we should have gone in earlier. We're all about to drown," Andrew said while the others nodded in agreement.

Jesus smiled at his friends. "You have seen everything I have done and heard what I have said, right?" he asked them.

"Do you honestly think that I would let anything happen to us?" From many people, this sarcastic question would sound condescending, but Jesus was honest, yet sincere.

To ease his friend's fear, he looked up towards the sky, and the huge waves and thunder stopped, even though the rain persisted. Everyone looked at Jesus, fully understanding the magnitude of his presence.

They stayed on the boat for hours after the storm ceased, fishing and enjoyed each other's company. With the people always tailing Jesus, they hadn't had much time to talk alone with Jesus and were filled with the Holy Spirit when they did. They were all thankful for the calm moment to share their friendship, and for a break from the craziness of the life on land.

After a while, they went back to the harbor and docked the boat, of which the owner had deceased two days prior and all of his possessions would soon belong to the state. Hearing their stomachs growl, Jesus decided they should eat some supper.

While his friends cut and cleaned the fish they had caught that day, Jesus wandered into a shopping center near the booming fishing harbor.

"I'll be back in a little bit," he hollered back at the guys as he walked into an office labeled 'Wrage County Tax Assessor.' The office was small and narrow, and Jesus walked in like he owned the place. The receptionist was getting her things gathered up and getting ready to go home for the weekend.

"Can I help you?" She asked as she grabbed her empty lunch container and piled it on top of her other files. "We are actually closing for the day, but I can get your name and number and have our tax professional contact you on Monday." She had obviously said this statement too many times.

Jesus smiled at the lady and kindly disobeyed her, walking towards the back of the building, towards Matthew. Matthew had been employed with the internal revenue service for sixteen years, and easily got tired of bringing bad news to people and demanding their hard earned money.

Matthew looked up with weary eyes when Jesus walked in.

"Do you want to have supper?" Jesus asked.

Not sure why the famous preacher had come to see him, Matthew agreed. They went to a small bistro-type restaurant next door and sat on the patio, under the big fans, enjoying the ocean breeze and smells.

As they ordered, Jesus motioned for a teenage mother and her baby, who were walking down the sidewalk to sit down and eat with them. The young girl obviously had her child when she was very young, and couldn't be older than fifteen.

Unsure what to do, but grateful for the kindness, the girl sat down and held her toddler in her lap. The three people ate and talked, listening intently to Jesus and aspiring to become a better person just by being in his presence.

After James and the others were done cleaning and gutting their catch, they left the harbor to see where Jesus had wandered off to. They had become accustomed to Jesus meandering out, finding people to talk with and listen to.

When they spotted him in the restaurant, they headed that way, but were stopped by a passerby.

"Hey, you are the guys that follow Jesus around, right?" the pedestrian asked.

They nodded and smiled, knowing that Jesus was turning heads with his new found fame.

"I thought he was supposed to be God's son or something," the man said in mockery. "If you were so high and mighty, would you be eating supper with someone who works for the freaking internal revenue service, and some kid who has a baby?" The man smirked, glad that his theories about Jesus being a fake were proving true.

John was about to speak up when Jesus interrupted, hearing the questions that the man had raised. He spoke loudly, as he was about thirty feet away, and had to shout for the man to hear him clearly.

"Sir, if you were not sick, would you go to the doctor anyway?" The man looked down at the ground and stared blankly.

"I did not come here and begin preaching for the people who do not need forgiveness, but for the sinners who need me most." Jesus was convincing with his words, and made his point to all of the people within hearing distance.

After years of seeing Jesus in the news and spotlight, everyone was beginning to become accustomed to him. A small group of people believed and followed him, but most people did not. They finally got over the feeling that someone was pretending to be their God, and simply accepted Jesus as a false prophet.

17

One day, when Jesus and his friends had left one church and were traveling to another, James' cell phone rang. After a short conversation, James turned to Jesus in disbelief.

"You'll never guess who that was!" he said excitedly.

Jesus smiled his kind smile. "Who?"

"The president!" James blurted out before Jesus had even finished asking. "His daughter has leukemia and has been given two months to live. She is only twelve, and he is begging that you go and heal her."

"Is this the same president who went on the news, saying that Jesus is blasphemous and warning everyone not to listen to him?" Simon asked, making a point with his tone.

"I guess he changed his mind," James said.

Jesus seemed to consider the question for a while before deciding to go see the little girl. The group suddenly changed their direction, with Jesus in the lead.

It took two weeks for Jesus and his friends to arrive at the presidential home. The many secret service guards reluctantly let them in, but obviously worried about how the public would receive this scene, and how it would affect their popularity. When you are a high political official, you must be worried about your image and reputation at all times.

They were let into the massive home, and when Jesus began walking towards the president, a young woman leapt onto him. Startled, Jesus was taken aback for a moment. The woman, a janitorial employee of the mansion, wanted to simply touch Jesus in the hopes of being healed.

She told Jesus that for years, she had been experiencing chronic hemorrhaging, but did not have any insuranceor enough money to see a physician. She had been dealing with the pain and bloody discharge the best she could.

Jesus smiled at her faith.

"You have great faith, my dear," he told her. "Please don't worry anymore. You will not be in pain any longer."

The woman hurried off, crying, knowing that she would be fired for stepping out of line in front of the president.

The man stood in a dark blue suit in front of Jesus, in his faded slacks, once-white button up shirt, and dirty tennis shoes. The president was obviously nervous, and at a loss of words.

"Um…" the president paused. "Follow me. My daughter is in here."

Jesus followed the man into a room adjacent to the entryway of the house. The girl's mother was lying on the bed with her, distraught from their long battle. Jesus could tell that she was the one who asked her husband to contact him.

Without speaking, Jesus walked towards the girl, who was asleep. She had no hair, due to her chemotherapy, and was very pale and meek. Jesus looked at the suffering young girl and placed both hands upon her.

Jesus prayed while he held the girl, and then left the room without speaking. He knew that the doctors and physicians would find the girl in perfect health, and hoped that this would help bring around more people's faith in God.

The group continued on, and Jesus decided that he needed to find more faithful friends to walk with him. James, Simon, Andrew, and John were already trusted friends, and to them Jesus added Phillip, Thomas, Matthew, Lebus, Thad, James S., Simon P., and Judas. Jesus found the other guys in the same fashion that he found the first four young fishermen, and was once again glad for their faith and trust in God.

Once Jesus' twelve new friends and colleagues had traveled with him for a month, Jesus decided it was time to send them out to continue his preaching. He sent them all in another direction, in hopes of reaching more people individually than they could as a group.

Jesus and all of his friends went out on their own paths, bringing the word of God to all different types of people. During his stay at one large city, Jesus was speaking to a group of people when someone shouted a question he had not been asked during his years of preaching.

"So are you trying to bring world peace to everyone?" The female voice came from the middle of the crowd.

Jesus smiled at the question, and at the asker. "Please do not think that my purpose is to bring peace to the world. Although I think world peace would be wonderful and pray that countries and their people will someday accept each other's differences, that is not my job here.

"I have come to turn children against their parents, married couples against each other, and grandchildren against their grandparents. A man's enemies will be the people who live in his own house." Jesus spoke the words, despite what the crowd of bystanders would think and the gasps he knew would follow. He was not here to win a popularity contest with the media, but to deliver the truth.

As expected, everyone gasped and was taken aback by Jesus' answers. He continued on, to further explain.

"Anyone that puts any person or thing before God or myself is not worthy of us. When I say that I am going to turn children away from their parents, I do not mean that I will ask them to run away or disobey their parents. The same goes for married men and women.

"The point to be made here is that while loving your family is wonderful and should be a priority in life, you cannot put anyone before God. Not even your husband or wife. You have to love God first, because he is the one who gave you love. You have to be willing to forsake all of your worldly goods, including other humans, to sacrifice for me and my father."

With a little more understanding, the crowd nodded their heads. Jesus had a way of getting people's attention.

While Jesus and his pals were busy bringing the word of God to the world, the government officials of the country were busy arguing about what they should do with this situation. People were really beginning to listen to Jesus, and follow him.

The president, whose daughter had miraculously overcome her leukemia, told his advisors to leave Jesus alone, for the young man was not breaking any laws. But his co-workers believed that this man would continue to gain power until he had a whole army full of followers, and then overthrow the government. They believed Jesus' goal was to become powerful in politics.

The president had not told anyone about Jesus coming to his house during the night, and when people asked how his daughter healed from her disease so quickly, he thanked the wonderful physicians in the hospital.

It was hard to justify his reasons to his political friends now, but he insisted that they leave Jesus alone, for he technically wasn't breaking any laws set forth by the country. While the president made his decision, the rest of the government officials met privately, after the country's leader left the room.

They decided that while they had not been given the authority to arrest Jesus yet, they could try to bring down as many of his friends as they could, in hopes of scaring Jesus into ceasing his preaching.

"He is just going to take over the country when he has a big enough army," an older man argued to the group.

"Have you ever heard one of his sermons?" another man asked. "He doesn't say anything negative about the country or its leaders. He just wants to bring people closer to God. He doesn't care about overthrowing anyone.

"Either way," a young woman spoke up. "We cannot let some person go preaching around the country, doing whatever he pleases. We do not allow cults in this country and will not allow this nonsense. Until we convince the president otherwise, we cannot override his decision. We can, on the other hand, find reasons to arrest as many of Jesus friends and followers as we can, until he backs down from his preaching."

Most of the others nodded their heads, including the ones who previously disagreed and wanted to leave Jesus and his friends alone. They took a vote and were unanimous, in agreement to alert the police officials about the names and address of some of Jesus' well known friends.

18

Two weeks after the closed door decision, there was a knock on John's door late at night. The same door that had been opened for the baptism of Jesus so many years before. John opened the newly painted door, and smiled at the remodeled building. It had taken everyone five and a half years, but the place was finally finished.

"John?" a policeman asked.

Stunned, John answered, "Yes."

"Did you baptize a young boy a couple of years ago in the pond behind this church?" A harsh policeman asked.

"Jesus? Yes. Why?" John was obviously confused.

"All I can tell you is that the boy had run away from home at the time you took him in for the night, and his parents are pressing charges on you for harboring a runaway minor," the officer told John before reading him his Miranda Rights.

John was stunned. He knew Jesus' parents would never press charges against him. He had personally met them before and they understood to the fullest extent who Jesus was and what he was doing. They supported him and would never go through this legal process. Besides, if they really were upset about the situation, they would have done something about it five years ago, not now, when Jesus was almost twenty years old.

John began to panic as the officers placed handcuffs on his wrists and began walking him towards their black and white car. What would his family and congregation think? Would they be fighting to get him out of jail? He had never been to jail, and started to hyperventilate at the thought of going.

He had always heard that other inmates beat each other up, scream, yell, and even rape new inmates. Especially ones who are convicted of any crime connected with children. John had the overwhelming urge to cry as he was being placed in the back of the car, but instead, he decided to pray.

Pray for safety in prison, and pray for his hasty return. He prayed that his family and congregation would have the faith to know John would never do anything wrong, and trust that God would take care of all of them. John was still praying when they arrived at the county jail.

After Jesus traveled many miles to preach God's word, he finally was close enough to his childhood home to stop and see his family. He only had to knock one time on Mary and Joseph's front door before it was opened, and Mary was shouting for everyone to come see who it was.

Mary ushered Jesus into the house, and he smiled to himself as he noticed the toddler toys were slowly being replaced with pre-teen and teenage electronic gadgets. Joseph came into the room with a huge smile on his face, shaking his son's hand.

"Man it has been a long time. How are you?" Joseph asked as he put down his tongs on the kitchen counter, as he was in the middle of cooking hamburgers for supper.

"I know," Jesus said with a familiar smile. "It's so good to be here."

"How long can you stay, honey?" Mary asked the way any mother would after seeing her son, pleading with him to stay longer than she knew he would.

"I can only visit for a minute," Jesus told them. "I was on my way to the church before hitting the next town." There was a small silence for a moment. "Where are my brothers and sister?"

Jesus' question made Mary suddenly remember her other children. She jumped up and walked towards the sliding glass door beside the kitchen. She slid it open and hollered at the kids, who were jumping on the trampoline in the wonderful spring weather.

The kids came in and jumped on Jesus, attacking him with their smiles and questions. They were a family once again, however short it was. Jesus agreed to stay for supper and was elated to be around the wonderful people again.

Sadly, three hours later, Jesus knew he had to leave. He could not stay any longer, although Mary begged him to. As always, Mary and Joseph both cried when he left, but Jesus, with his wisdom and knowledge, simply nodded and gave them both a hug.

He went to his hometown church, the church where he had grown up. He was excited for the familiarity and looked forward to seeing some of the old preachers and church elders. He walked in the unlocked doors during a business meeting, which had just begun.

When the men saw Jesus standing at the door of the Sunday school classroom in which they were seated, everyone stopped their conversation.

"Can we help you, son?" the leader of the meeting asked.

Before Jesus could answer, another man, who had been staring curiously at Jesus, looked like a light bulb had just gone off in his head. "That is Jesus. You know, from the news. The guy that does the miracles and preaches to people," the man said. "He is Mary and Joseph's son."

"If he is Mary and Joseph's son, how does he have the ability to do the things that he say he does?" another man asked. "His dad works for that construction company, building cabinets in cracker box houses, right?"

All of the men in the meeting stared at Jesus now, waiting for him to speak.

Disappointed at the unexpected, unwelcome reunion, Jesus responded to their criticism. "History shows us that great warriors and leaders receive honor and glory, except in their own houses and city. I guess this is no different." Jesus left town that night and did not heal any illnesses or diseases, as he had planned. For the first time in his ministry, Jesus had been turned away.

While Jesus continued to minister, John was being transferred to a state penitentiary. Still not sure why he had been arrested, he tried his best to comply with the guard's orders.

After asking for a lawyer for the seemingly millionth time, John was told that this was a homeland security issue, and under the rendition law, the government leaders could imprison or expedite anyone who was suspected of terrorism without right to an attorney.

John had argued the absurd accusations, but there was nothing he could do. He was stuck in state prison. His own kind had betrayed him, and now all he had to do was pray that God would watch over him.

A couple of months into his imprisonment, John was allowed to have special privileges on account of his good behavior. He was assigned to clean the warden's office on a daily basis, along with walking some of the prison dogs.

Chris Herod, the warden of the prison, was a laid-back man who was sometimes more concerned with the luxuries of life than running the prison. One day, Herod happened to be working in his office when John came in to clean it.

"So you are John?" Chris asked with a wide smile.

"You must have really done something bad. The president's advisors requested that you come to my prison. Isn't that something? He wanted to make sure that I would keep an eye on you." Herod winked at John.

The warden leaned back in his chair and propped his feet up on the desk while he began twirling his burly mustache.

"Yep," he said. "I'm supposed to keep an eye on ya. You don't seem that horrible to me, though. What exactly did you do, anyway?"

John put down his broom. "Well, sir, when they arrested me, they told me that it was for harboring a minor fugitive, but now they tell me it is for terrorism. I have never committed any crimes. I don't even speed for crying out loud! So to answer your question, I honestly have no idea why I am in here." John tried not to show his anger through his answer, but everything was beginning to go to his head.

"Huh," Herod said. "We'll just have to make the best of it while we are both here."

"Easy for you to say," John mumbled under his breath.

"Well, since we have nothing to kill but time here, tell me a little bit about yourself," the warden probed him.

Talking about his arrest and prison sentence brought anger, but speaking about his life prior to prison was easy. John smiled and began to tell the warden about his church and wonderful congregation, and about God's grace.

This relationship went on for months, and John and Chris became friends through their odd circumstance. John thanked God for giving him his new friend, and started to accept his situation in prison was a little more ease.

When John had been in the state prison for six months, he heard through the grapevine that it was Chris Herod's birthday. With the help of the other inmates, who usually left John alone as long as he didn't start trouble, John bought a Cuban cigar, a type that he knew Herod would love.

John was excited. He loved to give people presents and see the joy it brought them. He carefully wrapped it up and placed it on the warden's desk when he went in to begin his daily cleaning routine. When Chris never showed up, another guard informed John that he had taken the day off in celebration of his fortieth birthday.

19

On the morning of Chris Herod's birthday, he awoke to his beautiful wife standing over him, holding a small cupcake with a single candle. He smiled drearily and pulled her onto the bed beside him.

"Happy birthday, baby," she whispered seductively in his ear.

Chris and his current wife Helen were still experiencing their newlywed phase, as they just recently got married. Helen had been working for the prison as a secretary, and Chris Herod had just gotten promoted to warden.

Every day, Helen's skirts would get shorter and shorter, and her tempting offers would get more promiscuous. One day, Herod finally gave into the sexy woman and they began having an affair. The affair went on for a couple of months before Helen filed for divorce and convinced Chris to do the same.

Helen's husband and Chris' wife were both devastated when they found out the news, but all that mattered to the two prison employees was their lust for one another. Helen moved into Herod's house the day after his wife and son moved out. With her came her eighteen-year-old daughter, a senior in high school.

Helen's daughter Sarah was a very pretty girl, but did not have the best reputation, nor the best morals or values. She used her appearance to get whatever she wanted, and up until this point, it always worked. Helen had taught her daughter everything she knew, and the two women once had the nickname of "Tag Team Mother and Daughter."

Before Helen had gotten divorced from Sarah's father, she joined a sacrilegious cult that based its beliefs on a non-religious life style. Helen had a friend in the cult who had been trying to recruit her for years, and finally succeeded.

Once Helen's last name was officially Herod, her mission set for the by the cult leaders was to take down John, the man in jail for baptizing Jesus. They wanted to start with the source of all the new God fearing people.

On the night of Chris Herod's birthday, Helen had a huge surprise party planned. Hundreds of people were coming, and it would be in the mess hall of the prison. At seven o'clock on the dot, Chris walked into the room to run his nightly checks as always, and was taken by surprise as everyone began shouting and streamers starting to flood the air.

The room was decorated in bright colors, with balloons everywhere that said "Over the Hill," and "Happy Birthday, Old Man." An elongated table stretched twenty feet on one side of the room, covered with every food you could imagine. On the very end of that table was a birthday cake the size of Texas, patiently waiting for everyone to begin eating.

After shaking many hands and talking to all of his friends, Chris wound up in front of his new wife. He looked down at her and smiled.

"How is it that you planned all of this without me finding out?" he asked in a hushed, sweet voice.

"I'm just good like that." She winked at him before engrossing herself in a passionate kiss with him. "But," she stopped. "That is not all of the surprise." Helen winked, and as if on cue, the lights began to dim, and a spotlight show started while some seductive music began to play.

Herod laughed. "Oh my, what have we here?" he asked Helen.

"You sit down here in the big birthday boy seat and enjoy the show." She bit his ear and walked away, shaking her hips and clanking her four-inch high heels.

Suddenly, as the song began to progress, Helen's daughter Sarah appeared in the doorway. She was wearing a black, men's overcoat, fishnet panty hose, and black heels, higher than her mothers. She stood seductively, with one hand rested high on the doorframe and her body leaned to the side. When the spotlight flashed onto Sarah, the real show began.

She was all the way across the huge room, with Chris Herod seated in the opposite corner. Sarah began to slowly walk towards her stepfather, her eyes never leaving him. After three steps, she ripped off the overcoat in tune to the music, showing her black lace bra and matching panties.

Sarah started to crawl on the floor, twist and turn, and perform a stripper dance as she worked her way towards her new stepfather. Sarah was not ashamed of her body, and had obviously pulled stunts like this before.

"Gross," one of the guests said to another. "Isn't that Chris' new stepdaughter?"

"Yes!" the other replied. "I am appalled. But this is like a car wreck. I am disgusted, but can't stop watching."

Conversations like this were popping up all over the room, and the faces of the bystanders were pure disgust and embarrassment. Many of the elder guests left the room, and others backed up towards the walls and exits.

The whole time Sarah was doing her dance, Helen was smiling, knowing that their goal would be accomplished. The look on Chris' face told her so.

Sarah kept making her way to her stepfather, doing her seductive dance the entire time. Thanks to the alcoholic beverages in his stomach, the lack of time spent around his new stepdaughter, and the dim lighting in the room, Chris Herod did not realize that this entertainer was Sarah. He thought she was simply a girl hired from an entertainment company, to come and entertain the party.

As Sarah got within inches of Chris, her dark eye make-up and curly hair wig her identity hidden from her stepfather. She inched towards his face until she was straddling his lap. She stuck the lollipop, which she had carried with her this whole time, in her mouth and pulled it out slowly.

Loud enough for everyone to hear, she asked him, "Now that I have danced for you, what are you going to do for me?" Sarah continued to suck seductively on her lollipop.

Chris Herod looked around and smiled at his buddies. "Anything you want, darling."

With that answer, Sarah looked over to her mother, who was nodding. "I want you to make sure that your prisoner, John, is not alive in the morning." Her seductive tone was gone and she was standing up in front of him now, instead of sitting on his lap.

"What?" the warden asked, confused. "You want me to kill someone. What kind of strip dance is that?"

"I don't want you to kill anyone, daddy," Sarah's voice suddenly turned innocent and manipulative. Chris' jaw dropped as he realized who the girl was.

"I just want you to make sure that your other prisoners show John a good time. Come on, Herod," Sarah said. "Inmates get murdered all the time in prison. Drug deals gone wrong, gangs, hate crimes. It doesn't matter. Just get someone to do it. Understand?"

Chris looked around at his friends, some of them politicians, and some wardens from other prisons. He had let John get close to him, but his reputation and appearance towards these people was more important.

He looked at the floor and mumbled, "I'll make sure it gets done tonight."

Sarah smiled and walked out the same door she walked in. Helen motioned for the house lights to come back on, and for the regular party music to begin once again. After a moment of shock, the guests began to continue to mingle around and sample the food.

Helen embraced her husband and kissed him hard on the mouth. Herod looked at her with betrayal in his eyes, harshly shoved her arms off of him, and walked out the door.

When Chris' friends gave Helen questioning looks, she shrugged and walked over to flirt with the other men.

Late that night, with the knowledge that he would be rewarded and given special privileges during his time served, an inmate who was in jail for murder and theft went into John's open cell and strangled him with a telephone cord until he was no longer breathing.

20

With the news, media outlets, and common gossip pool, good news travels fast and bad news travels faster. Some of the local news stations caught wind of John's story, probably from attendants from Herod's birthday party. The story was aired on a local news channel, in a special edition on what life is really like in prison. It was called "Inside the Prison Walls," and really got the citizens talking.

Like everyone else, Jesus eventually heard the news and was devastated. John had been a true friend to Jesus and he mourned the loss. He tried to continue preaching, but could not overcome the sadness he felt for John. Jesus decided to go into solitude for a while, to pray for John and the people who planned his death.

About a mile away, Jesus had seen a flat bottom boat sitting on the banks of a large lake, and decided that would be the perfect, serene getaway for a little while. The lake was away from the city and seemed to be secluded and peaceful. After walking around a while, since Jesus had forgotten the exact location of the lake, he finally found it and saw the boat still sitting in the same spot it had been.

Other than a couple of fishermen and some recreational water-skiers, the lake seemed empty and Jesus was excited in anticipation of some quiet alone time with his father. As he began to push the boat off of the banks and get into it, Jesus heard people shouting at him. He turned to see mobs of people who had followed him to his secret hideaway.

Jesus thought about being mad, but instead smiled. He was so glad that so many people had such great faith, that they would hunt him down in hopes of hearing a sermon or getting an ill family member healed.

Jesus tied the boat back up to the metal stake and walked towards the people. Jesus' two friends Simon and James were also in the crowd, and feared that they were the ones who led the people to him.

"I'm sorry," Simon told Jesus after he had pushed his way through the crowd. "We didn't realize these people were following us. Most of them were in cars, but left them parked at the marina. Do you want us to tell them to leave?"

Jesus smiled at his friend. "No, they have come this far. They should stay."

"But Jesus," James argued. "We didn't realize it was so secluded out here. It will be dark in a while and all of these people will need to have supper and go home. There are a lot of little kids out here, and they probably have school in the morning. We'll just tell everyone to go home and name a place and time tomorrow or the next day where they can come listen to your sermon. OK?"

Jesus seemed to think for a minute. "No," he replied. "They can eat supper right here on the lakeshore. We'll all picnic." He smiled at the peaceful thought of a picnic by the lake at dusk.

Simon laughed. "A picnic with what? The closest Wal-Mart is more than ten miles from here. There's a gas station up the road, but they don't have enough food in stock to feed all of these people. My gosh, there must be thousands of them." Simon looked around, as if scanning the crowd, counting heads.

"More than four thousand," Jesus told him without even looking at the people. "They came here for worship, and that is what they are going to get."

Before Simon or James could protest anymore, Jesus turned to the crowd. "I'm so glad you all came. This is such a lovely, peaceful lake, and I think it would be lovely if we all had a short picnic before I deliver a sermon." Most of the people simply looked at Jesus, waiting for more instructions.

Jesus sent Simon after a small child down the shoreline, feeding bread to the ducks. As instructed, Simon asked the boy if he could take the thin white bread, packaged in the recognizable Wonder © blue, yellow, and red polk-a-dot cellophane.

Simon brought not only the bread back, but also the little boy and his grandfather, who wanted to see why the large crowd of people had gathered. Another man from the crowd had lunch meat in his cooler, obviously from a camping or boating trip.

Jesus took the turkey meat and small loaf of bread and prayed for the food. Everyone bowed their heads, and joined in. When he was done, Jesus began to pass the bread and meat to the first row, and instructed them to pass it on after they had received some.

He then took a young girl's grapefruit juice pack and began to bless each person, giving them communion with the juice. It grew dark outside and the hours crept on until each person had received and eaten a sandwich.

No one was sure how the small amount of food had fed everyone, and most of them figured that people were adding to the supplies as they were passed around. Many people, mostly women, would not eat anything on account of it previously being touched by others, but were simply happy to be in the calming presence of Jesus.

After everyone had eaten a snack, some of the men started a fire in a large fire pit and one of them started to play his guitar. Many people started to sing old Gospel hymns and sway to the music. Everyone was full and happy, and Jesus was glad to have the company. He said a short prayer, thankful for the faith and convictions of so many people. They all had comfortable beds in warm houses, and the obligations of school and work in just a few short hours. But they had put Jesus as a higher priority than those, even if just for the night.

Around three o'clock in the morning, the last couple people of the crowd dispersed and left only Jesus and his friends. As they heard about the meeting, more of his close friends came out to join in.

Once again abandoning the luxuries of life, Jesus and his friends found luxury in nature and decided to sleep by the lakeshore, in the peaceful night air. It was a beautiful night, and they were thankful to be able to enjoy it together. They stayed up a couple more hours, talking and relaying to each other stories from their travels and preaching.

Around six o'clock the next morning, the bright sun began to wake all of the young men up. The lake began to get crowded with early fishermen and some recreational enthusiasts.

After eating leftovers from the night before, Jesus and his friends were cleaning their makeshift campsite when a large red boat flew by close to the shore. It circled and came back, slower this time. As it got closer, some of the men recognized it as a Tahoe Ski and Wakeboard Boat, and remembered their days of recreation.

"Hey!" the young driver shouted. "Aren't you guys the ones with Jesus?"

They nodded, and the driver asked if they wanted to tube and wakeboard for a while. "Please don't think I'm a psycho and going to kill you or anything," he laughed. "I just think you guys are doing a good thing and deserve a little fun time. This is my dad's boat, and he is gone for the weekend. All of my friends are busy, and I don't have anyone to hang out with. What do you say?" His voice was pleading.

"You guys go ahead," Jesus told them. "I want to be alone to pray this morning."

No longer reluctant, Jesus' friends walked to get onto the ski boat. Once they were all in and life-jacketed, the boat took out of sight. Jesus, thankful for the quiet solitude, cleaned the rest of the campsite and walked away from site to pray.

Jesus was deep in the state park, which was adjacent to the lake, seeking prayer when the clouds overhead became dark. It started to rain, but Jesus did not let the rain stop his mission. He continued praying and thanking his father for the amazing faith of all those people the night before.

Soon mixed in with the rain was lightning and thunder, and then the loud pelting sound signaled hail mixed in the storm also. The only downfall to leaving all electronic devices behind was the lack of access to the weather channel or other weather alerts.

The storm had blown up out of nowhere and Jesus decided to go find his friends, before it got worse. The lake was not a big one, and it did not have any coves, so boats were usually easy to spot.

Jesus stood on the shore, getting constantly smacked by frozen balls of rain and trying to see through the raging wind and rain. The lighting struck a tree five feet away from him, and the tree instantly set ablaze. The tremendous rain put out the fire as quickly as it had started, as Jesus kept scanning the lake for the red boat.

The boat did not have a cuddy cabin or interior living quarters, so if they had not come in to the marina, there would be no cover for anyone on board. Jesus walked closer and closer to the shore, steadily looking for the boat, his eyes never leaving the lake, scanning it for the bright red color.

He saw black boats and blue boats and a green boat, but no red one. He continued walking the shoreline, faster now, looking for the boat. He caught a glimpse of the blood red boat and starting walking along the shoreline to reach it, or so he thought.

It seemed that the boat was just within reach, and Jesus, in an attempt to get to his friends, inched closer so that he would not fall in the water. Jesus finally touched the boat, and wondered why they had not just gotten off of the vessel if they were this close to land.

As he reached for the railing on back of the boat, Jesus suddenly noticed that everyone on the boat was staring blankly at him. They were being beaten by hail and rain, but did not even try to cover their eyes. They were staring right at him, almost in shock.

"What?" Jesus asked.

When no one answered, Jesus looked down. He was standing on the surface of the water, in the middle of the lake. They were in fact nowhere near the marina or the shore, and it seemed that Jesus had walked all the way out to the boat.

"Oh my God," said the young driver of the boat.

"Oh my God is right," Jesus smiled at him. "Through God, you can do anything." He winked as his friends helped him onto the boat. Once Jesus climbed up the ladder and onto the anchored boat, the hail stopped and the rain began to slowly die down. The summer storm was ending as quickly as it blew up, as summer storms always do.

Peter and Phillip started to get towels from the storage containers under the seats, and passed them around to everyone while the rain finally gave way to the humid day. While everyone started to dry off, the young boat driver continued to stare at Jesus with a blank look.

Finally, he spoke up. "You really are God's son, aren't you?" The words and the realness of it brought the man to tears. Jesus smiled at him, and began to pat the young man's back with a towel, rubbing it hard against his shivering body.

Once everyone was dry, they all looked at Jesus, who had just walked half way across a lake to get to them. No one knew what to say. Finally, Jesus decided they should pray, and they all agreed.

21

While Jesus and his friends were enjoying the peacefulness and solitude of the lake, the president's advisors were secretly meeting once again. The president had informed them that Jesus was not breaking any laws, nor hurting anyone, but the high government officials honestly believed that Jesus would continue to gain power until he overthrew the government.

They were scared for not only their jobs, but also their families' lives. They did not know what the future held, but wanted to be prepared to protect it at all costs.

"We need a law that says we can arrest someone, even if they have seemingly broken no laws, to stop what they will do in the future," one of the government leaders said.

"We have one," another spoke up. "Rendition. But you know the president won't let us arrest Jesus. I honestly thought that he might back off with his sermons after we arrested John, but he didn't. What now?"

"Make him break the law." A young girl in her early twenties spoke up this time, probably a summer intern and college student. She had been staring blankly at the table, and no one had even acknowledged her until she spoke.

"What?" an older man laughed.

"Write a law that prohibits preaching, or whatever it is Jesus is doing that you don't like. Run it through the system, like super-fast. Then, he will be breaking the law. After you have arrested him, take the law out of circulation." The girl explained her theory like it was a no brainer, and was very nonchalant in her description.

Everyone was quiet for a minute, not sure if they should agree with this young person.

"It seems to be a reasonable solution to the problem," the leader of the meeting finally said. "It will take a couple of months to write the bill and make it a law, but I think it is a wonderful idea." The man turned and smiled at the girl in the corner, followed by smiles from everyone else in the room.

"Frank," the man starting giving directions right away. "Start writing the bill. We are going to have to make our purpose as subtle as possible, so hide the clause about illegal preaching in a four hundred-page bill about education. The readers of the bill will pass it on without even reading the fine details."

When Jesus and his friends left the calm and serene lake hours after the storm, they were all refreshed from the peaceful silence. They missed each other's company and decided to travel together as they continued preaching the word of God.

All thirteen friends were staying at a large church, sleeping in the gym when the media caught wind of Jesus' whereabouts. The church was a massive one, and aired a special on television every Sunday, where the preacher's sermons were not only on the local news, but nationwide.

When people heard Jesus and his friends were staying there, huge crowds flocked to the church, usually at nighttime, after work and other obligations. They sat squished in the pews and seats, trying to hear anything he said. While the growing number of people pleased Jesus, he still felt that he needed to reach out to more of them.

Due to all of the media attention the church was getting, the preacher decided that it would be a good idea to let Jesus perform the sermon on Sunday instead of her. When she asked him, he smiled at her and thanked her for the opportunity.

Sunday was four days away, and Jesus thought and prayed hard about what his sermon should entail. On Sunday morning, the sanctuary was more packed than it had ever been, with standing room only, even in the hallways leading to it.

After the song service and prayers, Jesus got up to walk towards the pulpit. While he had been preparing his sermon, he thought about a question that an old man had asked him during the week. The man had wondered why Jesus and his friends wondered all over the country instead of buying or renting a house. He said they were a drain on the economy and he was tired of paying taxes for people who had no money and would not work. Jesus smiled as he thought about the man, and knew that his question would be the driving force behind the message he was about to give.

"This week, a man asked me why my brothers and I travel around, and do not have a place of our own. He said he was tired of paying taxes for people like us, who do not work and use government handouts.

"I think the idea behind this is a great lesson that we can all learn from. This man was so frustrated with his financial situation and the financial trouble of the country that he lost sight of the reason I travel around.

"We get so caught up in our materialistic lifestyles that we forget the big picture. Our only purpose on this earth is to worship God. He does not tell us that we cannot love our families, we cannot work, and provide for ourselves. He does not tell us not to enjoy life and find happiness. But if you are not worshiping him along the way, therein lays our problem.

"Defilement is a fancy word for denying God or I. Defilement starts within your heart, and you must not harbor it.

"To further explain, everyone eats food, right? The food you eat travels through your body systems until reaching your stomach. After drawing all of the nutrients from the food, your stomach eliminates the rest of the food substance through fat storage or waste.

"All of the organs, intestines, and blood inside of your body are unimportant. The food I just described, the body systems, and even the outwardly body appearance are unimportant, compared to what comes out of your body.

"Not the waste you might be thinking of, but out of your mouth. Defilement comes through your thoughts, your words, and your actions. Every day, you might tell a little white lie, or slip out a curse word, or have harsh encounters with other people.

"These words and this form of defilement, which come from your mouth, are sometimes the hardest to suppress. We think that a curse word here or there or yelling at your spouse or other family members is OK, but this hurts my father and me. We want you all to be as kind to one another as we are to you.

"Heed the example I am setting and treat one another with a little more kindness. Try to start small and get bigger. Give someone a smile throughout the day, and experience the joy that kindness can bring you. You never know what someone else might be going through, and your small smile or short word of encouragement could change his or her whole outlook on life.

"In our society today, the worst form of defilement is as common as running water, and I am pleading with you to stop. This form of defilement is using my father's name in vain. Every time someone stumps their toe, their car won't start, the loose their keys, or a million other scenarios, I have found them using God's name in vain.

"I want you all to think about your fathers right now. Think about all of the nice things they did for you when you were growing up and think about how much you love them." Jesus paused for a moment.

"Now imagine people hollering your father's name every time something negative happened in their life, and blaming him for it. For example, say your father's name is David. Now say that I dropped my cell phone and it broke. Instead of dealing with the minor inconvenience, I shout out, "Damn it, David!" and I curse your father every time something negative went array.

"It would physically hurt you to hear the words. Your father did nothing to cause that person a small inconvenience, just as mine did nothing to cause any misfortune in your lives.

"You must stop using my father's name in vain. This pains us more than you could know and I pray that you find another way to take out your frustrations. I don't blame you and holler, 'O Peter!' when I step on a sharp rock or my shoe breaks. Please cease hollering out my father's name when you do."

Jesus stepped off of the pulpit and walked back to his seat on the front row. He smiled at Peter, who was sitting four people down from him, thanking him for being an example in the day's message.

More songs were sung and an offering plate was passed around before the final prayer was said. As the congregation milled out of the church, Jesus did not have many people coming to talk to him as he usually did. Many of them did not make eye contact with him and seemed to be ashamed of how they treated him in the past.

Jesus was walking through the long corridor towards the open doors of the church, greeting people along the way. The building had been so crowded that he had not noticed a middle aged, blatantly uncomfortable woman nervously waiting to speak with him. She seemed to be trying to shield her face from anyone who might recognize her.

When Jesus was almost to the door, the lady grabbed him and pulled him into a receded part of the hall that held a water fountain and the doors to a woman's and men's bathroom. The bathroom entrance was visible to the rest of the hall, but the woman seemed to feel safer in the smaller area.

"Hi," the lady said, keeping her back to the church-goers in the hall. Her eyes stayed peeled on the floor and she spoke so quietly, Jesus could barely hear her. His friends started to lead the woman away, but Jesus motioned to them that everything was OK.

"I'm sorry that I am so uncomfortable and uneasy. I am the mayor of this town and a proclaimed scientologist. I have publicly spoken out against people who believe in God and believe you, and for that I am sorry." The lady really seemed sincere.

"I don't know what I believe now, and that is not why I am here today, regardless. I have a nineteen-year-old daughter who needs your help. I am at my wit's end and don't know who else to go to.

"She has been addicted to methamphetamine crystal ice since she was fifteen." The lady started to cry. "She was such a good girl, just fell in with the wrong crowd, you know?"

"Anyway, we have sent her to rehab seven times and she will stop for a couple of months. But as soon as she runs into a user, she'll start using again. We've moved clear across town and hired a full time caretaker to keep her from running into any other crystal ice users, but they are everywhere.

"It's like she's possessed by this demon that won't let her go. These drugs are so powerful and so strong that she just can't break the cycle. If she doesn't stop, she'll be dead within a couple of years." The lady stopped crying and tried to pull herself together, looking into Jesus' eyes for the first time.

"I want her to lead a full and long life. I want her to wake up from this horrible nightmare, and she does too. The drugs are just too powerful. I don't know if you can, or even would help her, but you are my last resort." She was pleading with her eyes for an answer from Jesus. One that said he would help her daughter and all would be right.

James, who had been standing off to the side and talking with members of the congregation who were gathering around the door, suddenly recognized the woman and had an angry look in his eye as he walked towards the two.

"Jesus," he said with a tight mouth, almost under his breath. "This is the mayor. The scientologist who publicly curses you and God." He did not even attempt to speak in a tone in which the lady could not hear him. She looked at the floor as James attempted to make Jesus walk away from her.

"James," Jesus said in a calm voice, trying to soothe James' anger. "I was not sent here to help the people who already worship God. I was sent for the lost sheep." He looked with compassion upon the lady.

"Where is your daughter?" he asked her.

"She is in the car!" the lady almost shouted with delight and hugged Jesus hard. She had a small stature and had to jump just to reach his neck.

"Bring her to me," he instructed.

Jesus continued to visit with other guests while the lady went to get her daughter. When she arrived back, she was leading a young girl through the door, holding her hand and supporting her back. The lady no longer seemed to care that people saw her, and focused more on helping her daughter than the stares she was receiving.

The girl looked like she weighed about ninety pounds and wore baggy jeans that probably fit at one time, and a large T-shirt. She was very pale and had deep, dark circles around her eyes that looked as if she had been punched in the face. Her hair was very thin, and you could see her scalp in several places. Her arms were covered in blotches and bruises, from years of poking needles through her veins.

The girl did not have enough strength to walk alone, and had to utilize her mother's help. Most of the people still in the church could not hide their repulsion from the mother and daughter, but Jesus smiled with compassion at them.

"You have greater faith than most, mam," he told her. "I don't know what you believe in, but not many people are so strong that they would seek help outside their comfort zone. I hope this helps you reconsider some of your choices in life."

The lady nodded her head, and Jesus knew that she would. She helped her daughter sit down in a metal chair, and the girl began rocking slowly back and forth.

"It's part of her withdrawals," the mayor explained. "Her body is so used to the drug, that when she goes without it, she physically pains."

Jesus held the teenager's hand and said a short prayer out loud for her.

"Father, please heal this girl. Let her be free from her prison of drugs, and let her live a full and happy life, worshiping you." The prayer was short, but accomplished.

The girl stopped swaying, and although it would take time to heal her body and look as she once did, she now had the power to overcome the drug that held her captive for so many years. She would go on to get her GED, receive her Bachelor's degree in religious studies, and proceed on to become a preacher, sharing her experience with her congregation. Her mother would continue to act as mayor, but drop her previous lifestyle, converting her faith and belief to God and Jesus, and would be devout in that faith.

Jesus smiled and hugged them both, knowing that their lives would be changed for the better. Jesus and his friends continued with their preaching, and Jesus kept healing people along the way, bringing more and more people to him.

22

After months of traveling and continual media coverage, Jesus decided that it was time to begin preparing his closest friends for the future. Although he dreaded the pain that he knew time would bring, he wanted his loyal believers to be prepared for it.

"Hey, guys," he said as they sat in a small church, eating their daily lunch of sandwiches and chips.

Mouths stuffed, they looked up, ready to listen to what Jesus had to say. All twelve of his closest friends sat at the table, with their mouths full of bread and sandwich meat.

"Not too long from now, I am going to have to suffer through a lot of stuff. The political leaders are planning it as we speak, and no matter what you do, you will not be able to fight what will happen. I just want to warn you guys and tell you not to worry. This is all part of God's plan, and is what he wants. It is the only way to save the people from their own sin."

The young men all stared blankly at Jesus, not sure what he was talking about. Peter finally spoke up, saying, "Nothing bad will happen to you, Jesus. Everyone loves you. And the people who don't love you just leave you alone. What could ever go wrong?"

"Peter," Jesus replied. "What I told you will happen. They will arrest me, beat me, and finally kill me. There is nothing you can do to stop it. Why would you have more faith in the human heart than you do in me? I am God's son, and if I say something will happen, you can bet it will."

Peter and the others looked at each other.

"But why would anyone arrest you? You cannot arrest someone when they have not broken any laws," Simon asked, confused.

"When you have enough political pull, you can do anything you want," Jesus said calmly. "I don't want you to worry about the future. I just want you to be prepared for what will happen. Understand?"

Jesus' friends could tell that the conversation was over, although they were scared for their leader's safety, as well as their own.

"If anyone, including you, wants to truly worship me and my father, he will have to give up everything and deny his own self to follow me. Worldly and material goods will not matter. Whoever tries to save his own life will lose it, but whoever gives his life up for me will save it. What does it matter if you gain all of the material goods in the world if you lose your soul in the process? You might be surprised to find out what most people would sale their soul for. Everyone will be rewarded according to his or her work here on earth."

Jesus could tell that his buddies were confused with his words, but he decided to leave them that way, and let them ponder the deepness of it.

After the guys ate their lunch, they sat at the tables, their stomachs full. They prayed and talked and laughed, enjoying each other's company, but not bringing up the future that Jesus had just described. It was a big white elephant in the room, and the tension could be felt although no one mentioned anything.

The thirteen men stayed at this church for another week, traveling close by to preach during the days, and staying on cots in the gym at night.

At the end of the week, Jesus asked James, John, and Peter to head toward the east end of town with him while the rest of their friends traveled in different directions, going door to door bringing the word of God.

The four of them walked until they were secluded on the world's tallest hill. The people in the town had told Jesus that their highest point, right outside of the heart of their small city, was two inches too short to classify as a mountain. Their claim to fame was housing the tallest hill in the world, and Jesus and the others walked the winding paved road that led to the top in an hour and a half.

The town below was small, and seeing how it was during the middle of the day during a workweek, the hill was deserted. There were scenic overlooks, places to pull your car over and look at the town, along with picnic tables and benches all around, but all were vacant.

"Sure is pretty up here, huh?" James asked as they stopped to take a break and enjoy the beautiful picture of nature painted in front of them.

James, his younger brother John, and Peter walked close to the edge to look out and enjoy the beauty of the world. It was a crisp fall day, and the reds, yellows, and oranges swirling around them made for an almost unreal sight.

They were just about to ask what they should do next when all three young men felt warmth on their backs. Slowly, they turned around at the same time and did not know if they should run or stand still. They were frozen in time, not sure what to do; a little scared and a little mesmerized.

Jesus, who had been sitting on a bench behind them, was now seemingly glowing. Light reflected from his face and clothes, making his dingy shirt and pants white as the light, and his face so pure and full of light it almost blinded them to look at it.

Suddenly, there were two other people standing beside Jesus, and they three shiny people were talking with each other. It seemed to be a pleasant conversation, and James, John and Peter continued to stare at the wildness happening before their eyes.

"Umm…" Peter finally spoke up. "What's going on here? Who are these people, and why in the world are you guys glowing? Should I be worried?"

Jesus smiled. "This is Moses, and this is Elijah."

"Like from the Bible? They died hundreds of years ago!" John was stunned.

Before any more questions could be asked, a lightning bolt hit the ground, not twenty feet from the scene. With no rain or even clouds in the sky, James, John and Peter's eyes became even wider and fear spread across their faces.

"This is my son, with whom I am pleased!" a voice came out of nowhere, like someone had planted an I Pod to play at exactly that moment. The three friends of Jesus became very scared, not sure of the situation.

They looked at one another, and seemed to agree with each other that they should leave. When they turned to walk away, Jesus put his hand on their backs.

James, John, and Peter turned around and saw no one but Jesus.

Still shaken, John looked hard at Jesus. "What in the world was that all about? You can't just go around talking to non-existent shiny people and expect us not to freak out!"

Jesus laughed as they all began to come back to reality. "Have you not realized yet that normal rules don't apply to me?"

They all smiled, knowing that Jesus had the ability to do anything he wanted. "I want you to do something for me. Don't tell anyone about this until I am gone. You'll understand later."

"No one would believe us anyway," Peter laughed and everyone's mood lightened.

"People killed John, the man who baptized me. They have killed many, many people for reasons that might not even know themselves. The same will happen to me. Don't fight it; just know that this is God's plan."

They all nodded, knowing not to question Jesus' wisdom. They started the long road down the hill and were silent as they walked.

By the time the four men arrived back in town, they saw a large gathering of people in the Wal-Mart parking lot, which was on the outskirts of the loop, the first thing that Jesus would walk by.

Catching a glimpse of one of their friends, the men walked off the hill and into the crowd, curious to what was happening.

While Jesus was trying to walk to the front of the crowd and meet his other friends, an older man grabbed him.

"Jesus!" he cried.

Startled, Jesus answered him as he tried to wriggle loose from his tight grip. "Yes?"

"My son suffers from severe epilepsy. None of the medicine the doctors give him works. He cannot go to school, for his outbursts disrupt the other students, and the special school that our district sends him to is awful, with minimum wage employees who have eight hour lunch breaks while my son and the other students sit or lay around all day, doing nothing.

"My wife is dead, and I cannot do this alone anymore. I just want my son to have all of the opportunities he deserves. I don't want him to be punished for his epilepsy anymore. Is there anything you can do? Nothing else I've tried works."

The man was begging Jesus with his eyes. Jesus seemed tired. "How long will I be here to help people? What will you do after I am gone?" He paused and sighed. After no answer, he said, "bring him to me."

Jesus held the little boy, who was seizing and shaking all over. Jesus prayed, with the boy in his arms, and handed him back to the exhausted father. Knowing that he would never seize again and the father or son would not suffer any more epileptic pain, Jesus met his friends at the front of the crowd.

"I tried to help that man and his son," Matthew said. "If you would make it where we could heal people too, maybe you wouldn't be so tired all the time."

"You do not believe like I do," Jesus explained to them. "You cannot because you do not have the father that I do." He smiled. He then dropped his head and seemed to contemplate what he was going to say next. All twelve of the men moved in closer for support.

"I will soon be betrayed and killed. They will arrest me, and kill me, but three days after my death, I will be raised."

"What? No?" protests from his friends cried out.

"Arrested for what? That is crazy," they all said. But Jesus was finished with the conversation and walked away from them, into the crowd to talk and pray with the people.

23

Five hours later, when Jesus was finished speaking with everyone that begged and pleaded for his attention, he and his friends retreated back to their temporary home for some rest and relaxation.

Some of them were sitting on their cots while the others helped the young preacher's wife make supper. She had made easy meals while they were there and was obviously still new to the cooking world. As the timer signaled the spaghetti was ready to eat, everyone bowed their heads to pray before digging into the feast.

Before Jesus could get a word of prayer out, there was a loud knock on the door. No one probably would have heard it, except for the fact that they were all silenced. The banging was coming from the front entrance, through the gym where Jesus and his friends were staying, and the sanctuary.

"I'll go see who that is," the preacher said. "It might be one of our youth group members. They come over a lot to play basketball and hang out with us."

When the preacher came back, a woman and man in professional clothing followed him. Everyone looked uneasy, not sure what they were there for.

"You sure are hard people to find," the man said in a condescending voice. "I guess when you don't have a place of residence or address, you can outrun us." He smiled a cocky smile.

No one spoke until the woman explained the situation. "We're with the Internal Revenue Service, and it seems that none of you-well, not you two," she said, motioning towards the preacher and his wife. "Have paid taxes in the past five years. We are here to set up a payment plan or settle on an amount that needs to be paid within a month." The lady was not any nicer than the man, although she seemed to be unconcerned with her job.

"We don't have any money," Mark spoke up.

"Well I guess you better find some," the IRS man said.

"We have set up an appointment for all thirteen of you. Next week, Tuesday at 9:00 am. Our office is downtown on Sycamore St. All of the information is in this packet. We will set up a payment plan or you can pay it all in a lump sum. All thirteen of your back taxes are shown in detail in the packet. Just show up. I found you once, and I will find you again." The man threw a manila folder down on Luke's cot and the couple walked out.

Worried glances were exchanged around the group. They did not know how they would pay taxes; they had no jobs or money.

Seemingly all at once, everyone turned to Jesus for an answer.

"Simon, do you think the IRS is more concerned with our paying taxes or their own children paying them?" he asked.

"Us," Simon replied.

Jesus seemed to think ponder the situation for a minute. "O well, we need to pay our part so that we don't offend the government more than we already do." Jesus' friends looked around at each other, confused and unaware of the government plans and building hatred.

"Peter, go to the lake we were on during that stormy day. Remember? The one where I walked across the lake?"

"How could I forget?" Peter smiled.

"Go find the young man whose boat you guys were on and get back on it. Bait and cast a line, and catch the first fish you can. Clean and gut the fish, and inside of him you will find a zip lock bag with enough cash to pay all of our taxes." Jesus gave him the instructions like they were no big deal, and things like this happened every day.

Peter looked at Jesus like he was crazy. "Are you serious?" he laughed. "Even if there was money in a fish, how would I know which fish to catch?"

Jesus smiled at all of his friends. "You just keep on doubting me, don't you? You have seen me perform miracles and heal thousands of people. I have provided food and shelter for all of us. Do you not think that I would provide money for our taxes to be paid?"

Peter looked at the floor, remorseful for questioning Jesus. After supper and eight hours of sleep, Peter did as he was told, and found the money in discussion. He could not help but smile when he waltzed into the IRS office and placed the exact dollar amount in a pile on the cocky agent's desk.

That night, after all of their taxes had been paid, Jesus and his friends were lying on their cots, with their few belongings packed and ready to leave in the morning.

"Hey Jesus," John said with thoughtfulness.

"Yes?"

"I have a question. There are so many Godly people. Preachers, teachers, you. Who is the best in the eyes of your father?" The rest of the crew turned to look at John, for no one had ever thought to ask that question.

Jesus seemed to think about the question for a minute. "Children," he finally answered. "Children have the strongest faith and do not question God. They are humble and do whatever they are told."

Jesus explained further. "If a child's parents or teacher cause him or her to turn away from me, by teaching other religions or disobeying my father, that adult might as well hang himself. Furthermore, if your right hand causes you to sin, you should cut it off."

Jesus' friends starred at him in disbelief.

"Say you are addicted to pornography and your right hand is the one that hits the "buy" button on the computer, or turns the pages in the magazine. It would be better to dismember yourself than to pay for that sin. The same with your feet. It is better to be maimed than to be condemned to hell for eternity."

The guys still looked confused.

"That is a metaphor, right? You don't really want people to cut off their hands and feet?"

"Of course not," Jesus replied with reassurance. "But they do need to understand that sinning against my father is far worse than losing a limb."

There was silence until everyone fell asleep as they thought about the seriousness of what Jesus had just told them.

When Jesus and his friends woke up, they started to gather their belongings in their old, faded duffle bags. The majority of them, including Jesus, had not purchased new clothes or items since they began their journeys, so the small amount of clothes and personal hygiene items were slowly falling apart, after years in suitcases.

They took off walking north, in the direction of cooler weather. Their traveling seemed random and unplanned to Jesus' friends, but he had a divine plan the whole time. They walked for nine hours, and made good time.

The human body is uniquely made to be able to adjust to almost anything. When Jesus and his friends first began to travel the country, their feet ached severely and were swollen and bruised from constant pressure and weight of walking.

Years later, their feet had grown so accustomed to the long walks that they probably could travel on the blacktop pavement barefoot, although none of them would ever want to. They were always thankful for the support from their followers and the general public. When their shoes would fall apart, or their clothes got too ragged and ratty to wear, they graciously accepted the donations they were given.

When they arrived at their next destination, Jesus led them to their new temporary home, a large church in the center of town. They dropped their belongings and went out to mingle with the townspeople, and speak on the local news, which had already spotted them and sent a camera crew out to monopolize on the celebrities.

It was a Friday evening, and most of the nine to fivers were off work, milling around the square at restaurants and shops. When people saw the camera crews and news van, they flocked to the scene in an attempt to be part of the action.

Jesus walked through the people, holding the children, shaking hands with the adults, and praying with everyone. People came out of the woodworks, looking for a miracle for all of their ales.

After hours of "politicking," as his friends joked, Jesus sat down on a curb in front of the large, old courthouse. It was a beautiful building that had probably been restored from its 1800's interior. It sat in the center of the square, and everything else seemed to thrive from it.

Jesus began to preach, as he always did when large groups of people gathered around him, and brought the good news of his father to them.

"We have all had someone wrong us." He smiled as he continued to play with the small toddler on his lap. He was bouncing her on his knee and smiling at her while he spoke into the microphone the local newscaster handed him.

"People try to get ahead to make a buck or better themselves, and stomp on others in the process. Maybe someone steals your sippy cup on the playground at daycare," he spoke directly to the small girl and the crowd laughed as she began waddling over to another venue of interest.

"Maybe your spouse lies to you. Maybe a co-worker gets you fired so he can get a promotion. Whatever it is that people do to sin against you, you must not harbor hatred towards them.

"You should pull them aside and speak about your issue privately. Discussing it publicly only causes embarrassment and rage from both parties. You need to tell that person that what they did was wrong and how it has hurt you.

"Now I realize that many people have oversized egos and will not listen to you when you try to bring up the topic of criticism or discussion of something they had done wrong. If they will not listen to you alone, you should bring two or three mutual friends or colleagues into the discussion and further address the issue.

"If the person still refuses to listen, then you can take the issue public and tell your boss or family, or whoever the issue involves. But before the last resort, you should try to talk to the person who has done wrong against you and tell them how you feel.

"I talk a lot about harboring anger and getting rid of your rage. This is another step into becoming anger free and forgiveness bound. When you learn to forgive other people, you will truly be forgiven by my father."

The crowd was quiet for a minute, and Jesus waited patiently to how people might react.

After a couple minutes of silence, an older man who had been listening in the back of the mob began making his way to the front. The cameras zoomed in on him, anticipating some drama.

"I have been married for thirty years," the man told Jesus, loud enough for many of the people to hear. He seemed weary and tired, like he had been through a long journey recently.

"We have two children and had five grandchildren. Two years ago, our youngest grandchild was playing in the garage and my wife didn't know it. She ran over her and killed her. Since then, my wife has gone crazy, yelling all the time, breaking things, cutting herself, and trying to kill herself. How am I supposed to forgive her and live with her? You say not to get a divorce. Live in my shoes and tell me you wouldn't get divorced."

The crowd was silent and showed looks of sadness and empathy on their faces.

"My dear child," Jesus said. "I never said life would be easy. But this is why I am here. Of course you should forgive her and continue living with her. She blames herself for what happened and will never accept peace until she forgives herself. But what she does not know is that she is already forgiven.

"As for divorce, hear me out." Jesus got louder so that everyone could hear. "We live in a society that teaches us the mindset of a light marriage, one in which you can just get a divorce if it does not work out.

"Have you not read the bible? Man and woman were created for one another in the beginning and God's plan was for them to be joined in flesh monogamously. What God has joined together, do not let men separate.

"Permitting and entering into divorce is committing adultery, and marrying a divorced person is also committing adultery. The only reason for divorce should be sexual immorality. People need to begin working with their spouse and working problems out instead of getting a decree of divorce at the first sign of hard times.

"God gave you each other to lean on for support and hard times. Do not turn away from your spouse. If you put God first in your relationship, your marriage will last forever."

A woman in the crowd spoke up next. "You have so many rules. You have never been married or done any of the things you preach about. You don't know how hard it is to be a good person and do all of the things you tell us not to do." She had a little anger in her, and Jesus guessed she was divorced.

He smiled at her and calmly told them, "I know. This is why I am here. To save you from all of the sin and the hard things in life, and to bring you joy and forgiveness."

The lady turned and walked away, obviously not satisfied with that answer. The camera zoomed in on her walking away and scanned the crowd one last time before shutting off to chase the next big story.

24

Jesus and his friends headed back to the church after the crowd dispersed and planned to settle in for the night. Little did they know, vacation bible school was taking place all that week at night, when the temperature was cooler and the volunteers were off work.

Puzzled by all of the cars parked at the church on a Monday night, the thirteen young men walked into the foyer and were greeted by woman with hula skirts on top of their blue jean shorts, pink and blue leis, and Hawaiian shirts, signaling a beach theme for the event.

They smiled and made small talk with the men and told them that if they walked left, they could go around the excitement and have a nice, quiet evening in their bunks. After the vacation bible school workers had discovered Jesus and the other men were staying at the church, they moved the arts and crafts booth to another Sunday school classroom so that the men could rest after their long days.

Jesus' friends started to go as directed, but Jesus lagged behind. "No," he told the bubbly women. "I want to be with the children."

The other guys seemed irritated with Jesus' decision, and had obviously wanted to call it a night. Most of them had never been around young people and were overwhelmed by their screaming and crying and running in circles.

"In that case, take a right and go on down. I'm sure the kiddos would love to see you," one of the ladies directed Jesus.

He walked down the hall, which had been decorated to look like a vacation destination, and he could tell a lot of hours of manpower had been put forth. He walked into the gym, where most of the children were gathered, probably to close out the first night of VBS.

When Jesus walked in, everyone turned to look at him. The speaker, who was the preacher of the church, spoke up into the microphone.

"Teachers and students! It looks like we have a change of plan tonight. This is Jesus, and I think that instead of breaking off into age groups, we should all stay and hang out with him." The volunteer teachers nodded in agreement and Jesus began to mingle with the children.

Their ages ranged from two to twelve year olds, and Jesus was obviously elated by their presence. He let them sit on his lap and play with his hair and, for the first time his friends had ever witnessed, seemed care-free.

Jesus sat with the kids, playing and laughing until all of their parents came to pick them up. He seemed happier that night than he had in a while, and when the preacher asked Jesus what made him what to come into the gym, he answered, "The little children own the kingdom of heaven. We should all learn to be as trusting and loving as them."

The preacher nodded his head with a smile as Jesus and his friends finally headed off to bed after an extremely long day.

After learning about the events going on at the church all week, Jesus decided to forgo their plans to leave the following day. They stayed in that same location for the entire week and were active volunteers with vacation bible school.

By the next night, all of Jesus' friends began to let their guards down and enjoy the children as much as Jesus did. After helping the women clean up on Saturday, the crew finally left and moved on to their next destination.

The thirteen young men traveled on foot for thirteen hours in one day, and were eternally grateful when Jesus finally told them they could stop. Although their feet became accustomed to walking, their fast pace for all those hours caused unexpected sores and blisters on all of their feet.

Unbeknownst to the guys, Jesus knew exactly where they were headed and why he was needed. They finally stopped traveling in front of an extremely large, well-manicured house. Jesus' friends were a little stumped, seeing how they usually stayed the night at churches or preacher's houses, and this was on the other end of that spectrum.

The house had a paved, blacktop driveway that wound through decade old pines up to the house. There were small lights defining each side of the driveway and elaborate flowerbeds overflowing on the sides.

Once they finally walked the long way up the drive, this stone and brick house seemed a lot bigger. It had a five-car garage to the left and was four stories tall. Like the long drive to get to it, it was perfectly manicured and had flowerbeds and bushes like you might see at the queen's palace.

"Ummm," Peter finally spoke up. "Dorothy, I don't think we're in Kansas anymore."

The other guys laughed, although no one specifically asked where they were, nor did Jesus put forth any information to their whereabouts. He simply walked up to the large wooden front door, under the forty-foot tall porch posts, and knocked.

A few moments later, a young woman answered the door, dressed in black and white work attire.

"Yes?" she asked politely.

"Hi," Jesus replied. "I would like to see Teddy. Is he around?"

"Can I ask who is calling?" the maid asked.

"Someone he has been wanting to see."

The young woman obviously recognized Jesus and his friends from television and the Internet, and was obliged to go find her boss.

Moments later, a young man, seemingly in his twenties came to the door dressed in a suit and smoking a cigar.

Once the other guys caught a glimpse of him, they realized they knew the man. He was a high political official who had scandal and gossip following him everywhere, for his newfound position at such a young age was rather rare. It didn't help matters that his father was the president of the country.

"How did you know I wanted to talk to you?" the man asked Jesus with no formal introductions.

"I know where I am needed," Jesus calmly replied, smiling.

For the next couple of hours, Jesus, his twelve closest friends, and the young political leader talked and prayed. The man had many questions that had been troubling him and wanted answers. Despite his public reputation of being a partying ladies' man, the young leader was a smart person who genuinely wanted to do the right thing, especially when it came to his country.

He had questions about life in general, and questions about how he should rule with the power he had been given.

"My whole life, I have had stuff given to me," he told them. "This house, all my cars, everything. It was all given to me. I try to work hard, but there is such corruption in government, I feel like I am just treading water.

"I just need to know if it is OK to have all of these material things. I mean, can I still get to heaven if I have them? If not, what should I do so that I can go?" The man was legitimately concerned about his life and where it was headed.

"It is OK to have nice material things," Jesus reassured him. "But if you are not using those material blessings to serve God, you need to change.

Maybe host bible study in your home or song service once a month. As long as you keep the commandments and know God in your heart, all will be OK," Jesus told him.

"Which commandments?" the man asked, searching for answers and security in the afterlife.

"You shall not murder. You shall not commit adultery. You shall not steal. You shall not bear false witness. Honor your father and your mother. Love your neighbor as yourself."

The man thought a minute, trying to see if he had abided by these commandments throughout his life.

"Since I was a young kid, I have never broken any of those rules. I of course have never murdered, and I have never cheated on my wife or any of my girlfriends from the past. I have never stolen anything, and have never prophesized against God. Other than normal teenage stuff, I never dishonored my mom or dad, and I have always tried to love others and treat them with courtesy and respect. But I still do not feel good enough to be worthy of going to heaven. What more do I lack?" The man was still hunting answers.

"As long as you do these things and worship my father, you have nothing to worry about, friend," Jesus told him. "But if you want to be perfect, sell your house and all of your cars, give all of the money from the sell to charities, quit your job, and come preach with my friends and I."

The man did not say anything for a long time. His head was facing the ground and he was swinging his legs like a little child. "I can't," he finally said when he looked up at Jesus. He got up and walked inside, leaving the others out on the porch alone. Before the shut the door behind him, Jesus could see tears in his eyes.

25

The thirteen men sat on the porch for a little longer in silence, until Jesus spoke up.

"It is harder for a rich man to get into heaven than to find a needle in a haystack."

"But a lot of people have money," James spoke up. "Who is good enough to get into heaven, if that is the case?"

"With men, it is impossible to get into heaven, but with my father and me, anything is possible."

Peter spoke up next, saying, "We have given up everything to travel with you. So are we better than men like this one who will not? We have sacrificed more than anyone else, so are we going to be rewarded for this?"

Jesus smiled. "Of course you will be rewarded. Once we are dead and gone from this earth, I will be sitting beside my father in heaven, and there will be twelve seats to my immediate left, for all of you. Anyone who has left their homes, mothers, fathers, children, or spouses in my name will receive eternal life."

The guys soaked in the information and simply accepted their reward, with no more questions for the evening.

"Come on," Jesus told them. "Let's go to the church and get some rest."

It was almost midnight before Jesus and his friends were settled in their sleeping bags in their new home for a week. They were almost asleep when Jesus said something.

"Soon I will be betrayed, arrested, and condemned to death. I will be mocked and hated and spit upon. But after three days in the grave, I will rise again. Soon. Very Soon." This was the third time Jesus predicted his death, and his friends were extremely worried and concerned, although no one said a word.

With the sunlight beaming through the windows, the men were awake in just a few short hours. They were so exhausted from traveling last night that they did not recognize where they were.

The guys stepped out on the porch of the church and James and John looked at each other with questioning, yet excited glances.

The sunlight and rested eyes allowed them to see that they were home. Their hometown and all of the people that they had left behind so many years ago was right in front of them. They turned and looked at Jesus and did not have to say anything. Jesus, along with everyone else, could tell how grateful they were just by their expressions and excitement.

The two brothers hurried to get dressed so that they could go visit old family and friends. While James and John went visiting, the others went preaching. As always, the local media caught wind of the celebrities and rushed to the scene. Jesus' sermons and teachings were broadcast on the local channels, and everyone was tweeting and facebooking about seeing Jesus.

Hours later, back at the church, James and John returned with a lady seeming to be in her fifties. She was beaming from ear to ear.

"Jesus," John said. "This is our mother. She wanted to meet you."

"So here is the man who has taken my sons away for the past ten years," she joked. "I am so glad to meet you, and can't tell you how excited their father and I are to see them. Thank you for this."

After much small talk, James and John left again to go visit old high school friends, leaving their mother alone with Jesus.

"Jesus," she said, wanting to ask a question. "My sons have given up everything to travel with you. We have not seen them in all these years, and they have sacrificed everything for you. They do not have a family or any of the joyous things that families bring. Please reward them by letting them rule with you in heaven." Her request was genuine, although she did not understand the complexity of it.

"Mam, no one can rule in heaven except my father. Things like this are only for him to decide. I did not come to this earth to be served, but to serve, and to give my life as ransom for the world," Jesus tried to explain to her.

The mother nodded her head, although she still did not seem to understand. She was like any mother, wanting what was best for her children, and wanted James and John to be rewarded for all they had given up. Those men were her only two children, therefore when they left and followed Jesus, they not only sacrificed their lives, but any future daughters-in-law or grandchildren that their parents might have gotten to enjoy. She was not fully satisfied, but knew that she must accept Jesus' explanation and be happy knowing that her sons were serving God.

The next day, Jesus and his friends were still in James and John's hometown, and were preaching to a large crowd. Instead of splitting up, all thirteen men were together, standing in front of a crowded restaurant, preaching the word of God.

When the thirteen of the spoke together, people were surprised at how nice the speeches flowed. None of their sermons were ever scripted or rehearsed; they instead would say whatever came to them and talk to the people about how to live their lives and worship God.

After the men had finished talking and answering questions, they started to walk through the crowd and greet people, as they always did. They could hear some loud shouting, but people were trying to muffle the shouting and shush it.

When Jesus made his way to the shouts, he could see two men sitting on a curb, whereas everyone else was standing up.

"What are you shouting for? Do you want me to do something for you?" Jesus asked them.

"Jesus," one of them said. "We live in an assisted living facility here in town. I was born blind, and my friend here lost his sight in a fire when he was four years old. We are only twenty and twenty-two years old and have to live in a nursing home because we cannot take care of ourselves. Of course there is eye replacement surgery to reverse our conditions, but we cannot afford it, and we cannot get health insurance because we cannot get jobs that provide it. I'm not asking for a pity party here, but if there is anything you can do to help us, all I ask is that you try." The man was begging, and had lived a tough life of rejection and neglect from society.

Jesus had compassion on the men and felt sorrowful that they had suffered with no help from others. He knelt down to get on their level. He could see the pain and years of suffering in the man's eyes.

He held one hand from each man and said a prayer with them. When he stood up again, the men both still had their eyes closed, continuing to pray for healing. Jesus was walking away when the men opened their eyes and were taken aback at how bright the world was. As their sensitive eyes adjusted to the light, they realized that for the first time in a long time, they could take in the world around them with their sense of sight and shouted their "thank you's" at the man walking away.

26

Jesus continued his travels, knowing that his time on earth was coming to a close. He and his friends walked from town to town, usually staying in churches and preaching the word of God.

After a long day of traveling one brisk October day, they had finally arrived at their destination and were ready to have a meal and relax. They had arrived at a large evangelistic church, which was featured on national television. Their weekly show seemed legit, and the church seemed to be doing well for itself.

When Jesus and his friends neared the entrance, they could see a sign that said, "Yard Sale," and saw people milling around, looking at items on tables.

"Look, they are having a fundraiser," Simon said. "That's great. I love how more and more churches are sponsoring these types of events to raise money for their needs. With money so tight today, I bet many of the congregation members can't tithe as much as they used to."

The other guys nodded their heads in agreement, and although they were worn out from their journey, they put themselves to service, helping with the sale. They asked the woman in charge where they needed help, and immediately started loading big items in peoples' cars.

While his friends helped with the fundraiser, Jesus went inside to find the preacher and let him know that they had arrived.

Jesus recognized the preacher immediately from his advertisements and billboards. He and another man were standing in the foyer, with their backs to Jesus, and unaware that they were being watched.

"This is your cut," the preacher told the other man. He handed him a large amount of paper bills while the man put them in his pocket.

"I'm keeping the rest, and we'll tell the church that the yard sale only made fifteen hundred dollars. All of the items were donated from members of the church, so we don't have to pay anyone anything else. No one kept up with the money except for us two, so no one will notice any missing," the preacher told the other man.

126

For the first time since he was a young boy, Jesus could feel his face get red and his arms lock and begin to shake in anger. The two men still were unaware of his presence, and each began to count their money.

With clenched teeth and a face as red as pure blood, Jesus said, "The bible says that the church is to be a house of prayer, but you have made it a den of thieves."

Without another word, Jesus went outside where the sale was taking place and started overturning the tables of items for sale. There were only a few customers there, but they were all, along with the women working for the church, noticeably scared. They did not know what to do, and were frozen in time as Jesus continued to overturn tables until not a single one was standing upright.

Jesus' twelve friends stared at him in shock, not believing what they just saw. Jesus never acted like that, especially not in front of innocent old ladies. Everyone was frozen in time until Jesus spoke up.

"Get your things. We're leaving," he told his friends. For the first time in all their years of traveling with Jesus, the crew stayed in a motel. How the rooms were paid for, none of them knew, nor asked.

Although none of the elder woman working the yard sale had a camera or a cell phone with a camera device, the story still made the news that night, and media all over the area becamea frenzy on this new turn of events.

Jesus had always been portrayed as a docile man, simply teaching the word of God. Now, the media began spinning his reputation into a power hungry man who assaults elderly woman.

The president's advisors saw Jesus' outburst as a perfect example of why they must act quickly. Since Jesus acted out at the church, the president was coming around to the theory of his colleagues. This was the start of his overthrowing the government.

As the government officials met one night, the young intern updated everyone on the status of the bill. The one that would cause Jesus to break the law by his preaching.

"I finished writing it, and it should be passed through within a month. Like you told me to, I disguised it as an education bill and threw the small clause in the middle," the young girl announced, nonchalant about the whole thing.

"Good," an older man said. "Now we just have to wait until it passes, and then we can arrest him, just like his friend John." The man turned toward the president, who was standing in the corner, not sure if he wanted to be a full participant of this conspiracy just yet.

"Do you see why we advised you to stop Jesus? Do you now believe that this man will eventually try to dictate our nation? No one simply travels around preaching, with no motive of his own. We believe his 'followers' are his army that he is training. He will begin a war and, if he has enough soldiers, overthrow our way of life. We are simply trying to protect it."

The president's hands were tied. He nodded his head, knowing that he would support his colleague's ideas. Before he signed the letter, which would push their bill through the system faster, his young daughter, healthy and running, flashed through his mind.

While the government officials were plotting against Jesus, he was preaching in the streets of a new town, one in which he had never traveled, and was very welcomed.

After his sermon on faith and doubting, Jesus went into the church to rest with his friends. Just as he laid his head down on his cot for a small nap, some men came into the Sunday school room where the thirteen men were sleeping.

The preacher was hurrying behind them, obviously trying to stop them from speaking with Jesus.

"Young man," an elderly man said in a gruff voice. "You travel all over the world preaching and supposedly healing people from their suffering. What authority do you have to do such things? I was not raised to believe in scams like you, and just what to know why you think you have the right to lie to all these people?" The man had anger in his voice as he spoke, and was obviously supported by the two elderly men with him.

"We saw what you did to the last church you stayed at. I watched it on the news. I don't think you should be here and I don't want our church destroyed and our wives scared," another spoke up.

Jesus was silent for a minute, taking in the anger directed by the men. "When someone is baptized in this church, is it through that preacher standing there, or through God?"

The men turned to look at the preacher standing behind them. "He baptizes people in the name of God."

"That is the same person who gives me the authority that I have. If you have no more questions, please go away now." Jesus turned his head away from the men and lay back down on his cot, signaling the end of the conversation.

Jesus' friends did not say a word, but followed Jesus' example and also lay down. The elderly men looked at the preacher, asking him to intervene with their eyes. The young preacher simply shrugged his shoulders and took off down the hall, leaving the men and their anger alone in the hall.

Jesus was getting tired of continually fighting this long battle on earth, and began to prepare more and more for his future.

The next morning, after a long ten hours of much needed sleep, Jesus awoke to knocking on the classroom door.

Sleepily, he wiped the sleep from his eyes as he went to open it, after seeing the preacher's face through the half glass.

"Hey. What's up?" Jesus asked, still groggy from over-sleeping.

"I promise I did not bring more nay-sayers, and I am truly sorry about the men last night. But some of my congregation had a couple of questions and I told them they could ask you."

"Sure. Let me brush my teeth and wake the rest of the guys up. I will meet them in the sanctuary."

Ten minutes later, the thirteen men were walking into the large cathedral when the questions began to fly.

"Jesus!" one woman shouted loudly. "I do not make much money. I try to save most of it and tithe to the church. I get so irritated at our government system, giving handouts to people who don't work for it and taking over one-third of my paycheck.

"Should we even pay taxes? Shouldn't we be giving all of our money to the church? Can you get us out of paying this corrupt government?"

Jesus almost laughed. "Young lady, whose picture is shown here on this dollar bill?" Jesus took one of her bills and held it up.

"A dead president," she replied.

"Then give the government the things that belong to the government, like this bill I have here in my hand, and give to God what is God's. Glory, honor, and service. Don't use my father as an excuse to get out of paying taxes. I hate to break it to you dear, but there is no way around that and there never will be. You are young. Better get used to it," he winked at her and laughed at her attempt to get out of paying the government.

There were about twenty people in the group, smaller than Jesus was used to speaking to. Soon another man spoke up, asking, "Jesus?"

After Jesus addressed him by looking in his direction, the man continued. "Say a woman was married two times, and her first husband died. After all three are dead, who gets the wife in heaven? See, my wife lost her first husband, whom she was very much in love with. But after she and I are dead, I don't want her to leave me for eternity to be with her first husband. It might be selfish, but I love her and want her forever."

Jesus almost laughed. He shook his head. "Have you read your Bible or studied God's word? In heaven there is no marriage or husbands and wives. You will be angels of God."

The man looked at the floor, embarrassed for asking such a silly question. Next was a man dressed in a designer black suit, and hair gelled to a T.

"Jesus, I am a lawyer," he said, like lawyers always do. "I need to know which is the most important commandment of all, in the Ten Commandments."

"If you abide by the first and second commandments, you will abide by them all. Love God will all your heart and love others as yourself. If you follow these two commandments, you will never break any of the others, because you will not be murdering, committing adultery, or dishonoring your mother and father if you are treating them as you would treat yourself."

The question and answer session continued for hours, until each person in attendance had asked a minimum of two or three questions, including some of Jesus' friends. When a long pause signaled the end of the questions, Jesus thought that he would leave them with a question of his own to ponder.

"Why do you think God sent me to this earth?" he asked. "What do you think my purpose is?"

"To preach to us.""To help us.""To heal us." The answers came from all over the room.

"I am here to die for you." After Jesus spoke the words, he left the scene and went for a walk through the streets of the quaint town. His friends did not follow, nor did mobs of people, and Jesus was thankful for his momentary solitude. Silent time to pray and think.

27

Hours later, Jesus returned to their home for the week, calm and at peace with his future. His friends were gathering their belongings because Jesus had told them before he left that they would be leaving that afternoon.

Without a word, Jesus began folding the sheets on his cot and cleaning up his items. Through the large, open window, the streets of the city could be seen, with people milling around and buildings and houses standing in the setting sun.

"See all those buildings?" Jesus asked his friends. Without giving them time to answer, he went on to say, "Soon, not one brick will be standing. These earthly buildings will be torn down and all of the worldly things gone. Why don't people start believing in and worshiping something higher?"

It was a rhetorical question that did not require a direct answer. Lately, Jesus had been asking questions like this aloud, and his friends wondered if Jesus' prediction of his death was coming faster than they thought.

Before leaving, Mark asked the question that was on everyone's mind.

"Jesus, when will all of these things happen? The things that you keep telling us about; like your death and all of these buildings collapsing? How can we be prepared?"

Jesus answered, "Friends, do not let anyone deceive you, for many people will come claiming to be the son of God, but you know that I am his only son. You will hear of wars all over the world, but do not worry with them, because they will pass with time.

"Nations will rise against each other, and there will be a lot of suffering. These tragedies are only the beginning of the problems to come. People will arrest you and kill you for being my friend, and many people will hate you.

"Hate will run rampid in the streets, and many people will deceive others. Lawlessness will abound, and love will grow cold. No one will be able to trust anyone. The people who endure all of this will be saved, and rewarded for their suffering. Then the gospel of God will be preached all over the world, and the end will come."

Jesus' friends looked at each other with wide eyes. What Jesus had just told them scarred the living tar out of them. Surely all of that would not happen? Why? The world was great the way it was. Why make everyone suffer and endure all of that pain?

Jesus seemed troubled and knew that his friends did not entirely believe what he told them. Just the way people did not believe that he was going to die soon. Faith is a hard thing to come by in today's world. People always want to see things for themselves in order to believe that they are true.

Quietly, almost in a whisper, Jesus added, "After these hard times, I will come again and show myself from heaven. All of the people who remain alive will mourn. No one knows the day nor the hour that all of this will occur. Only my father and I. People will be eating in restaurants, at their workplaces, at the lakes and other recreational venues. The person beside them will be taken to heaven and they will be left here on earth to endure what I just described to you.

"If you knew your house was going to be robbed at a certain time, you would probably be sitting up, watching your door with a rifle, ready for him to break in. But you don't know when someone might break into your house, so you have to be ready all the time. Sleep with a gun by the bed, or lock the doors and deadbolts.

"The same can be said for the end of times. If anyone knew when it was going to happen, they would live the life they wanted, and then ask for forgiveness a day or two before. You have to be ready at all times to die and go to heaven. Read your bibles and pray. Follow the ten commandments and you will not be one that sits and worries, not knowing if you will see me in heaven or not."

Jesus' friends were not sure if he was addressing them personally or the rest of the free world. He seemed to be staring off into the distance as he spoke, speaking to many more people than just the ones in the room.

These warnings and conversations with Jesus were becoming more and more frequent and were really starting to scare the guys, and Luke, the youngest of the group, usually changed the subject when Jesus started describing the desolate future. It was easier to dismiss the thought than to consider such a grim life.

"So," Luke piped up energetically. "Where are we headed next? I hear the new water amusement park opened up a couple of towns over. I think we should go there," he joked, and everyone laughed.

Luke's breaking of the tense ice lead to other conversations popping up over the room as the finished packing their bags. Jesus sat in silence. He did not laugh and joke with the others, because his life was coming to an end, and he knew it.

He knew that when he died, he would be eternally happy with his father and would judge the millions as they died, deciding if they would enter heaven or eternally burn. He was just burdened with the people he had not yet touched and the people who would not sacrifice their lives for God. He felt that he needed more time, but there was no more to give.

"The bill just passed sixty-two to forty-eight," the young intern announced at the meeting. Most of the other attendees looked relieved and overjoyed.

"So what is our next step?" the president asked.

"We arrest Jesus, bribe his friends to testify against him in court, and put him away for a couple years. Just enough to change his way of thinking," an older man explained.

"Sir, I don't know what your hang up is about this whole situation. But this is what is best. If we were not to protect our country, men like this would overthrow our way of life, as we know it. This is our job, sir," another man told his leader in an understanding voice.

"People in our positions have protected our country and freedoms for years. They have made decisions just like this one a thousand times over. Is it better to arrest one man, or to allow our country and government to be risked?"

The president nodded and told his advisors to let him know when Jesus had been arrested. After two more orders of business were discussed, the meeting ended and papers began to shuffle around as the people packed their things and left the conference room.

Soon, the only people left in the elongated room were the president and the young intern, whose idea it had been to orchestrate this whole plan. She was on her laptop, pretending to be working but actually on her facebook account. The president sat, starring out the window, not moving, the same way he had been sitting for the past thirty minutes.

The twenty-two year old girl did not want to break into the man's deep and troubled thoughts, but felt an overwhelming urge of sympathy for him as she glanced in his direction. She had not spoken directly to the man yet, and still felt too inferior to do so.

Still, she said, "Are you OK? You sure seem upset about something."

The president looked up, startled. He glanced over at the girl, unaware of the fact that anyone else was in the room. His thoughts of remorse and regret had drowned out the pecking sound of fingers hitting letters on the keyboard, and he had not bothered look around the room to see if anyone was still left.

"I don't mean to get in your business," she continued to make small talk. "It's just that I've been an intern under you for six months now. I've seen you give orders to go ahead with a war for crying out loud! But I've never seen you so upset over a decision that you obviously did not want to make."

When the man did not answer, the girl shied away from the topic. "Sorry. I know it's none of my business. I was just trying to help."

She continued typing on her laptop while the man sat and continued to stare out the window. As the intern typed and read the gossip of her friends, she glanced over at the president of her country.

She couldn't help but notice how old and frail he looked, even though he was only forty-three years old. He took a deep breath, realizing that the girl had no intentions of leaving the conference room.

"He saved my daughter's life," he said, almost in a whisper.

"What?" the girl asked, almost in disbelief that her country's leader was confiding in her, a measly young intern.

"Did you know that my youngest daughter had leukemia?"

"Yes, I remember hearing about that. The media said that she was terminal and only had a couple of month to live. You never talked about it or brought it up, so no one here at the office did either. But I remember feeling really sorry for her. I even prayed that she would be OK."

"You prayed for her?" The president looked up at the girl for the first time since he started talking to her.She nodded.

"My wife heard about Jesus healing all of those people and started following him on the news and Internet. She researched every aspect about him, and could not find anything negative, other than critics who had never met him.

"She told me that she was going to find Jesus and ask him to come into our home and heal our daughter. I told her that it was not a good idea, with this being a reelection year and all. But she would not hear of it.

"Our youngest daughter was dying and all I could think about was the election polls!" The man started bawling uncontrollably and the young woman could tell that he had kept this information bottle up for a long time. She guessed this was the first time he had discussed it.

After the president caught his breath, he continued.

"I got one of Jesus' friend's cell phone numbers through the national database and called him the next day. My daughter was so weak that she could not breathe on her own, had a feeding tube, and was as white as a ghost.

"She is only eight years old. Her life is ahead of her, and I thought we were going to lose her forever!" He was in tears again, not caring that the intern could see him in such an emotional state.

The man was gasping for air in between his heavy sobs. His speech was almost uncomprehend able and his body was still shaking.

"He came. Jesus came in the middle of the night. He held our daughter's hand and prayed for her healing. I was skeptical the whole time and knew that she was going to die soon. I did not have faith in him, faith that he would heal her weak body. Her organs were already shutting down, you see. Stopped responding to the chemotherapy.

"Two years we had gone through the cancerous battle with my daughter, and I was so tired of it. Exhausted from trying to deal with our country's battles and my own family's battles at home. I was ready for it all to be over.

"My wife had such faith. She never left Alisha's side and really believed that Jesus could rid her little body of the leukemia. After Jesus left, I did not notice any change in Alishia, and her home health nurse said that her vitals had not changed.

"We stayed up for most of the night, until both my wife and I feel asleep in our daughter's bed, and the home health nurse went to her bedroom that we provided for her." The man stopped again, but this time he did not cry. He looked the intern dead in the eyes.

"When we woke up, Alisha's color had been restored in her face, and she looked healthy again. Over the next week, my wife took her to every specialist in the country, and not one of them could find a single health issue with Alisha.

"None of the doctors understood what happened, or how she healed overnight. One minute, they had released her to come home and die in peace, and the next, she was running through the doors of the clinics, smiling and laughing."

The president looked more troubled than the young intern had ever seen. "That man saved my daughter's life, my marriage, and my own life. Do you have any idea what I have let you people do to him? He has done nothing wrong."

The president began to tear up again, and the intern was in total shock from the overload of information presented to her. She did not know what to say or how to react to the man.

Following her instinct, she went over and sat close to the president. She held his hand and told him that it would be OK, that you couldn't fight the way of the world.

"I never thought Jesus was guilty of anything," she confessed to him. "I had seen him on TV and stuff, but it never occurred to me that he was trying to take over the government. He just seemed like a nice preacher, minding his own business and preaching to people. He sort of reminded me of my childhood youth minister," she said, and paused to momentarily reminisce about her past. "I just got the idea for the bill, you know to pass it, make it law, therein causing Jesus to break the law. I shared it because I want to do a good job here so that I can start a good career. Working in politics is all I have ever wanted to do."

The president looked at her hard for a moment. "Then we have both helped kill the man who saved my daughter," the president said angrily, jerking away from the woman and standing up.

"I know they will accuse him of being a terrorist. They are going to seek the death penalty." The president turned and looked at the intern. "And he has done nothing wrong." He stormed out of the conference room and slammed the door behind him.

The young intern had never been an emotional person before, always able to separate herself from her emotions. But for reasons unbeknownst to her, tears came that she could not stop. Hundreds of miniscule beads of salty water ran down her face for the first time in two years, since she found out of her fiancé's other girlfriend.

She almost could not bear the thought of this kind, good man being arrested for terrorism. He had healed the president's daughter and countless other people, and she alone had come up with the idea to remove him from the free world and place him in jail with murderers and thieves. That decision would haunt her for the rest of her life.

28

Jesus and his friends had been traveling for hours when, at last, they made it to their next destination. They walked into the church, greeted the preacher and couple of congregation members, and sat down in the designated area for a nighttime meal.

They ate and talked with the people, enjoying their time together. Soon, the sound of the front church door could be heard opening, and the preacher got up to see who it was.

"Deborah," they could hear the preacher's voice. "What are you doing here at this hour?"

"I heard that Jesus was traveling through our town and staying here, at our church," a woman's voice replied.

"Yes, he is. Do you want to come join us?"

Moments later, the two were walking in to join everyone else. Deborah seemed very nervous, and unsure of how to act. She looked about forty-five years old, and like life had dealt her a tough hand. Noticeable calluses on her hands and arms were proof of her years of hard work, and she seemed embarrassed to suddenly be the center of attention.

"I'm sorry to interrupt," Deb said quietly.

"Don't be. I'm glad you joined us," Jesus said with a smile, although the expressions on some of the other congregation member's faces proved otherwise.

"Look, I don't want to intrude. It's just…" she paused for a moment, looking around at her peers. "Jesus, can I talk to you in the hall?"

Taken aback, he followed her away from the other people.

"I'm so sorry. I just get really nervous around big groups of people."

"No need to apologize. What can I do for you?"

"You see, for the past twenty years, I have been employed as a massage therapist. I'm licensed and everything. Business used to be good, but with the economy these days, I hardly have enough money to make ends meet. I'm a single mother of three and spend every cent I make on bills and gas.

137

"I just thought that maybe, since I can't offer you anything of monetary value, you and your friends might enjoy a massage. I brought my most expensive oils, fused with shea butter and cocoa trees.

"You just do so many nice things for other people; I wanted to do something nice for you. What do you say?" The lady seemed glad to have blurted it all out, and waited for his reply.

Jesus smiled a big smile. "That is the best thing anyone has ever offered me! I would love to have a massage. It sounds great." Jesus was happy to see how elated he made her with his acceptance.

"I brought my massage chair. It's in my car. I left in out there in case you didn't want a massage. I'll go get it!" The lady was so happy to be able to do something for Jesus.

While she ran to her car, Jesus' friends poked their heads out the door to see what was going on in the hall. He explained to them what she had offered, and most of them couldn't wait to get in line for a relaxing massage. Most of them except Judas.

"If she is as poor as she says she is, why doesn't she use this time to charge a paying customer for a massage, instead of giving them to us for free?" he said with disdain.

Jesus looked at him with pain in his face. "Why are you concerned about it? She is doing a good deed for us. Don't bring negativity into this situation. She is excited to do something nice for us, so take advantage of it and be appreciative."

Judas looked down in shame while the other guys got ready for their wonderful relaxation.

Years of stress and worn bodies from traveling were pampered and rubbed until four o'clock in the morning. Deborah massaged each man for a full hour, until her hands were sore and aching from use.

The men could not imagine how wonderful and rejuvenated they would feel after their hour with Deb, and discussed how they should have gotten massages before now. Deborah left, after a thousand thank you's, and was obviously happy to have been able to give Jesus and his friends something.

The men fell into deep sleep an instant after Deborah left, and got the best sleep many of them had in a long time. The first one to awake was John. His laughter woke everyone else up, because it was loud and silly.

"What?" his brother asked him.

"We all slept until one o'clock in the afternoon."

With that, everyone looked at the clock and also laughed and smiled. They were always awake by six o'clock, at the latest, and could not believe they slept so late.

"Those massages were better than we could have expected, I guess," Simon joked. "And to think Judas tried to turn them down." He played with his friend, and everyone looked at Judas and laughed.

In a group of thirteen friends, everyone plays their individual roles, and it is not hard for someone to be forgotten or overlooked. In this group of thirteen, James was the practical one, Simon was care-free, Andrew was the serious one, John was the goofy one, Phillip was the old one, Thomas was the young one, Matthew was the kind hearted one, Lebus was the quiet one, James S. was the jokester, Simon P. was the bubbly one, Thad was the dry humored one, and Judas was the forgotten one.

Judas never said much, and kept a lot inside, bottled up. He never could fully get past the life he could have had with his finace back home, and began to resent Jesus for taking him away from her and his could-have-been life.

Judas probably would have kept his resentfulness hidden longer, but the previous night, he had felt embarrassed when Jesus criticized him for trying to stop Deborah from giving her massages.

Most people can take a joke, but Judas was not one to play around with. That morning, when another comment was made in relation to the situation, his anger was too much to control.

Judas decided to go for a walk by himself. Get away from everyone else for a while. He would return a different man, never to be the same again.

He took off towards the middle of town, and walked into an Internet café, which he had passed earlier in the day. Judas sat down at a computer, something that none of the other guys ever did, but he checked into the digital world anytime he was alone around the Internet.

Signing into his e-mail account that every one of Jesus' other friends gave up years ago, Judas clicked on his inbox and read his latest e-mails. Notes from families, letters from friends, and a reply e-mail that caught his attention.

The reply e-mail from Jacob Rosser, a political advisor to the president. He had been returning Mr. Rosser's e-mails since the man had found his digital address on a whim and started talking to him.

Jacob Rosser was a fifty-one year old man who had been working in politics for twenty-two years, and had diligently worked his way up the ladder of success until gaining his current position, senior advisor to the secretary of defense. He had been married for twenty-eight years and had three children in their teens. Mr. Rosser would go to just about any lengths to keep his reputable job intact and his family living the life they had become accustomed to.

It was Jacob Rosser's job to find weaknesses in terrorists and get his team's mission accomplished. After doing thousands of background checks of Jesus' closest friends, Jacob had chosen Judas as the weak link he needed. His mission was to get one of Jesus' closest friends to testify against him in court.

Jacob had gotten Judas' attention with an e-mail asking if he could interview him on television during a special about his days with Jesus. Knowing that Judas would enjoy the attention, he took the bait and had been reeling him in ever since.

It took fourteen e-mails and twenty days before Jacob Rosser saw his chance and took it. He and Judas had been discussing Judas's days traveling with Jesus and the other men. Judas had confided in Jacob the embarrassment he felt by Jesus and Simon's joking with him the previous day. Jacob could feel Judas' tension hundreds of miles away, through the screen of his computer.

Judas read the e-mail carefully, taking it all in and thoughtfully considering the question at hand while he read.

"Good to hear from you again. I'm so sorry to hear about your public humiliation yesterday. I have been in your position, working hard with someone who I thought was my friend, only to be betrayed or backstabbed by him in the long run.

You have sacrificed so much to travel the country with Jesus, and he is not appreciative of what you have done for him. You could have a normal life with your girlfriend, who would have been your wife by now.

A couple kids, and half way up the career ladder. You could have the life many people dream of, but instead you are giving all of that up to travel the country and preach God's word.

Now I know that when you first began traveling, you honestly thought that you were doing the right thing, and felt that God was calling you into this ministry. We all start out with the best of intentions, but sometimes those intentions fall by the wayside.

This is what has happened with your friend, Jesus. My colleagues and I have discovered that Jesus is planning to overthrow our government and control our country, probably in hopes of expanding that control to other countries also.

I know this is shocking news to you and you might not be able to fathom such a betrayal by one of your closest friends, but you have to trust me. You cannot see the things that we have discovered because Jesus hides his true goals from you and the other men.

Judas, I am only confiding all of this in you because I want what is best for you. I do not want you to go down with Jesus when his crimes come out into the public eye. If you are convicted of begin a conspirator with him, you will get a minimum of ten years in prison.

I feel like we have become close through our e-mails over the past couple of days, and I am only warning you of these things to look out for you. I know that you are deeper in this thing than you know and it will be hard for you to get out.

If you want to be proactive and think about what is best for you, I have a solution. I can offer you redemption if you agree to testify against Jesus in court. He will soon be arrested for his terroristic actions, and I don't want you to go down with him.

All you have to do is testify, under oath, that you have personally witnessed Jesus plotting to overthrow the government or create his own army and you will be free from all charges.

Judas, please consider what is best for you. You have already given eight years to this man. Do you want to sacrifice ten more in jail? You are only twenty-eight years old. You could still have a normal life. I could even offer you a job if you would like.

Please consider this thoroughly and let me know what you decided."

Judas read the e-mail with mixed emotions. He loved the attention Jacob was giving him, but found it hard to actually believe that Jesus was a terrorist. Regardless, his thoughts kept returning to his feelings of regret for the life he left behind and the loneliness from his life on the road.

Judas sat in front of the computer for a long time, weighing his options and the immensity of his choice. Twenty minutes later, after staring blankly into the empty computer screen, Judas had made his decision and began to write his reply e-mail.

He left out his usual pages and paragraphs of random stories and feelings. These e-mails were his only outlet of emotions and secrets. This e-mail was different though, as it was hard enough to write, without adding all of the extra small talk.

"Ok, I will. Just tell me when and where I need to show up."

29

Back at the church, Jesus had requested a big dinner for the evening, knowing that it would be one of his last. The preacher's wife had so kindly obliged and fixed two hams, mashed potatoes, cream corn, and green bean casserole.

Jesus had helped her prepare the meal, and they laughed and talked together as they worked, with the radio playing softly in the background.

They were mashing the freshly boiled potatoes when Judas walked in the back door. The other men were napping and playing a board game in the gym, anxiously anticipating supper.

"Hey," Jesus said to him without looking up. "Where have you been?"

Judas fumbled his feet as he tried to walk straight passed the man he had just agreed to testify against.

"Umm…Just walking," he stuttered.

No more words were exchanged between the two, as Judas got away from the kitchen as fast as possible and joined the other men in the gym. He lay down on his cot and pretending to be asleep, so that no one else would speak to him or probe him with questions of his whereabouts.

Half an hour later, Jesus was hollering at the guys to come and eat. Much to their surprise, he had taken out the small children's tables in the kindergarten Sunday school classroom and replaced them with one long table.

There was a pretty, white fabric tablecloth on it adorned with hunter green fabric placemats and napkins neatly folded into napkin holders. Instead of the usual buffest style paper plates and plastic cutlery, real plates and silverware were sitting on top of each placemat. There were thirteen place settings, as the preacher's wife had faked prior engagements, sensing that Jesus wanted to be alone with his friends for the night.

The men were so accustomed to bringing their paper plates through a buffet style line that they did not know what to do when they saw their huge feast, steaming in serving bowls in the center of the table.

John smiled. "Wow!" he exclaimed. "What is all of this for? Is it someone's birthday?" John's happiness was illuminated through his voice resonance and the other men were showing their own appreciation through their facial expressions.

"No," Jesus replied. "I simply wanted to have a nice dinner tonight." No more explanation was offered, and no more questions were asked.

The men all took their seats and could not wait to dig into the food. Jesus usually said the prayers before meals, but this time, he asked Andrew to bless the food.

"Father," Andrew prayed. "Thank you so much for the food sitting in front of us. Use it for the nourishment of our bodies, to make them strong so that we can continue traveling. Forgive us where we fail you and our brothers, and help us to be strong in our faith. We pray that we will be an example to others, so that they may come to know you. In your name we pray, Amen."

Amen's were heard all around the table as the men sat down and started passing the bowls of food around. The noise level rose as conversations of surprise and pleasure were shared concerning their surprise meal, and the clinging of silver on hardened and painted clay rung out as the food was dished out of the bowls.

Jesus had not spoken since the prayer was said, and he sat in silence, waiting for everyone's plates to become full. Once the food had been passed around and the men began to eat, Jesus spoke up.

His friends could tell that something was weighing on his heart, and had been for the past couple of days. He no longer joked or kidded with them, and he did not speak as much as he used to.

"Look guys," he said, almost in a whisper. Everyone had to stop chewing and moving in order to hear him. "This is hard for me to say, but I want you to be prepared for what is going to happen very soon.

"Soon, I will no longer be able to be with you. I will be arrested, as I have told you before, and will be placed in jail. And one of you will be the sole reason for that arrest. Someone among you will betray me and testify against me. You all need to be prepared for that, and have a right to know what will soon happen."

The men looked at each other in disbelief.

"We would never do anything like that," Thad said, almost appalled that Jesus would accuse one of them of such an act.

Jesus had a blank look on his face, all emotions drained from it. There was no anger, no hurt. He was unblinkingly starring at Judas, his eyes never leaving his face.

"One of you already has," Jesus replied, his eyes still locked on Judas. In unison, all of the other men turned to stare at him also, aware of the fact that Jesus was indicating him as the man who was going to testify against him.

Finally, Jesus stopped starring at Judas and went back to eating his food. The rest of the men followed suit, and not another word was said. All you could hear was the clinking of forks and spoons.

Throughout the whole forty minutes that the men sat and ate, Judas never looked up. He simply starred at his plate. When all of the other men got up to help clear the table and wash the dishes, Judas continued to sit, with his face to the floor. He thought that if he pretended he was not there, everyone else would pretend the same.

After the dishes had been washed and the table wiped clean, Peter caught Jesus walking through the hall, headed to the gym for a peaceful night's rest.

"Jesus," Peter said, talking low so that the other men would not hear him. "I don't know what Judas has done, or any of the other men, but I want you to know that I will never, I mean never, do anything to hurt you."

Jesus smiled softly. "Oh, Peter," he softly shook his head. "You will deny that you know me or have ever met me not just once, but three times."

Peter was disgusted that Jesus would say that about him. "Even if I am arrested and tried for terrorism with you, I will never do anything to make your sentencing or arrest worse."

Jesus just looked at Peter. "If that is what you want to believe," he said before walking into the gym to sleep.

Judas was not a man who liked negative attention or public embarrassment, and knew that he could not handle another situation like the one that night. He packed his small bag of belongings and waited for everyone else to fall asleep.

When the deep snores began, he knew his chance to leave was at hand. Judas left the church on foot and walked the two miles towards the Wal-Mart, which was open twenty-four hours a day.

When he arrived, he pulled a faded and wrinkled piece of paper out of his pocket, one that he had been keeping for ten days. Jacob Rosser had given Judas his phone number, in case Judas ever "needed anything," or so Mr. Rosser put it.

He walked to the customer service desk inside and asked if he could use the phone. The giant superstore no longer had a payphone, on account of lack of use due to the surge in cell phones usage.

The lady working the night shift reluctantly agreed to let him make a quick call.

"Hello," a groggy lady's voice sounded through the ear piece. Judas could tell that his call had woken her up and he started to regret his decision.

"Is Mr. Rosser there?" he asked softly.

Judas could hear some scuffling trough the phone. "Jacob," the lady said. "It's for you."

The man was also in a deep sleep and his speech could barely be understood as he pulled himself out of his REM cycle.

"Hello," he said, almost irritated.

"Jacob?" Judas said, scarred to say anything else.

"Yes. Who is this?" he said gruffly.

"I'm so sorry to call you," Judas began. "It's just that you gave me your number and said that if I ever needed anything to call you. He knows about our e-mail. I don't know how, but he knows. I can't go back there. I'm scared for my life."

Jacob could hear the fear in his voice, and recognized who the person was immediately, though he had never spoken to him before.

"Are you OK now?" Jacob asked him, becoming more and more awake, and fearing that Jesus might get violent with the man if he found out about their e-mails.

"Yes, I am just scarred and don't have anywhere to go."

"What town are you in right now?"

"Cyprus, remember? I told you that in our last e-mail!" Judas was beginning to get discouraged and regret his phone call even more. Just how well did he know this man? He had left his friends, had no money, and was depending on someone he had never even actually spoken to, to help him and take care of him?

"Right. I'm sorry, I'm just a little scattered from waking up in the middle of the night," Jacob told him, helping to ease his mind a little.

"OK, there is a nice Holiday Inn Express in that town. I traveled there a couple of times for some conferences a couple of years ago. I'm going to give you a credit card number, and all you have to do is tell them the number and they will get you a nice room. I want you to go get some sleep and I'll call the hotel in the morning." When the man spoke, he spoke with authority.

Judas wrote down the number and got directions to the hotel from the employees at Wal-Mart. An hour later, he arrived there and was asleep in ten minutes, exhausted from the huge new spike in his stress level.

30

Jacob Rosser could not sleep the rest of the night. He had never heard or met Jesus, and, according to his colleagues, Jesus was a power-hungry man looking to overthrow the government. Jacob was honestly worried about Judas, wondering if Jesus would become violent with him after discovering their e-mails. He had seen the news stations broadcasting Jesus' violent behavior towards the elderly ladies at a church. He couldn't imagine what Jesus would do to a man that was planning to aide in his arrest.

Jacob knew that they had to act quickly, before Judas was hurt or even killed. The bill had passed through the system, so now they were just waiting on someone to turn Jesus over to the authorities. That someone was in the Holiday Inn Express.

When Jesus awoke the next morning, his mind was troublesome and heavy. He wanted to be alone. To pray, to think, and to calm his spinning mind. The town in which they were staying was a large one, of about three million.

In the business district of this town, there was a beautiful garden that the city had spent millions of dollars replanting and designing after the hurricane the previous year. Usually, the garden was swarmed with people, but Jesus figured that at this early hour in the morning, not many tourists would consume it.

"Hey, guys," Jesus said, loud enough to wake everyone up. "I'm going to the garden. Do any of you want to come?" Jesus noted Judas' empty cot, but did not mention it to the others.

Thomas opened his mouth as far as it would stretch as he yawned from sleepiness. "Sure. What's the big hurry, though?"

"Just come on if you are coming," Jesus said as he grabbed his toothbrush and headed towards the bathroom, leaving the other men to put on their clothes for the day.

Ten minutes later, they began the thirty-minute walk to the huge garden. They had performed a sermon there just two days before, so they were familiar with the location. The sun was not up yet, and James looked at his cell phone to show him the time, four forty-five a.m.

They walked to the garden in silence, some of the men still half asleep. Once they arrived, John immediately found a bench and lay down to enjoy some more sleep. Some of the other men followed suit and found similar benches.

Jesus, who had been walking in front of the group, looked back and rolled his eyes. He turned and shouted at them, "Are you seriously going back to sleep? I asked you to come here and pray with me!"

Jesus' friends could hear the anger in his voice, but the fluffy cushion tops on the benches were a welcoming feel at the early hour in the morning.

"Let us just lay here for a minute," Matthew said. "These are so comfortable."

There were four benches in all, and the eleven men were sharing them and leaning up against them and each other. Noticing that Judas was missing, Thad pulled out his cell phone and began typing Judas a text message.

"Hey. Where are you? We came to the garden." He wrote. Seconds later, his phone was buzzing and beeping.

"Taking care of some business. I'll see you in a little while."

The other men asked what Judas had said, showing concern about his absence. While they continued to sleep and relax, Jesus walked farther into the colorful blues and purples and greens and reds and yellows to find solitude and be closer to his father.

The full moon was reflecting off of the plants, and it almost seemed like the afternoon, with the bright light shining in the pool in the center of the garden. When Jesus was sure he was away from everyone and out of hearing distance, he began to cry.

Heavy tears rolled down his face and sobs were unstoppable.

"Father," he cried softly. "Are you sure all of this is necessary? I don't know if I will be strong enough to endure it." Jesus sat in silence for a long time.

"I know it is your plan, and I know I have to be strong. Please give me strength to get through the next week!" He was crying again, in agony of his knowledge of the future.

Jesus sat in the center of the beautiful garden for almost an hour, thinking and praying and silently crying. When the first yellow and orange array began to sneak into the big dark blue sky, Jesus knew it was time to leave.

He got up and walked back towards his friends, only to find them all knocked out in a deep sleep. Unsure why, Jesus became angry with them.

"Really?" he said, loud enough to wake them all up. "I can't believe you are all still sleeping. I ask you to do this one thing with me and you can't even do that! If you knew that this was the last time you would spend with me, you might not have been so apt to sleep through it!"

Jesus' friends looked around at each other with questioning eyes. As if on cue, the amazing yellow and orange sunrise was blended with blues and reds. The sounds of loud and whining sirens started coming from all directions, getting louder every second.

The eleven men's eyes were wide with fear, but Jesus was emotionless, standing tall while his friends tried to hide from whatever was coming.

Although Judas had felt safe in his hotel room, he did not sleep at all. He was scarred, although not quite sure what of. Every little noise or scratch made him jerk up from the bed and his heart race.

Judas had sat up all night, flipping through channels on the television to occupy his mind. When that did not work, he called Jacob Rosser, who was also awake and devising and plan to protect his source, Judas.

Judas and Jacob figured that once someone realized he was missing, they would text or call him. When Thad did, Judas immediately called Jacob to tell him where Jesus was, who in turn contacted the local authorities and told them where a terrorist was. He gave them strict orders to arrest Jesus and hold him for questioning. Then, Jacob and his colleagues got on a plane.

An hour after the text messages were exchanged, police cars had the garden surrounded. A voice came over a loudspeaker, saying, "Jesus, if you are in the garden, come out now with your hands on your head."

The men were panicking, not understanding what was happening, and scarred for their own lives. They began scrambling under the benches and flowers, unsure if shots would be fired.

When Jesus did not walk out of the garden entrance, men dressed in all black, with the words S.W.A.T. and trained in heavy-duty combat began closing on the garden. The quickly rising sun allowed everyone to clearly see the scene play out.

Jesus stood, unarmed and peaceful, at the garden entrance. The men were shouting, "Clear," and kept walking towards the garden, leading with their automatic weapons.

Within seconds, the S.W.A.T. team entered the garden. Two of them grabbed Jesus and threw him face first onto the floor, handcuffing him, while the other men continued to search the garden and shout, "Clear."

After seemingly looking for bombs or weapons, the highly combative officers began picking up all of the other men and began handcuffing them also. In an attempt to get away, James fought back and punched one of them in the face with all his might.

The man retaliated and slammed him hard into the ground, bloodying his noise and knocking out three teeth.

"James," Jesus said calmly from the floor, with a knee in his back. "Those who use violence will be treated with violence."

Then Jesus turned his head as far as it would stretch to look at the man forcefully holding him down. He looked deep into his eyes and instantly recognized him as one of the men from his sermon in this exact spot not seventy-two hours before.

"Why are you doing this to me? You have heard me preach and know I am a non-violent person. Why did you not arrest me before, if I am apparently breaking the law?"

The man looked torn. "Look, man," he whispered. "I'm just doing my job. I got a family, you know. I need my income."

With the area clear of any external threats, the S.W.A.T. team began motioning for the regular police officers to come in and take over the situation. As more uniformed men rushed the scene, with guns held high and ready, Jesus' friends began to panic again.

The men came in, forcing Jesus up and leading him towards the waiting barred car. Although they recognized the other men from television, the police chief did his job and asked who they were and why they were in the garden.

No one spoke until Philip, the oldest and wisest of the group spoke up for all of them.

"We don't know what is going on," he said. "We are volunteers, cleaning the garden before the crowds of people start coming in. This man walked in and sat down. He did not bother us and we did not bother him." Phillip looked the man straight in the eye, waiting for a response.

The police chief shook his head. "Yea, that is what I would say too," he told them, chuckling a cocky laugh. "Well get out of here." He motioned to his men to take the handcuffs off of them.

The police chief knew that Phillip was lying, but he had the man they needed. There were bigger fish to fry than accomplices to terrorism. Besides, they could always find them again if they needed to.

After the men were free of their metal locking bondage, they walked to the backside of the garden. Once free of the strategically placed petunias, they began running, all of them. They ran as fast and far as they could, not sure where they were going to what they were going to do. All they knew is that anywhere is better than jail.

As they ran, Phillip had tears stinging his eyes. He had been the one to make that decision. Of all the emotions running wild through his mind, he could not break free of the thought that he never thought lying would be that easy.

Jesus was shoved up the concrete sidewalk, and into the waiting car. The policeman walking with him banged his head into the top of the car as he unnecessarily manhandled him in the backseat, blood running onto his face from the open wound.

"I love this country," the officer told him through clenched teeth. "And I don't take too well to terrorists. None of us do. You think we want to see our children or wives being blown up on television from assholes like you? You got another thing coming is all I have to say." The man was chewing tobacco and spit his brown saliva into Jesus' eye.

Jesus began blinking profusely, attempting to get the tobacco and blood out of his open eyes, as his hands were unable to wipe them. The officer slammed the car door shut and started high-fiving his fellow officers.

"Where did you find that?" the police chief asked in astonishment as one of his deputies walked towards the cars with a vest rigged to blow up an entire city block.

"Good thing we got this prick in time is all I have to say. No telling where he was planning on going with this," the deputy replied, avoiding answering the question.

He gave the vest to his boss and walked over to talk with his other colleagues.

"Jesus really had that? Wow, they must have been right about him. I've heard him preach, and he just doesn't seem like the type that would be a real terrorist, you know?"

"Well, we may have planted the vest," the deputy replied with a grin. "Just thought it might help in the trail, you know?"

When one of the other policemen looked at him like he was crazy, the man attempted to justify his actions. "Look, we protect this city every day. From thieves, murderers, and now terrorists. If that vest helps put away a terrorist and save the lives of children he would end up killing, maybe even your own, don't you think it was a good idea?"

The other deputies stopped to think about the lesser of two evils for a moment and ended up shaking their heads in agreement. Little did they know, Jesus was the farthest thing from a terrorist. He loved them, despite what they were doing to him.

31

As the police officers finished their job in the garden, they began loading all of their equipment and themselves in the taxpayer's cars. Turning off the sirens, the cars pulled out one by one, headed to patrol the streets and do their civic duties. Only two cars turned north, in the direction of the police station. One with Jesus, bleeding from the head and smelling of chewed tobacco, in the backseat. The car behind it, with Judas in the front seat.

Jesus was placed in a solitary holding cell until his first trial, in three days. With no means of providing his own, the government assigned an attorney to Jesus' case. He was a young lawyer, fresh out of school and just having passed the bar exam.

Micah Anderson met with his client after finding out his latest assignment. He was sitting in the dingy meeting room, waiting on Jesus, when a guard finally shoved him through the door and pushed his weakening body into the metal chair.

On first impression, Micah thought that Jesus looked frail and weak, a little pale with dark circles under his eyes. This was only the fourth case that Micah had ever presented in court, and he was still a little weary about first meeting the criminals.

"So," he said in monotone, flipping through Jesus' paperwork, looking for something to rebuke the charges. "You are on trial for terrorism against your country and the possible threat of communism control. Is there anything you can tell me to help our case?" Micah looked up at Jesus, trying to read his eyes.

"You might as well stop now," Jesus replied. "They will convict me of whatever they want to, despite whatever you may do to try and stop them. I have nothing to say, nor will I have anything to say in the courtroom. I just want all of this to be over and done with, and for them to decide how long I have to stay in here."

Micah looked up from the files. His expression was anger. "Look," he said, with a violently mad expression on his face. "My grades weren't that good in law school and I was more concerned with partying than studying. Because of this, I didn't get a job with a good firm, or any firm for that matter, and I am stuck making close to minimum wage working for the government.

"They give me three days to get a case together on poor scum like you, and now you want to treat me like I'm not needed? Please!" Micah threw the file in his face. "I'll see you in court." With that, he stormed out the door and slammed it shut behind him.

Three days later, in the preliminary trial, there was standing room only. Chaos was running rampid as people were shouting and hollering, arguing their opinion on the case. When the judge's gavel could be heard, silence surrounded the room so people could hear.

Jesus was sitting at the defendant's table, with Micah Anderson by his side. The table directly across from them housed the representatives from the state, the men fighting for a conviction.

The rest of the room was filled with media crews, Jesus' believers, family, and friends, and government officials and supporters who believed him to be a terrorist.

The judge was never looked up from his papers, flipping though them and familiarizing himself with the case at hand. Without looking up, he spoke into the microphone.

"You are being tried for being involved in terrorism against this country." He looked up and glared at Jesus. "How do you plead?"

Jesus said nothing and neither did Micah, who was still peeved from the last meeting with his client.

The judge opened his eyes wide and shook his head, as if to say, 'What is your answer?'

"Not guilty." Micah had to fight to get the words out of his mouth. He hated that he had to defend the man who disrespected him.

"Do you have any evidence to rebuke the charges?" the judge asked.

"No," Micah said, bound and determined to put forth as little effort as possible in this case.

The judge rolled his eyes. "Would you like to present any evidence or witnesses?" He turned to ask the state representatives.

"Yes sir," the man in the dark blue suit answered. The lawyer held up the bombing vest that was found in the garden with Jesus.

"This is a vest that was found in Jesus' possession when he was arrested. We don't know where or whom it was intended for, but now we will never have to know. We will not have to watch innocent people dying on the news because of this vest.

"We have witnesses who will testify that this man has plans to create an army with the people that he preaches to, kill the men currently in governmental positions, and create his own government, a communist nation.

"Our government system is set up to protect us from this very scenario. If we do not take action now, we are killing ourselves in the long run." The man sat down, signaling the end of his speech.

The judge looked at Jesus and Micah. "Let me guess," he said irritably. "Nothing?"

Micah shook his head while Jesus continued to blankly stare straight, like he had been doing during his time in the courtroom.

The judge's glare transferred to the other side of the room. "Let's have your witness."

The defending lawyer nodded at the men standing near the door. They opened it, revealing Judas standing directly behind it. He starred at the floor and never looked up.

Judas shakily walked all the way to the stand and was in a daze through the swearing in process, in addition to the questioning. He never looked up, in fear that he might lock eyes with Jesus.

"Is it true that you have been around this man quite a bit over the last couple of years?" the lawyer asked.

Judas starred at the mahogany floor and nodded his head.

"Yes or no?"

"Yes. I traveled everywhere with him and lived wherever he lived."

"Did you ever witness this man conspiring to kill leaders of the government and create his own form of communism?"

Judas had tears in his eyes as he nodded his head.

"Yes or no?"

"Yes."

"Did this man plan to blow up the president's house with that vest?" the lawyer pointed to the bombing vest sitting on display in the side of the room.

"Yes."

"Did you escape this man's accompaniment on account of fear for your own life?"

"Yes." More tears.

"Thank you. That is all."

Judas' whole body was shaking and his eyes were red and puffy. All of the color was gone from his face, and he found himself asking why he was doing this. Just because of a little joke and embarrassment? He started running and ran out of the courtroom. He did not stop until he was almost two miles away from the courthouse.

Back inside, the judge was making a ruling. He looked hard upon Jesus for a while, as if trying to figure him out.

"I see no remorse in you, Jesus. No attempt to prove you are not guilty and no emotion through this whole ordeal." The judge kept looking at him questioningly.

"In most cases like this, I would set bail. But I find myself hesitant to do that, since you are a threat to my country, and seem to show no respect to me or any concern for what you are in my courtroom for. Your trial is set for forty-five days from today. No bail, and I am sentencing you to general population. Maybe your prison mates will knock some sense into you."

The courtroom went wild. Jesus' friends and family starting shouting in protest, and crying for the falsely accused. Their screams for help did not accomplish anything, as Jesus was escorted, in handcuffs, out of the courtroom and moved to the county jail.

Outside the courthouse, Jesus' closest friends tried to blend into the mobs of people to await the verdict. They had slept and lived outside for the past three days, hiding out in fear for their own lives.

After hearing the verdict from Jesus' preliminary trial, they were devastated. The eleven of them found each other in the crowd, and all had tears in their eyes.

"You are one of Jesus' friends," a little girl in the crowd said loudly, looking at Peter. She was loud enough to gain the attention of the people closest to them, which started gaining the attention from the news camera crews close by.

"No I'm not," Peter said quietly, trying to hide away from the stares.

"Yes you are. I've seen you on TV." The girl was about ten years old, probably in the third grade. She had jet-black hair and was dressed in a hot pink jumper.

"You must have me mistaken with someone else," Peter replied as he pushed through the crowd in an attempt to get as far away as possible. He still was not sure if the authorities would arrest him and the other men for accomplices to terrorism, and was scarred for his life.

"Yes you are! I've seen you on TV. You were always on my favorite channel, preaching with Jesus!" The girl was being persistent, and her determination was attracting even more attention.

Peter's face was flashing on ever news station as the scene played out.

"Honey, I don't even know that man. Like I told you, you have me mistaken with someone else!" Peter took off running. Trying to get away from the chaos, and running from a potential arrest.

When Peter was far away from the courthouse, he took initiative and sent a mass text message to the other ten men that had traveled with Jesus for years.

"Contact your families and go home to them. Have them send you money for bus or plane fares and go stay with your parents or siblings. Stay there until we can figure this thing out. Watch out for yourselves and pray for Jesus."

As Peter sent the message, something Jesus had said to him a couple of days ago brought him to his knees. Jesus told Peter that he would deny knowing him three different times. His predictions were right.

Peter fell to the ground and started dry heaving, as he had nothing left to throw up. He cried out in agony and wondered why everything was happening.

32

After testifying in the trial, Judas had to get out of that room. He could not look up, could not look Jesus in the face. He asked himself why he was lying and could not come up with a good reason.

He left the witness stand in the front of the large, mahogany room and dashed out the back doors. Outside of the courtroom, media and people crowded around, waiting to hear the verdict. Judas had to get away from them.

He burst through the exterior doors, only to discover more people. This time, the media news crews stormed him, thrusting cameras in his face, trying to get an interview for television.

Judas shoved the cameras away and began running. He did not know where he was going, but he continued running, attempting to run away from his lies and destruction.

Judas had nowhere to go, no one to call, and nothing to do. He began panicking and wondering what he should do next. Running straight through town and into the outskirts of the suburbs, he found a wooded area and pushed through the brush, trying to get even further away from his problems.

Once Judas was completely alone, he lay down in a fetal position and began to sob uncontrollably. Jesus had been not only a good friend to him, but he also knew in his heart that Jesus was God's own son.

What had he done? How could anyone ever forgive him—especially God, Jesus' own father? After twenty minutes of uncontrollable bawling and screaming in agony and self-pity, Judas stopped and looked around, panicked and wondered what he would do.

The wooded area that surrounded him was spotted with old tools and knick-knacks, half buried in the dirt, the other half rusted and rotting. Being located directly behind a neighborhood subdivision, Judas theorized that the area probably once belonged to a mechanic or carpenter.

Still in a frenzy, Judas began rummaging through the rubble, not quite sure what he was looking for. Buried in an old metal box of motor oil, a long, dirty lariat rope stuck out, grabbing the attention of Judas.

Unsure of what he was doing, Judas scrambled for the rope, tears streaming down his face. His mind was spinning, and his emotional state was unstable. With a surge of energy, Judas found a strong, thick tree with many branches surrounding its bottom and middle.

He began climbing the tree, shouting, "I'M SORRY!" at the top of his lungs as he climbed. He continued to shout, although his sobs were making the speech uncomprehendable.

Forty feet up, Judas tied a slipknot around a heavy-duty limb. He fed the other end of the rope through the eye, creating an expanding and decreasing loop. His hands were shaking, and his mind would not allow him to consider what his body was mindlessly doing.

After securing the knot and checking for a clearing in limbs below, Judas slipped the looped end of the rope around his neck.

"I'm sorry. I'm sorry," he said over and over, hoping that he might be forgiven for his actions. Judas' whole body was shaking and his body started to convulse from anxiety.

Looking towards the sky, Judas jumped off of the tree limb upon which he was standing. The rope stretched almost to the ground, and Judas' toes scratched the dirt below as he struggled through his short death.

Jesus had been in jail for three days, awaiting his trial. He was placed in county bi-state, and thrown into a cell with a man named Barabbas. Barabbas had been convicted of auto theft, assault, and battery, and was sentenced to ten years in prison.

The third day of Jesus' prison stay; Barabbas caught a glimpse of the district attorney walking through the jail, on his way to meeting with another inmate. Barabbas was headed to the community room to watch television, when he saw a chance for freedom.

"Hey!" he hollered at the man, who was dressed to the nines in a designer suit with jewelry to match.

The district attorney glanced over at Barabbas, but kept walking.

"You don't have any hard evidence against my cell mate. If you want to keep your ninety-eight percent conviction rate strong, you might want to come talk to me."

The man turned at looked at the dirty inmate. He stopped for a minute, thinking. Finally he made a three-sixty and walked towards Barabbas.

"What do you know about my conviction rate?" he said with disdain.

"I know that my cell mate is Jesus," Barabbas said with an evil smirk. "And I know that you do not have a case against him, and still won't in another forty-two days. You do something for me, and I can guarantee you a win on that case. I'll get you a taped confession." Barabbas smiled, showing his four blackened teeth encased in a grungy mouth.

The district attorney glared at him, considering the situation. "And just how can you promise me that?" he whispered in a low, malicious voice.

"Don't worry. I'll get it."

The man who had recently gained his new position of DA considered his options. He looked deep into the smirking man's eyes. "What do you want?" he asked.

"Get me out of here and clear me of all charges."

The district attorney looked at Barabbas and laughed. "Yeah, OK. I'll bring you a steak dinner too." He took off down the hall in the same direction he was headed two minutes earlier, seriously considered the offer.

After his planned meeting, the district attorney walked into the community room, accompanied by two guards for safety. Much thought and consideration concluded that Jesus' case was a big political and media covered case. Barabbas was a no one, no name.

Not many people would be concerned if Barabbas was loose on the streets, but the country would be in danger and feel unsafe if a known terrorist was set free.

With disgust in his eyes, the lawyer walked over to the accused thief and squatted down on his knees, getting on eye level with the man in the broken and rotting recliner.

"Alright," he said, low enough so that no one could hear. "You take this," he handed Barabbas a small tape recording device. "Give me what I need, and consider yourself a free man."

Barabbas started smiling and laughing, spitting saliva on the man's clean suit through the wide gaps in his mouth. The DA left the prison, hoping that he had made the right decision.

While the DA and his colleagues climbed into their black suburban to head back to the office, Barabbas went into the laundry room, where the dryers would mask his voice, and spoke into the recorded, trying his best to imitate his cellmate's voice.

"Yeah, I planned it," he said in his best imitation voice. In school, Barabbas' teachers always told him that he could pursue a career with his voice imitations. "I just got arrested a little too early. I was going to take over the government next week, and kill anyone who got in my way." Barabbas cut off the recorder and smiled to himself.

"Freedom," he whispered and smiled a genuine and happy smile.

33

Two days later, Barabbas was a free man, and Jesus was deeper into the web of lies he had been cast into. Learning of the latest confession, the prison guards and fellow inmates began to harbor anger towards Jesus.

There are two things that are intolerable in prison: child molestors and terrorists. Men convicted of such horrid things are beaten, raped, tortured, and threatened until they beg for solitary confinement.

From the outside, state penitentiaries give the impression of a good and just place for criminals. Inside, a different story is portrayed. One of gangs, drugs, rape, and murder. Not only from the inmates, but the guards and wardens alike.

Bribery, money, and fear run the lives of the employees and prisoners, and almost all of them obey the orders of the vicious gang leaders. They know that disobeying means torture or death.

Murder is an everyday happening in a prison system. The news does not cover the violent stories of awful killings inside the barbed wire fences, and many times the family of the dead inmate is given no explanation. No one questions the system, but rather accepts it. Prisons are their own cities, with leaders more powerful than leaders of the country. Only in a prison, there are no laws or rules. It is do or die.

Anger towards Jesus began to flow through the prison like a rapid waterfall, crashing into the jagged rocks below. The gang members saw their murder and drug empire as necessity and only killed rival gang members when they deserved it. But to betray your own country and plan to kill innocent women and children was heartless and cold, and the ringleaders in the prison began to pass on their hatred to everyone else. The guards, the janitors, the other prisoners, and even the warden.

While obscenities were shouted towards him from every direction, Jesus sat in his lonely, concrete cell and tried to block out the screaming. He softly sang hymns to himself and prayed continuously for the men shouting at him.

Knowing that his time was running short, Jesus pleaded with his father to find another way to save the world. He knew that the pain and suffering he would soon endure would be almost too much to bear.

"Father," Jesus prayed silently as he heard the sound of heavy steel boots walking heavy on concrete, towards his cell. "If there is any other way, please show me." Jesus looked up. Nothing had changed, except the sound of boots was becoming clearer every second. Jesus still sat, innocently, in his jail cell, awaiting the guards.

"Warden says you're wanted in the courtyard," a deep and monotone voice came out. Four uniformed men stood waiting on him, in case force was needed.

Jesus stood up slowly and closed his eyes, praying and staying calm. In between short prayers, Jesus focused on his breathing, trying to keep it deep and slow.

Taking longer than expected, two guards went into the cell and shoved Jesus hard into the metal bars. "Hurry up!" one of them shouted in a loud voice, causing cheering and clapping from adjacent cells.

Jesus' head began to bleed from the force of the metal bar and a pounding headache blurred his vision. Instead of giving into the pain and wincing or flinching, Jesus stood strong and kept his mind focused. He did not show any signs of weakness or pain, and simply followed the orders he was being given.

"Open your eyes, boy!" another guard shouted at him. "You're the son of God right? Ain't nothing bad going to happen to you!" He screamed loud enough for all of Jesus' cell mates to hear, and they began shouting and scraping cups against their metal bars in approval.

When Jesus did not obey the order, another guard slammed his body into a metal staircase, producing more blood, this time from the knees, and shouted, "You better listen to my friend here, boy! He said OPEN your eyes!" The man stuck his thumb into Jesus' right eye, almost an inch deep.

Jesus tried to open his eyes, but could not. The pain, blood, and damage to his right eye forced it shut. Seconds later, when he finally opened them, he was blinded in his right eye, but could not tell if it was from the blood or the damage.

The guards were walking slowly with Jesus, punching him in the stomach, legs, face, and arm every couple seconds to get a rise out of the other inmates. Jesus' cell was on the end of the row, so the guards had to walk him in front of all of the other men to get out.

Many of the guards did not know where their anger towards Jesus came from. Maybe it was having power over another human's life, or maybe it was anger from other situations in their lives bottled up like a shaken soda pop, ready to spew. Regardless of where the anger came from, the guards were lashing out at the moment at hand and taking it out on Jesus.

Once they walked to the middle of the rows of cells, the guards stopped so that every inmate had a view of the action. The screams and shouts of approval were deafening, and sending vibrations through the concrete floors. The other inmates were alive with violence and wanted to see it, whether they thought Jesus was guilty or not.

One guard kicked Jesus' legs out from under him and another punched him in the mouth. Jesus was bruised and bleeding from all over his body, and was becoming too weak to move.

One guard walked away while the others continued to hold Jesus up to his peers and beat his weakening body—all to the shouts of the others. The guards felt like they were heroes, and all of the men were shouting for them and their good deed.

The fourth guard returned with a wad of fabric, and the other men began stripping Jesus of his state penitentiary clothes. Once he was naked, in front of hundreds of murderers and thieves, Jesus could not hold himself up from the stifling pain in his legs. His knees and calves had been punch and kicked so much that they refused to stand under his body weight.

Two days before, when the guards began to plan their unthinkable beating, one prison employee who would take no part in the violence came up with a plan of his own. He planned to secretly video the whole act on a small camera and send it to the news stations, in hopes of spurring reform of the prison system. He was tired of the lack of discipline and obedience in his place of work, and tired of fearing for his own life.

As his fellow employees began to carry out their plan, he was also carrying out his. He pretended to be cleaning a cell on the opposite row, and set his camera up in a direct line of view of Jesus. With all of the attention focused on the five men across the hall, no one noticed the man cleaning the cells, or his electronic device.

After beating Jesus' naked body senselessly, the four guards forced him into the wadded fabric, which resembled a robe of some sort. They grabbed his arms and pulled his body up, forcing him to stand on his wobbly knees.

One guard stuck out his left arm and spun it around, signaling silence from the men in the cells. Once it was almost quiet, the guard shouted,

"Alright, you 'son of God!' You want us all to worship you and your 'father,' well now we will do it!"

The men let go of Jesus' arms, but he began to falter and shake. The lead guard nodded at another to hold him up, and as one guard supported him, the other three kneeled down on the ground and pretended to pray to Jesus.

The men clasped their hands together and flattened their fingers, pretending to pray, and held their hands and eyes up towards Jesus. As the men pretended to pray to him, they suddenly stopped their actions and began spitting on Jesus instead.

After witnessing the mockery, the inmates went wild. The sound of laughter and screams was louder than any of them had ever heard, and the guards began to fear that the sound waves and vibrations might actually crack the foundation of the building.

They jerked the cloak off of him, forced his clothes back on, and led him out of the hall. The men had to practically drag Jesus to the courtyard, since he could not stand or support himself. This led to more anger and punches and kicks, shouting at Jesus to get up all the while.

The courtyard of the prison was on the back of the state property, surrounded by rows of barbed wire rolled fences, three lines deep. There were basketball goals and a soccer field for recreation, and weight lifting benches and bleachers.

In the twenty minute time period it took the guards to escort Jesus to the courtyard, the video camera, streaming live footage to the local media, resulted in mobs of people heading in the direction of the prison. Instead of entering the state facility through the main gates, the bystanders snuck through the old man's property adjoining the prison to avoid being turned away.

As instructed by the prison employee aiding them, the media and curious locals hid in the thick brush surrounding the prison grounds, in attempt to not scare away the guards from their violent intentions.

With a nod from the warden, watching the scene from the tall watchtower, his assistant reached out his index finger towards a large black button. The button was directly beside a large red button, both inside a clear plastic case under lock and key.

The red button was designed to lock down the prison, during riots or gang killings. The black button was designed to open all doors to all cells.

"I want them all to see the punishment for being a terrorist against this great nation," the warden told his assistant while the man held the black button down until he heard the loud one-beep siren that signaled the opening of the doors.

The four guards leading the massacre pushed and drug Jesus to the middle of the courtyard, continually punching and kicking him in the head, sides, stomach, and groin the whole way.

By the time they reached their destination, Jesus' body was already starting to turn purple and blue from the whelps popping up. He was bleeding profusely from his head, while small amounts of blood were seeping out of his other scraps and scratches.

His knee was broken and the bone was jutting out towards his calf, from a powerful kick to the bone. He could not stand or put pressure on the leg, nor the other leg, which was convulsing under stress.

Jesus' right eye, which had been poked with the guard's thumb, was swelled shut, while red tears poured out of it. The entire right side of his face was beginning to swell and turn purple, from blood bubbling under the skin while the eye bled from the inside as well as the outside.

Jesus was breathing heavy and his body was convulsing from the huge amounts of stress it was being placed under. He kept his head down, never saying a word, trying to focus on staying strong through his violent humiliation.

Jesus' left arm was pulled out of the socket, from being jerked against his own body weight as the guards drug him by his arms. While they were laughing and mocking Jesus, another guard came towards them, saying, "The guys in the metal shop just finished making this. He is supposed to be the son of God, right? And we are all supposed to worship him? Well, a man of his standings should have the proper attire. A crown!"

The man shouted the words loud, feeling proud that he contributed to the act. With him was a makeshift hat, made of rusted and neglected nails, probably rejected from old projects of the inmates.

The nails were welded to an old hat band, and the rusted, pointed ends stuck out just far enough to puncture the head of the person wearing it. In the front of the headpiece, nails roughly spelled out the words SON OF GOD, although you could not see them unless you looked closely.

The guards looked pleased. One of them took the hat and pushed it hard onto Jesus' head, pushing the nail heads further than they should have gone. The puncture wounds instantly brought blood to the site, and Jesus winced in pain.

Head wounds bleed more than wounds from any other location, and the blood ran into his open left eye. Jesus tried to wipe the blood from his eye, but the guards were jerking on his arms, forcing him to stand up.

As the crowd grew larger and larger, the guards began enjoying the attention. The violence escalated and the men seemed to be getting pleasure from inflicting such pain on another human.

When the screams and clapping got louder, the guards became stronger with their punches, putting on a show for the inmates they were supposed to be guarding. Behind three lines of barbed wire fence, the media and citizens left their post in the brush and rushed to the fence. With the inmates circling in on the men in spotlight, the outsiders needed a better view.

The rolling cameras broadcast the horrendous acts to their substations, which took the story national, unveiling the necessity for prison reform in the country.

In the town where Jesus grew up, his mother and father were eating lunch with their middle son, who was home from college for the weekend. The three of them were enjoying their food at a breezy, open restaurant, not paying much attention to the large flat screen television to their right.

When Joseph started choking on his food and a horror-stricken look spread across his face, Mary followed his gaze to the high definition screen he was staring at. At first, she did not understand what she was watching. As the realization hit her, Mary started to scream and cry, running towards the television, hoping it was not real.

34

Not understanding where their anger and violence was coming from, the guards continued to beat Jesus, while more guards came in to take their places, as the original guards grew weary from throwing hard punches and holding the weight of Jesus' one-hundred-sixty-pound body.

Soon, fourteen guards surrounded Jesus, wailing and hitting him. After one hour of beating Jesus, a siren's loud noise stopped everyone in their tracks. The guards turned to look towards the tall guard shack, where the noise came from.

They could see the warden stationed there, motioning them to lead Jesus back to his cell. He concluded that Jesus had endured his punishment, and would no longer participate in terrorism, once released from prison. Hard lessons - that was the warden's motto.

Instead of obeying the warden's orders like expected, the guards gave into the inmate's prompting and continued their acts of violence. Jesus' limp body hung motionless as two men supported his arms to keep his body high enough for their peers to continue punching it. Jesus was a live punching bag with no way out.

The warden sounded the siren two more times, but the guards and inmates kept on with their tactics.

In the meantime, media and bystanders were growing with curious people, as others all over the country and world were watching the horrendous beating portrayed by the camera.

The people who Jesus had touched, his friends, family, and followers of God, were mortified by what they saw. People everywhere began praying for Jesus, and praying that what they were watching was not true.

Jesus' family started their travels in the direction of the prison, five hundred miles away, to stop the insanity. They just hoped they would not be too late. While they rushed to the scene, the insanity did not stop. In fact, it grew worse. Violence that had not been seen before unraveled before the eyes of millions of people.

Jesus slipped in and out of consciousness, giving into the physical pain thrust upon him. After enduring an hour of punches, kicks, punctures, and broken bones, Jesus had not complained or fought back. He just winced in pain, knowing that his pain was necessary for all of the people of the world.

Every punch. Every kick. Every nail shoved into his head. He had to endure it, so that his father's people could be saved from their own sins. He was the world's free ticket into heaven, and he knew that he had to be strong enough to face the physical pain.

"I'm tired of holding him up. He's too heavy. Come on, I have an idea!" One of the guards shouted towards the others, over the deafening noise.

With sirens blasting and calls to the National Guard being placed, the prison guards drug Jesus towards two old crossed railorad ties near the outside bleachers that were once used as the bleacher foundation. The mob of inmates followed them, shouting in anticipation of the action they were about to see.

Led by unexplainable violent thoughts, the guards drug Jesus towards the heavy, rotting railroad ties. "Let's put him on these so we don't have to hold him up!" the man shouted.

"How?" another asked.

"That one is already stuck in the ground. Just put the other one on top of it and put him on them!" the man was shouting, proud of his own ingenuity.

One of the crossties was stuck vertical in the ground, sticking out about three feet, reaching for the sky. The men picked up the loose crosstie and placed it evenly on top of the other, creating a T shaped structure that would hold weight twice its size.

The men placed Jesus on top of the horizontal crosstie so that the mob could view him easier, and they could rest from holding his dead weight. Once Jesus was placed on the structure, two men climbed on top of it to hold him steady.

Inmates from all walks of life found themselves cheering from the violence in their hearts. Bloodthirsty, they pushed and shoved to catch a glimpse of the relentless beating of Jesus' body.

Once the guards grew exhausted from the endless punches they threw, they began to allow other inmates to get in on the action. The men swarmed the scene, trampling two other inmates in the process.

The two men clinging for life below the hundreds of stomping feet were convicted burglers. They happened to be standing closer to Jesus than any other inmates, and were thrown forward and down when the numerous men behind them ran forward with hundreds of pounds of force.

Grabbing sticks and rocks on their way forward, Jesus' fellow inmates began punching him, throwing rocks at his head and face, and poking him with sharp sticks until they pierced his skin and blood began to pour.

For the duration of three hours, the men took turns beating Jesus. He was slipping in and out of consciousness, trying to stay awake to fulfill the plans of his father.

Sirens all over the prison had been screaming since the warden told the men to stop. The warden's assistant's voice kept coming over the loudspeakers, "Stop immediately! Stop! The National Guard is on the way! Stop beating him!" But the men did not stop.

The media and bystanders crowd grew larger in numbers over the continued hours of beating, and many of the people cried, threw up, shouted at the men to stop, and sought out local authorities. Unlike the guards and inmates, they could not bear to see the life taken away from someone with such violence.

The inmates continued to punch, throw rocks, and use Jesus as a baseball, sharp sticks as bats. When a large, flat rock flew through the air at thirty miles an hour and slammed into Jesus' shattered skull, the force pulled his mind into reality again, away from the black world it was in.

With a pail and painful face, Jesus spoke the first words he had said since the senseless beating had begun. With all of his might, he shouted, "Father! Why have you forsaken me?"

As if on cue, the men who were taking turns beating Jesus to death stopped, and waited for what was to come. A couple of seconds later, the men exchanged glances, as if waiting for a lightning bolt to strike them all to the ground.

"Doesn't look like God is coming to save you!" one of the men shouted, followed by shrill laughter from the other inmates.

Suddenly, Jesus' body fell from the top of the crosstie. He had leaned over in his final second of life, and since no inmates were supporting him, his body hit the ground with a thud.

35

Within seconds, blue and red lights and louder sirens were screeching from all ends of the courtyard. Men covered in black with huge metal shields and black sticks were creating a circle around the violent inmates and guards, closing in fast.

A voice over the loudspeaker kept saying, "This is the National Guard. Do not fight or you will be taken down. This is the National Guard. Do not fight or you will be taken down!"

Outnumbered, the guards and inmates found themselves face down in the dirt, their hands handcuffed behind their backs and connected to their ankles, which were also handcuffed, a mere twenty minutes after the trained professionals arrived. The men of the National Guard each took down one man, and still had backup to guard the premises.

Once the scene was secure and the inmates and guards were being marched into their locked down cells, some of the outsiders who had been watching rushed towards the fences to aide Jesus.

The old man who owns the property they were standing on had joined the people a couple of hours ago, coming across the commotion while checking fences in his old pick-up truck.

In the truck were fencing pliers, cutters, and ties. He laughed when he saw the men trying to climb the three layers and chain link and rolled barbed wire fence. "Maybe these will help," he said as he held up a pair of fence cutters.

It took more than fifteen minutes to cut through the thicker than normal fences, but once there was a small opening, the crowd rushed to check on Jesus while the inmates and guards were rushed into locked cells by the National Guard.

Cameras rolling the entire time, people ran to Jesus. What was once a human body was indescribably mangled. Blood covered the courtyard, the crossties, and Jesus. His arms were broken and facing backwards, his legs were broken at the knees and stuck the wrong way. His face was so swollen, you could not see where his eyes or nose were, and his hair was matted with dried blood, giving the appearance of one big red blob.

The first man to reach Jesus picked up his lifeless body, hunting for signs of life. He felt for his pulse, but found none. Many of the people could not get close to his body, for the smell alone was too rank. They could not look at his dead body up close.

The man holding Jesus' wrist suddenly moved backwards and began dry heaving and throwing up blood, as did many of the other people. Soon, many of the people were being pushed out of the way by a short woman, making her way towards Jesus' body.

"I'm a surgeon," she told the people. "Let me help. I won't get sick; I do this kind of thing for a living." Some of the men nodded and moved aside as the woman came and knelt beside the broken and dead body.

She felt Jesus' pulse, to be sure the man had not overlooked the faintest beat of blood running through a small vein. Holding his arm and counting for two minutes, she declared him dead, and caused every witness to begin crying.

The people who did not know Jesus cried for the pain and violence they watched him endure. The people who did know Jesus cried out for justice, knowing that he did not deserve to be in prison in the first place.

The crowd sat in the hot air, crying and praying. No one was sure of what to do; where to take Jesus' body, how to fix the fence, how to get in touch with Jesus' family, or what they should do next.

Soon, three men in white coats rolling a stretcher walked through the back door of the wing closest to the courtyard. They wheeled the rolling bed closer, planning to place Jesus on it.

"We are with the city morgue. We take bodies from the prison and incarcerate them if no one claims them for a proper funeral," one of the men said in a kind voice.

"We're not sure what happened here, but the warden told us that this prison was probably going to be shut down, and he would lose his job or end up in jail with these hooligans," another one spoke up. "You know, this is not the first murdered inmate we've picked up from this prison. Things like this happen more often than you'd know. If I was you people, I'd walk right back through those broken fences and not come back."

The people began to exchange looks of fear, realizing that they were inside the gates of a maximum-security prison.

"What about the fences? Are these murderers going to get out onto my land?" the old man who owned the adjoining property said, obviously fearful of his life.

The men thought for a while, not sure of an answer. "We'll tell the warden about it before we leave with this man's body. I think they have the prison on lock down right now, so you don't have anything to worry about for a while. Surely they won't let the prisoners into the courtyard until the fences are mended."

"Just in case, I'd fix them myself and go on and get out of here," the third morgue employee piped up. "What are all you people doing here anyway?"

"This man," a man said, pointing to Jesus and fighting back tears. "Is Jesus." He could not get the words out without his voice cracking.

"The preacher from T.V.?" one of the white coats asked in shock. "What was he doing in this place?"

Everyone was quiet. "If I know him as good as I think I do," a man finally replied. "Probably preaching to his fellow inmates."

The city employees worked together to pick up the dilapidated and deformed body. With legs protruding in the wrong directions and arms facing backwards and mangled lifelessly, the men had some difficulty completing their job.

Onlookers cried for the man whom they had prayed with and worshiped not long ago. They could not believe the immorality and inhumanity they had witnessed, and many of them rushed to Jesus' side for one last touch, before the men wheeled him away.

The three men from the morgue finally laid Jesus' body atop the medical device and gave one last look of remorse to the large crowd. The men pushed the roll-a-bed towards the west wing door of the prison while the crowd, still crying, became vastly aware of their whereabouts.

With red, puffy eyes, the people began to slowly walk back through the fences, which had been cut almost six hours earlier. Some of the men offered to help the old man fix the fences, so that prisoners could not get onto his property.

The volunteers rode in the back of his old truck to the barn, to get more supplies for fence mending. The others slowly left, one by one, until the last person was left standing alone. It was the cameraman for the local news station, the one who got the tip about this violence from the other prison employee.

He had been strong in front of the hundreds of other people. He had not said a word, but simply filmed the horrid facts that were unraveling. Now, all alone, starring at the old stone building, he fell to his knees and began crying. The man had never seen a person die before, especially not a violent and tragic death.

36

An hour later, when Jesus' body had arrived at the county morgue and was being tagged and classified, Jesus' family was arriving at the prison.

Witnessing the violent beating of their son and brother on national television, Mary, Joseph, and their other children immediately got into their SUV and drove in the direction of the prison.

They had been planning on going to visit him the next weekend, and had already mapped out destination of how to get to the state penitentiary. The family had been devastated when they learned of Jesus' arrest, but he had assured them that he was OK, and not to worry.

When they pulled into the massive stone gate, they found no guard sitting in the guard shack, checking cars and people who drive into the parking lot. Mary, who had been crying non-stop since the discovery of the brutal pain her son was enduring, cast an unwary look at Joseph, who was driving the vehicle. She had an eerie feeling about the whole situation.

The oversized parking lot had been stripped clean of cars, and had twenty-eight black school busses, which read "National Guard" in their places. Joseph could see his children's horror stricken faces in the rear view mirror, and he knew he had to be strong for his family.

"Listen," he told them over his wife's sobs. "Your mother and I are going to see where Jesus is and if we need a doctor or something." His eyes were wide as he spoke. "I want you to take this," he told his second oldest son as he handed him a twenty-two caliber handgun.

The whole family looked at Joseph in shock. "Where did you get that?" Mary asked. "And what does he need it for? We are not a violent family. You put that back," she scolded.

"Mary, I don't think you understand the severity of the situation. This maximum security prison, with crooked guards and a crooked warden, is running wild. They had to call in the National Guard! Geez, we don't know what to expect. Some of the inmates might be running through those

171

trees beside us as we speak. Why do you think there are no cars in the parking lot? Everyone else left in fear. This is no safe place, Mary."

Joseph held the gun, showing his son what to do. "All you have to do is turn this from 'S' to 'F,' and shoot. It is automatic, so keep firing until you run out of bullets. Do you understand?"

The twenty-four year-old was speechless, with pure fear streaked across his face. He shrugged his shoulders and Joseph nodded. "It's OK. We're going to go get your brother. If anyone tried to break into the car, just shoot. Then drive away. Your mother and I will figure out the rest."

"Now get in the front seat, lock the doors, and all three of you keep watch in different directions. I love you."

None of Joseph's family spoke, including Mary. They were all in shock because of the circumstances, and scared for their lives.

Mary got out of the car and walked around the Joseph's side, holding on so tight to his hand that it began turning blue and purple. They walked through the front doors, where an information desk sat empty.

The sound inside the prison was deafening, with shouting and metal doors slamming and gun shots going off all around them. Without instructions or a map, Mary and Joseph did not know which way to go. Suddenly, the saw a person dressed in all black with a shield and a heavy metal stick walk past their right, down a dark hallway.

"Excuse me," Joseph yelled to the figure.

The National Guard volunteer turned around abruptly, stick held high, ready to strike.

"Identify yourselves!" shouted a woman's voice. They could see only her eyes—and they looked frightened. Before giving them a chance to answer, she shouted again, "We cleared this building thirty minutes ago of all civilians for safety reasons! Who are you?"

"The parents of the man who was shown on television being beaten to death. We came to get him," Joseph said, strong in his convictions.

The lady's eyes turned from fear to pure remorse, and began to fill with tears. "Oh I'm so sorry," she said softly. "I'm so sorry."

Being not quite sure what the apology was yet for, Joseph and Mary waited for her to offer more information.

"Follow me," she said and instantly turned in the opposite direction. They walked almost a hundred yards, past endless cells with concrete beds and small lavatories, until they came to a large room, probably the mess hall.

Mary gasped at what they saw. The warden, his assistant, and the eighteen guards involved in the beating of Jesus, in addition to all of the inmates housed in the prison, were handcuffed, laying on their stomachs, with a black uniformed person standing over each of them, ready to act if they attempted to move.

"We're waiting on another unit of the National Guard to take them to different prisons. You can't just beat someone like they did and get away with it. There is no telling how many cases just like that have happened here. We're just lucky that someone filmed this one, opening the country's eyes to the reality inside a prison." The lady boasted at her job, proud of what they had accomplished.

Mary and Joseph looked confused. "But where is he?" Mary asked timidly, scared of what the answer might be.

Realizing that the couple had not heard of Jesus' death, the lady's eyes filled with water once again. "The morgue," she said with a shaky voice.

Hearing the words, Mary's knees buckled and she cried out. Always the strong one, Joseph could not hold his tears back any longer. Picking his wife up off of the dirty, wet, concrete floor, Joseph cried with her.

Suddenly, Mary started to run. She ran in the opposite direction, running towards the door they had entered through. She could no longer be in the place where her son was murdered. Her emotions would not let her.

Through tears, Joseph asked for directions to the morgue, and the lady told him. Then he followed his wife, his face pale and body exhausted from the emotions flowing through him.

Jesus' brothers and sister knew what had happened to Jesus when they saw their mother, running towards the car. Twenty feet from their parking spot, she twisted her ankle and fell, scraping skin against asphalt.

Not far behind her, Joseph helped her up as Mary walked, barely supporting her own body weight. Their three youngest children began crying as they watched their parents struggle to get to the car, knowing the truth.

No one said a word as Joseph started the car and drove in the direction the woman instructed him. Tears filled all of their eyes, and Mary started banging her head against the window, softly whining and shivering.

The morgue was only a ten-minute drive from the prison, and Jesus' family was sitting in the parking lot minutes later, hesitant to get out of the vehicle.

"It's probably not even open," their daughter said. As if on cue, a man in a long white coat opened the door on the side of the building and fumbled in his pocket, finally pulling out a cigarette.

Joseph slowly got out the car and walked towards the man.

"Sir," he said as he approached. "I think my son is in this building right now. Can you let my family and I come in to make sure?"

The man looked around. "Well, we're not really supposed to do that. First the police have to check out all of the bodies, which won't be until the morning. Then, if they need a body identified, they will call the family to come in and identify." He flicked the butt of the cigarette.

"Who is your son?" he asked.

"Jesus," Joseph said. The man looked up at him with sorrowful eyes.

"I'm so sorry. He did not deserve that." Looking around, he added. "You can come in, but you can't stay long. And maybe just you and your wife should come. The less people milling around here the better, you know?"

Joseph nodded. "Thank you." He looked back at the car and hollered, "Mary! Come on!"

Three car doors began to open, so Joseph said, "Just Mom, guys."

Mary gripped Joseph's hand harder than she ever had during childbirth. Preparing herself for what she was about to see, they followed the man into the building, thanking him over and over.

"This will probably be really hard for you," the man said, looking at Mary. "Are you sure you want to see this?"

Mary nodded her head. "I have to."

"OK. Right through that door."

The smell of formaldehyde was stifling, and almost took Joseph's breath away. When the three of them were in the room, the man walked toward a wall of drawers. They were big drawers, and looked like a huge filing cabinet.

He walked to a drawer on the far left side, the second to last row from the bottom. He looked up at Joseph for confirmation before pulling on the handle. Once he opened the seven-foot long, three-foot wide drawer, something covered in a white sheet awaited them.

The man pulled back the sheet and Mary fell to the floor again. Joseph did not cry. He could not. He was still in disbelief.

"Can we take him?" Joseph asked.

"I don't think so," the man said. "Not for a couple of days anyways."

"So what do we do?" Mary cried.

"You need to go ahead and start arranging a funeral. If you want to have it in your hometown, you will have to fly the body. We cannot drive them more than one hundred miles," he explained.

"What if we can't afford that?" Mary asked in horror. After non-insured hospital bills for broken bones, braces, and a serious car wreck through the years, Mary and Joseph savings account slowly depleted and they found themselves with only two thousand dollars in savings. With the average cost of a funeral, there was no way they could afford to fly Jesus' body back home and pay for a funeral.

"Usually if no one claims the body or the family won't or can't take care of it, we incinerate it," the man told them sadly.

Mary started crying again, and Joseph tried to fight back tears. All three of them jumped when they heard slam of the door, brushing against the cold metal frame.

"Who are you?" the man working at the morgue asked.

"Sorry to scare you," the man said in a gently voice. He was an older man, probably retired, and dressed in a long overcoat and a suit underneath. The man was very tall and slender, and hunched at his shoulders, from years of supporting his upper body. He seemed kind, and smiled at them sweetly.

"My name is Joseph, oddly enough," he smiled. "Same as yours," he motioned to Joseph. "I have listened to your son preach for years now, and have become a firm and strong believer in God. I know that I am going to heaven when I die, and that I am forgiven of my sins." He smiled, showing the pleasure he received from a secure afterlife.

Mary, Joseph, and the morgue employee looked at the man, waiting for him to offer more information.

"I apologize for letting myself in. I owned a locksmith business for thirty-two years, so the front door was no problem," he laughed a deep, bellowing laugh. No one else found the humor.

"I have no wife or children, and no close family to spend my money on. My business did not make me filthy rich, but I am definitely secure in my old age. I am here to ask you if I might oblige in paying for the funeral of Jesus. I do not feel that I can make any other contributions, and I feel led to offer this."

Mary looked at Joseph in confusion. Was this man for real?

"Well I sure don't mind," the employee of the morgue spoke up, although with a little disdain towards the man who broke into his place of work. "But it will be three days before the body is released by the police and the state. After that time period, feel free to take it and have a proper funeral."

"Really?" Joseph asked, cocking his head as he looked at the man. "You would do that?"

"It would be my pleasure," he replied kindly.

"Well we need to start preparing things," Mary said through her sadness. "His funeral will be in our town. Nowhere else."

The man nodded generously. "Of course."

"In that case," Mary said, "thank you."

The three of them left the morgue employee alone with the bodies as they left the building and exchanged information. They began brainstorming places to have the massive funeral, since they knew thousands of people would want to attend.

37

Over the course of the next two days, the need for prison reform was addressed nationwide. Government officials along with members of the military were sent to every prison in the country with a checklist. Thousands of guards and wardens were removed from their positions and even arrested for abusing the legal system and creating their own.

The media went wild, showing the truth of the corrupt prison system. Wardens and guards did what they wanted, when they wanted, with no reprimand or punishment for their behavior. A call for change had been a long time coming, and the live coverage of Jesus' beating brought it even quicker.

For the time being, prisoners lost their rights to leave their cells, and inmates all across the nation were on lock down twenty-four hours a day. The few guards still employed by the prison systems could not control the thousands of inmates, forcing them to remain behind bars until they gained reinforcements.

The crime scene investigators went to the morgue where Jesus' body was kept and performed tests, took samples, and made conclusions. Since Jesus' case was getting so much media attention, in addition to the fame status Jesus had already achieved, they ordered a policeman to be stationed on duty at the morgue every hour until his body was gone. They could not afford to have someone move his body or tamper with their evidence; they had a case to build against the prison system, and it started with the evidence from Jesus.

After three days of testing and reporting, the local authorities contacted Jesus' family and released his body. His parents retrieved the business card that the old man had given him, accepting his financial help.

Joseph, the old man who offered to pay for Jesus' flight home and funeral costs, bought plane tickets for Mary, Joseph, and himself to fly to the city holding Jesus' body and fly back home with him.

They arrived at seven o'clock in the evening and caught a taxi to the morgue. Walking through the doors, they saw the employee who had let them into the morgue just a few short days ago. Nodding their heads in thanks, they kept walking down the hall towards the room, which held Jesus' body.

Once they entered the room, the uniformed policeman seemed ecstatic to be relieved of his duty, guarding a room of dead bodies. He said hello, and then walked out briskly. Mary walked to the drawer holding Jesus' body and took a deep breath.

She had arranged his funeral back home to the last detail. All she needed now was his body. As she opened the drawer, Mary looked back at both Josephs in questioning shock.

"Where is my son?" she asked as the tears started once again. They were as common as breathing these days.

Mary's husband shrugged his shoulders and left the room, hunting a person with answers. While he went in search of help, Mary pulled the drawer out to its full extent, wondering if Jesus' body had slipped to the back of the metal shelf.

Instantly, three morgue employees and the policeman on duty appeared in the doorway, with questioning looks on their faces.

"Where is Jesus' body?" one of the employees accused the policeman.

"I don't know!" he defended himself. "You think I open those drawers and look at the dead people? Heck no! I just stood in this little room for the last eight hours and no one came in or out except you people," he motioned to the workers. "And these people," pointing to Jesus' parents.

The tension in the room turned from anger to an eerie feeling, which was creeping up Mary's spine. Suddenly, Mary's husband began to smile. His smile grew larger and larger, spreading across his face.

The other Joseph scrunched his eyebrows in question, as Mary said, "What are you smiling about? Someone has taken our dead son's body. Haven't we been through enough?" She could hardly catch her breath between heavy sobs.

"Everything that Jesus told us he was going to do, he did," Joseph tried to explain. "I can't believe that none of us have thought about the fact that he told us he would rise again, three days after his death."

Everyone continued to stare at Joseph, still confused with the situation. Joseph continued to smile, almost laughing at his doubting heart.

"Every time Jesus told me something, or I watched him telling crowds of people on the Internet or news, I could not fathom the miracles or extravagant plans he said. And every time, he proved true to his word, and true to my doubt."

Joseph paused, staring off into space as if in disbelief of the facts laid out before him. "Can't you see that this was the plan all along? Whatever he was saving us all from, he has done it. Everything he preached and told us all came down to this moment.

"I'm not sure, but I think he has broken the barrier to heaven. It's like by his death and resurrection, we as humans are given a free ticket into heaven. We just have to try to lead a Godly lifestyle. He knows that we will sin, but now, through our son, it is OK. We have forgiveness and eternal life." Joseph was pacing, questioning himself as he said the words. Everyone in the room stared at him, waiting for more.

"This is what our son was preaching all along. Don't you get it?" He held Mary's hand and looked deep into her eyes? "He was never really our son to begin with." Joseph smiled a genuine smile while tears filled his eyes in awe of the sacrifice Jesus made.

Mary was still confused. "So there is not going to be a funeral?" she asked.

Her husband laughed. "No, dear." He seemed to suddenly have a thought. "We can still have a memorial to remember Jesus, and we can tell everyone what has happened. Keep all the plans you made, and we will turn the funeral into a celebration! A celebration and memorial for Jesus' life. We can ask his closest friends and his younger brothers and sister to speak and share some of their favorite memories with him," Joseph began to get excited.

"We are all free and forgiven of our sins. Does no one feel the empowerment about this besides me?" Joseph looked around the room. The morgue employees seemed to have already written Joseph off as a lunatic, and the policeman turned to go in fear of this seemingly crazy man.

Joseph, the old man who was assisting Jesus' parents with the cost of the funeral smiled. "You're right. This is what Jesus preached to us all along. I can't believe this. I feel liberated!" He began laughing in his deep voice, and smiling like a giddy school girl.

Mary and the two Josephs left the morgue, and traveled back to their hometown, to continue with their plans for the memorial of Jesus. Instead of a funeral, they would tell all of the attendees of the wonderful sacrifice Jesus made, and celebrate his life.

38

News of Jesus' disappearing body spread faster than the news of his death. Media outlets all over the world halted their stories on measly school cafeteria food or routine traffic stops to headline this story.

The social networking websites cast out their gossip of who was dating who, to be bombarded with opinions and thoughts about Jesus. People felt like they had grown up with Jesus, and knew him personally, thanks to all of his media attention. Everyone had an opinion about his resurrection, and they were not afraid to share them.

The world was abuzz with opinions and arguments about Jesus. His life, his preaching, his death, and the disappearing of his dead body. One night, a nationwide news station performed a poll, interviewing thousands of people. They wanted to find out how many people believed Jesus' story, and how many people thought he was a hoax.

In the poll, they discovered that only twenty-two percent of the world were believers of Jesus. The other seventy-eight percent had an astounding negative and harsh idea that Jesus was indeed what his nation's government thought he was; a terrorist looking for fame and followers as he started his new cult.

Watching the news, James and John, Jesus' old friends began to cry. "Those people don't even know him!" James said as he threw the remote down and slammed it into the coffee table. "Do they have any idea what he went through FOR THEM? This is ridiculous!"

James' mother rubbed his back, trying to comfort him. "I just don't understand why people bash Jesus' name or not believe him. My goodness, what is their other option?" John added softly as he looked down at the floor. John got up and walked towards his bedroom, trying to get far away from the television and its interviewees, shouting hateful things about his dead and risen friend.

One day before Jesus' memorial, the government officials who acted in the arrest of Jesus were sitting in a long meeting, nominating new candidates for an election. The dozen people who met just months earlier, planning Jesus' arrest were sitting in the back row, not paying attention and dozing off.

"Hey," an old man said, whispering to the others. "I think we need to talk to the city cops that worked at the morgue where Jesus' body was kept. We need them on record, saying that some of Jesus' friends came into the morgue and took his body the night before he was released.

"I don't know what happened to his body, but we don't want people believing that ridiculous story his parents are telling everyone, and some of his followers taking up where he left off.

"We have to be proactive and stop a problem before it starts. If people think that Jesus got away with this, they might try it also. Any objections?" With no word from his colleagues, the man continued. "OK. We will fly to the town and talk with the policemen. I'm sure we will have to compensate them monetarily, asking them to lie on national television, but that is what our security fund is for." The others could barely hear the man's whisper over the monotone woman talking through the loudspeaker.

As the respectable officials settled back into their chairs and the old man got on his Blackberry, booking flights and hotel rooms for the following day, the young intern who had come up with the idea to pass the bill that made Jesus' preaching illegal stared at the floor.

She thought about the president, and the day he had cried to her, telling her about Jesus healing his daughter. She stared at the floor, tears falling from her eyes and hitting the burgundy, Berber carpet. "When will I stop denying him?" she thought, as she excused herself to go to the bathroom and cry for the next ten minutes.

The next day, nine men flew to the city that held the state penitentiary where Jesus died. Their three-piece suits and long black and gray overcoats proved too hot for the climate, and they instantly began sweating in the humid air.

"We need to speak with the chief," one of the men said to the young woman working the desk at the police station.

"Sure," she replied. "Right in there." She motioned to a glass office to her left, and the men let themselves in.

"Can I help you?" the chief asked, without looking up from his computer. When no answer followed, he looked up and was taken aback for a minute. The chief smiled, recognizing the men and wondering why they were seeking him.

"Wow! What in the world are you men doing here?" He was obviously excited to have such high officials calling upon him.

"Well, we need a favor," one of them said coldly.

"Sure. What's up?"

"You are familiar with the case of Jesus, I take it?" the older man asked.

"Of course," the chief laughed. "Who isn't?"

The man speaking smiled a brisk, unfriendly smile. "Right," he said slowly, thinking they might need more money to offer for their bribery.

"Well, many of the people who protect this country every day have proof indicating that man was a terrorist. In order to prevent other people from getting crazy ideas in their heads, following Jesus' lead, we need the world to believe that Jesus' body was taken.

"Now Jesus' family is telling people that he rose from the dead." He said the last five words with dripping sarcasm, as if he were telling a fairy tale to a small child. "I need your deputy to say that some of Jesus' friends came to the morgue and bribed them, taking his body in the middle of the night to orchestrate this elaborate scheme."

The man stopped, waiting on an answer.

"I don't know," the chief said, obviously with a good heart. "I try to run a clean business in this town. We don't usually do anything illegal." He scratched his head, trying to get out of the situation.

The man speaking cleared his throat. "You know," he said. "My men and I are over homeland security. So, in a way, we are like your boss. The president is asking you to do this. You are not going to say 'no' to the president are you?"

The police chief made a face. "I guess not," he said softly.

"Good. I've scheduled a press conference for you and your men. There is an account set up for you and each one of your men involved in the Cayman Islands. Here is the information on how to access it." He threw the card on the police chief's desk, and the men left the building, smiling at their empowering authority.

The next day, Jesus' old friends met at James and John's parents' house. James had sent a mass text message to the remaining eleven of Jesus' closest friends, asking them to come to his house.

"I just wanted to see you guys again," James told the men, explaining his reasons for calling such a meeting. "There has been so much going on lately, sometimes I think I am going crazy."

The other men were in agreement and they discussed the horrible beating and death of Jesus, and the resurrection he had promised. They hated that the world was denying what had happened, but they could not fight it. They were the minority.

The men were all still extremely guilty for denying Jesus in the beautiful botanical garden that day, and prayed together for forgiveness. Right before saying a unanimous, "Amen," a voice from behind startled all of them.

"My friends," it said, deep and commanding. "You are already forgiven."

They turned around, and then looked at each other in disbelief. It was Jesus, in the flesh once again. But he looked more angelic, glowing more than a normal person.

"What in the world!" Peter shouted, rushing to hug his friend. "How did you get in here?"

Jesus laughed as he embraced him, smiling at Peter's unimaginative mind.

"I can go anywhere I want, now," he smiled, spinning around at inhuman speeds. "One of the perks of my new job, I guess." Jesus was beaming, glad to be reunited with his friends.

The men were still in shock. Jesus was standing before them!

"Look," John said, with his head hanging. "We are so sorry about what we did the last time we saw you. We were just so scared. I guess fear can do a lot to a man."

Jesus smiled and genuine and forgiving smile. "Don't worry," he told them all. "As I just told you; you are forgiven and it is forgotten."

The men began to return smiles to Jesus, knowing that they were truly forgiven.

"I can't stay long," Jesus told them. "I just wanted to show my truest believers that I have risen from the dead. I want you to tell everyone you know this great news. My father has given me all authority on heaven and earth. Go and witness to people of all walks of life, baptizing them in my name. Teach them and observe all of the things I have commanded you. Most of the people will not believe you, but the ones that do will be forever changed."

Jesus hugged all of the men and left, walking right through the closed back door. Jesus family, and other believers and friends received similar visits throughout the evening, making his memorial the next day grow even larger in attendance.

The civic center parking lot was already overflowing with cars, and there was still two hours before the memorial. Mary, Joseph, and their other children were in the kitchen, watching over the last details from the catering company.

Disgusted, Mary turned off the small television sitting on the corner shelf, which was broadcasting a national news bulletin. Policemen were claiming that people had taken Jesus' body during the night, creating more nay-sayers to the sacrificial act and wonderful life of Jesus.

Mary started to cry, but fought back the tears. No matter what people said, her son had given his life to save everyone from their sins. She couldn't be more proud.

Two hours later, people were standing in the parking lot, in adjacent parking lots, and in the middle of the road, watching the fifteen-foot tall port-a-screen, which had been wheeled outside the civic center, roling live footage of the memorial inside for the overflow of people to see.

Inside, there were row after row of crammed metal chairs, shoved together to maximize space. In the front of the building, tables of food outlined the stage, ready to feed to people buffet style.

On the stage were huge portraits of Jesus. His baby pictures, pictures from his childhood and teenage years, and pictures from his years of preaching God's word. His whole life was being told in print, for the entire world to see.

Of course, camera crews and media employees were stationed at the back of the building, ready to report the events of the memorial to the country. The massive, echoing chatter subsiding and the cameras began rolling when a petite woman dressed in black walked onto the stage. Her once red hair, which was now covered in splotches of gray, was pulled into a classic up-do, and her black pants suit completed her professional look.

Her short high heels thudded loudly against the wood planked floor. When she reached the podium, she fumbled for some papers. She looked over the papers for a minute, and then seemed to decide against them. She stood up straight, and began to speak.

"Hi," she said shyly. "My name is Mary. The last time I spoke in public like this, I almost got arrested." She paused and laughed into the microphone before continuing.

"I almost got arrested because I talked about God at my high school graduation. And now, here I am, speaking at my son's memorial, after he was arrested and killed in prison for the same thing. Ironic? I think not."

"My husband and I claim Jesus as our son, but he actually wasn't. We didn't adopt him or anything. I gave birth to him just like all mothers. But my husband was not his father. God was.

"This might sound strange and hard to believe. Trust me, I thought so too." Some people laughed in the audience. "You know, we think that miracles are things of the past, only from Bible times. But God still performs miracles today. You just have to be willing to accept them.

"When we found out that I was pregnant, we could not believe it. We had never had sex, and here I was, a young girl, pregnant and scared to death. Instead of focusing on that fear and the impossibleness of it, I focused on the gift that God was giving Joseph and I.

"If you believe in God and trust in him, you will receive rewards greater than you could ever imagine. Jesus brought me joy that I would never experience if I hadn't conceived a child by the Holy Spirit.

"When Jesus was a small child, my husband and I knew he was different. We had not been around children much, but we knew they were not supposed to be that angelic. We found that out with our other kids." More laughter in the audience caused Mary to cast a playful wink in her children's direction.

"I remember one day specifically when I found Jesus in our local church, talking to the preacher and deacons. He was ten years-old, and he had walked into a business meeting on his way outside from children's choir.

"Most children would have been scared and walked away, but Jesus walked into the meeting, sat down, and began talking with these elderly men. He explained things to them and told them things that they could not understand.

"When I finally found him, after frantically searching the entire church, Jesus was sitting in the middle of the men, and every one of them was crying. He never told me what they talked about, and I never asked. But for a young child to have enough knowledge and wisdom to bring grown men to tears moved me." She paused, remembering the day. Taking a deep breath, Mary scanned the crowed and continued.

"Jesus never sinned. He was a perfect human. None of us will ever be able to say that. Ever. Whether you let a small cuss word slip out, gossip about other people, have impure thoughts, or even beat someone to death, we all are guilty of sin."

Mary started coughing and had to turn her head when she spotted the warden sitting in the middle of the crowd. He had not been sentenced to jail, although he was not allowed to work for a government entity again.

With forgiveness in her eyes, Mary looked straight at the warden and continued talking. "When Jesus was fourteen years old, he left home. He didn't run away, my husband and I let him go.

"I know you are probably thinking I am crazy for letting my son leave home at fourteen years of age. Trust me, everyone thought that. Even my family, who told me so and gave me their opinions almost every day. But when you listen to God and trust in him, you will be able to do what he wants you to, not matter what other people think or say.

"When Jesus left, he traveled around the world, preaching God's word. God had a plan for Jesus all along, and that plan started with sharing his word with the world. He reached many people and made lots of friends.

"He used to call home and tell my husband and I about a new person he met at a different town, and delight in the joy and faith of people. Jesus also cured people. He cured them from physical and mental illnesses, as well as curing them from their own human nature.

"Thirteen years. That's how long Jesus was allowed to preach, heal people, and bring them the word of God. Thirteen years until the government decided they did not want his evangelism.

"Jesus was arrested and died a horrible death, but that is not what I want us to focus on today. I want us to rejoice in the full and happy life he lived, and remember the lessons he taught us.

"Don't be sad for Jesus, because he is in heaven with his real father. His life and his death were all part of God's plan for us. Before Jesus lived and died, not everyone could enter heaven.

"Only the people who truly knew God and worshipped him in their hearts. But now, through the sacrifice Jesus made, his blood had been shed so that the barrier between earth and heaven would be broken.

"Everyone, no matter what you have done in the past, and no matter what religion you claim to be, have a free ticket to heaven. All you have to do is accept Jesus as the living Christ and worship God the father.

"God knows that we cannot stop sinning. All he asks is that when we ask for forgiveness, we repent. This means that we honestly try to do what is right and live a Christian lifestyle, witnessing to others.

"I think what we need to focus on today is this great sacrifice that Jesus made. My son died for you. And for you. And even you," Mary looked at people around the room, and then at the warden. "We are all forgiven!"

People were crying, their emotions overtaking them.

"And when you think of Jesus, my son, God's son, you think of the love and compassion he showed to all of us. You show that same compassion and love to everyone around you. Give all glory and honor to God.

"Jesus was the light of my life. He still is, and can be the light in your life as well. All you have to do is ask him."